IT'S RAINING IN MANGO

Born in Brisbane, Thea Astley studied at the University of Queensland. She has published ten novels and one collection of short stories. Three of her novels have won Australia's prestigious Miles Franklin Award: *The Well-Dressed Explorer* (1962), *The Slow Natives* (1965), and *The Acolyte* (1972). In 1975 her novel *A Kindness Cup* won the Australian book of the Year Award. *Hunting the Wild Pineapple*, a collection of short stories, won the James Cook Foundation of Australian Literature Studies Award in 1980.

Thea Astley recently retired from the position of Fellow in Australian Literature at Macquarie University and is now living and writing full time in New South Wales, Australia.

Beachmasters, Girl with a Monkey, An Item from the Late News, and *The Well-Dressed Explorer* are all available from Penguin.

D0167747

IT'S RAINING IN MANGO
PICTURES FROM A FAMILY ALBUM

Thea Astley

A KING PENGUIN
PUBLISHED BY PENGUIN BOOKS

PENGUIN BOOKS
Published by the Penguin Group
Viking Penguin Inc., 40 West 23rd Street,
New York, New York 10010, U.S.A.
Penguin Books Ltd, 27 Wrights Lane,
London W8 5TZ, England
Penguin Books Australia Ltd, Ringwood,
Victoria, Australia
Penguin Books Canada Ltd, 2801 John Street,
Markham, Ontario, Canada L3R 1B4
Penguin Books (N.Z.) Ltd, 182–190 Wairau Road,
Auckland 10, New Zealand

Penguin Books Ltd, Registered Offices:
Harmondsworth, Middlesex, England

First published in the United States of America by G.P. Putnam's Sons 1987
Published in Penguin Books 1988

1 3 5 7 9 10 8 6 4 2

LIBRARY OF CONGRESS CATALOGING IN PUBLICATION DATA
Astley, Thea.
It's raining in Mango: pictures from a family album/Thea Astley.
p.   cm.—(King Penguin)
ISBN 0 14 01.1403 3
I. Title.
PR9619.3.A75I83   1988
823—dc 19   88-14308

Printed in the United States of America by
R. R. Donnelley & Sons Company, Harrisonburg, Virginia
Set in Bodoni

ACKNOWLEDGEMENTS

The author wishes to thank the Literature Board of the Australia Council for the Senior Fellowship on which this book was written.

Come with me to the point and we'll look at the country,
We'll look across at the rocks,
Look, rain is coming!
It falls on my sweetheart.

A song from the Oenpelli region.
From Aboriginal Australians *by Richard Broome.*

Cornelius Laffey, born 1838, vanished 1878, rediscovered 1924.

Jessica Olive, wife of Cornelius, born 1847, died 1927 reaching for the rosella jam.

Nadine, their daughter, born 1865, washed out to sea, 1879.

George, their son, born 1868, died 1928 while fencing.

Mag, wife of George, born 1896, died in flu epidemic 1926.

Harry, son of Nadine and wandering bushman, born 1878, brought up as a Laffey, died violently, 1949.

Clytie, wife of Harry, born 1884 and long-suffering till 1963.

Connie, daughter of George and Mag, born 1922.

Will, son of George and Mag, born 1923, committed sideways 1983.

Reever, son of Connie and American serviceman, born 1943 and last seen heading north.

Bidiggi (known later as Bidgi Mumbler) born 1860s, father of Jackie Mumbler, grandfather of Charley Mumbler and great-grandfather of Billy Mumbler.

IT'S RAINING IN MANGO

Even at the end of things she is still looking for a reason as she had been at the beginning, puzzling in a muddleheaded way while she watches that fool of a Reever, legs dangling from fifty feet up where he has lashed himself for the third day into the crown of a celerywood tree.

Along the new road being hacked through the rain forest, bulldozers grumble and snort and shove brutally at the matted green, blades skimming challengingly towards the heads of protesters buried up to the neck or nudging back a still chanting mob of greenies. She shifts the binoculars upwards and catches sight of Reever's straining face as he peers back down the track through leaves. There's a gummy smile on his mouth, the set look of martyrdom frozen into a kind of dubious bliss. His greying hair is blowing in jagged slices all over his lined and kindly mug and his hoicked-up skirt and the vulnerability of his middle-aged shanks make Connie want to weep.

She puts down the binoculars and gets her yard hat, cramming it over her own ashen plaits before blundering out and down the house track to the road.

Someone has to stop him.

Defiance has its natural sticking-point and it is apparent that that hot nest of leaves in the upper limbs of the celerywood is it.

Tough, sun-cured, she lets her anxiety and distress tumble her along that half mile of mud-rut from the house, reeling through downhill years of comers and goers, aware of herself as stayer, the last of the real stayers, she decides, falsely but proudly, as she trots, stiff-necked, to squawk sense into someone.

For the first time in more than sixty years her solitariness daunts her.

Sweet reason, she keeps telling herself against all reason, against the ticking of summer grass, against tree hiss, against the whooped

13

amusement of hidden waters. But the lewdly mouldering heat paws at her. She feels that the mob at the bottom of the slope is getting farther away even as she hoists herself across tussocks on the old car tracks; and though their shapes, the faces belonging to those shapes, become humidly vague, voices are clarifying and strengthening all round.

A hundred yards yet into heat-swing ferociously grabbing.

You okay?

A large and strange man is mouthing as he leans over her.

Has she fallen? She doesn't remember falling. Doesn't remember concussion, thud of bone into flesh into earth. There is the sting of grazed flesh, small pains fluttering along one leg. Her eyes, sundazzled, are squinting an examination of acres of florid skin close to her, curved in concern. There isn't a feature in that vast expanse she can recognise, although he is talking with a familiarity that once she might have reprimanded in a stranger.

You okay, Con old girl? You tool a hell of a tumble back there.

Old age brings weightlessness, *her lips pronounce.*

That's the old Con, *the face above her approves. And all its planes shift into laughter.* That's the girl.

The chanting has stopped. The bulldozer thrums into silence after a last chord-crash of tree. There are so many people all around, and voices are warning other voices to get back, move away, and then someone has hoisted her up in a fireman's lift and she is being rocked up the track again as if she had never left.

That was the point, her addle-brain tells her: never leaving; burrowing in; or, if leaving, the brevity of those intermissions gulped by return, by the continuum of the country she knows from the houses that have held her. There had been Europe for a while, the shortest of whiles. There had been America. She could give an intimate tour of unlikely places in southern France, in Denmark, in California, in Texas. There was even a section of street between Second and Third Avenues on the east side of Manhattan that might display its streamers of greeting the moment she returned. So many places like that, willing to be contained by, or to contain, the visitor. Yet she had chosen never to go back to those away places, to what was ephemeral because exotic. Wherever she went a sense of self lamented its lost sense of place, and though the idea of home persisted with the worn toothbrush, the travel-

ing clock dented on one corner, the handbag bric-à-brac, those deposi-tions of self soon lost their meaning in the impersonal rooms of motels or third floor walk-ups.

Under her closed lids, patterns form, tessellations of family.

She goes back to the start of things.

Bugger the reason, she says silently. Her mouth moves later than the formed thoughts that force their shapes upon her lips.

In this large and airy bedroom, figures prowl about, tinker with louvres, draw curtains.

You're cutting the sky, *she hears some old lady croak.* Don't do that.

The acre of face looms.

You're a card, Con, *its voice says.* Regular card.

There are numerous little irritating ministrations. Someone has placed a wrung-out flannel on her forehead. A knee stings viciously as someone dabs. Her wrists and hands are being sponged and then the palm of her right hand stings in chorus with the knee. She is conscious of water-sips and, under and over the taste of water, the crushed granules of aspirin, bitter on her tongue.

Get Reever, *she commands.* Get the fool of a man down.

But no one seems to hear and she isn't altogether sure if she has said what she intended saying. All her life has glittered with moments when the words uttered were not those meant, the phrase angled for caught up and wriggling on the hook of her tongue as something quite other.

She goes back to the start of things.

After all, despite all those by-chance places and their strangers who become intimates on North Sea or Sydney ferries, on trains to the Isa or Boston, the bus station encounters in Darwin and Manitoba, the el-derly Greek who ran an all-night diner on Second Avenue, the friends of friends in Kamloops, in Kerville, in Dirranbandi, the unexpected confidings of unknowns between planes in Athens and Melbourne, de-spite all that, only the family as she knows it has cohesion, provides a core.

As it was. Is.

Here here here, her mind mumbles. Here.

Cornelius Laffey.

Jessica Olive, wife.

Nadine, George, Harry, question mark, children.
Leroy, Duke, Bucky, someone or other, husband.
Will, brother. Self-fleeing brother brother brother.
Connie, me. Doesn't matter any more.
Reever, son. Uptree Reever, mattering, worrying me, Reever.
So closely meshed, all of us, the nature of our closeness bound up with this place. With family.
Laffeys. In this rainforest triangle, tented in green. Bedouins of the sticky leaf.
It had all begun so long ago and remains fresher in the aging memory, the way things always are for the old.

HOW TO
GET SACKED

Cornelius Laffey had slipped ashore, father told her often enough, from the dinghy of the sailing ship *Jeannie Dove*, one steamy late March day, onto burning sand in a place that would later be called Bowen.

The nothingness appalled him, quite apart from the heat, the mangroves, the flies.

His soft northern skin, attuned to the Canadian maritime provinces, crisped as if it had been placed on a griddle. He thought momentarily of the grey waterfront of St. John, but flies alone kept him busy. For days the ship's party had been camped offshore on Stone Island, because the mainland natives—foolishly, all the crew agreed—were preventing their landing.

Stone Island was nothing like the tropical nirvana his dreamy Celtic soul had imagined. His hands were pulpy from trapping fish in reef pools, his feet skinned and bleeding from coral. He was convinced of error, of misjudgement. He had celebrated his twenty-fourth birthday gutting mackerel hauled from the shallows of the most virulent blue waters he had ever seen. His scaling knife slipped and cut his thumb. Scales clung like spangles. From across the channel came the sound of rifle fire as officious colonisers showed the indigenous people what's what in a ratatat, idiot anticipation of another civil war half a world and half a week away.

It was 1861.

That early day in April when the township, cleared of black landowners, was proclaimed, Cornelius was looking for and expecting a frontier magic he still failed to find a month later. Scowling at the hopeless canvas village that scabbed the bay-line, he resolved his stay would be the shortest. He had come to this new southern land as a journalist, trained for something more than sandflies and heat, he thought aggrievedly. With a yearning affection he recalled his old newspaper offices in St. John.

He'd brought with him a small Columbian press that had been dumped in its crate outside his tent. Visionary plans for a journal unravelled as his days spent themselves in helping other settlers peg out land, dig storm drains and raise pole frames for the first of the slab-and-tin shanties. More distressing was to watch departing squatters riding north and west to select their kingdoms.

Should he follow?

At the end of four weeks he managed to bring out a broadsheet, the copy written by candlelight, the type agonisingly hand-set between building bouts in a half-finished shed he had whacked together. The broadsheet was a gossipy farrago of personal encounter and the sort of ferocious political complaint he imagined new settlers expected. He was wrong. They wanted encouragement. They wanted to be amused. His sympathy for the dispossessed blacks infuriated the eighty settlers left in town, and someone threatened to horsewhip him.

Cornelius pulled down his tent, repacked his little press and with the last of his money took passage on a ketch returning to Sydney.

"That's your grandfather, muttonchopped splendid, the cheeky devil," Jessica Olive had pointed out to four-year-old Connie, who had been nagging for a face, the photograph album dog-eared, pictures spotting with mould from too many Wets, grandfather caught up with after all those years in a magazine clipping of Sydney bohemians her brother had cut out and posted to Jessica Olive when it was too late for forgiveness.

Found! Sprung! The only nonstayer, sprung! Aging in Darlinghurst Road, some one-roomer lodging boxed round him, chilling in his underwear, the family all loyally hoped, when the plane trees dropped their leaves down the length of Hyde Park.

Look at him.

Take a good look. A nice face, really, and always a gentleman, George said Jessica Olive said, even when drunk, the Canadian accent thickening but still lilting. It was those tosspot evenings in Bowen started it, father explained to a glue-eyed Connie, those all-night sprees with drunken packers back from an overland stint. Or

18

farewelling those about to go, dragging sticks and bottles across ripple-iron walls to cheer themselves up while they belted out choruses of "Blow the Man Down."

What a training ground!

Father could still remember dapper Cornelius rolling home along Charlotte Street from the Cradler's Joy, shantying away in a pleasant tenor between the tent rows of Charco Harbour to tuck a little tune, as he put it, into Jessica Olive's next pregnancy.

Connie flicks over portraits in her half-daze between struggles to rise from the bed, mumbling warnings about Reever and Will. There was something to do with Will. She was more afraid for him than for Reever. She couldn't sort sense from it. Concerned neighbours keep pressing her back with stifling kindness into memories of that ancestor to whom she had never spoken.

He's a sepia stranger there, with those other strangers; but this photo, she understood, was taken just after the wedding, grandmother convent-fresh under his arm with five hundred and seventy-two weekly communions behind her and precious little else to come.

He'd charm the halo off a saint, Jessica Olive had insisted to Connie's small-girl dubious face as she dabbed at those muttonchops with a small damp finger. *Or at least make the saint wear it tipped sideways.*

How? the small girl had asked.

Oh easily, with his songs and his poems and his gallantries. When he sang "Macushla," Connie dear, I used to become quite faint. And Nana would laugh for the girl she once was.

These words were Cornelius Laffey's last testimony from the one who had known his early manhood best, for he died soon after the clipping unmasked him, and two thousand miles away Jessica Olive, perhaps missing the spleen that had sustained her, followed not long after, as she reached for the breakfast jam.

"I've come all the way from Canada, halfway across the world to find you," he'd flattered Jessica Olive, blushing in a Sydney tearoom, her brother watchdogging them both through a screen of manly laughter. It wasn't true, grandmother admitted. He'd come to make his fortune. But he had a way—a poet's way—of inflating the moment. These inflationary processes—summertime lunches in the Botanic

Gardens, strolling the windy beachfront at Bondi, horse-and-buggy picnics at Lane Cove—quickly became courting ploys.

There were single flowers with the emotive force of bombs. There were poems. "A little trifle, my dear, a little trifle for a nontrifling occasion." He turned a neat quatrain. "He's deep," Jessica Olive's mother had warned. But he wasn't. Jessica Olive was captivated by shallows. Her father, a barrister with a silken Trinity College, Dublin accent beautifully preserved for the colonies, toasted his bum before the fire in their Balmain house and swayed, hands in pockets, to and fro on feet cemented in reality, so used to being paid for opinions he had become socially reluctant.

"Newspapers!" Jessica Olive's mother nagged over toast, over morning tea, over lunch, over . . . "A journalist! My dear child, it's too . . ."

Nevertheless, there she was, dear Nana, in a spring cloud of white silk, orange-blossomed, virginal, nestled under the big Canadian shoulder like a white mouse. They moved to Birchgrove when it was fashionable and the Harbour was blue.

Instantly pregnant, poor Nana, with Aunt Nadine. About whom the family rarely spoke. Connie moans enviously in her half sleep, recalling a photograph somewhere of a ringleted puss with one of those heart-stopping mouths so fashionably drooping. Nadine at twelve, two years before she ran away.

"Where to?"

A compression of lips.

"But Nana, couldn't the police . . . ?"

"We don't talk about it, Connie. Not to little girls. Not about things like that." Rocking fifty years of resentment.

"But Nana!"

And after Nadine, George. Cornelius smiling, tipsy, down the late-night length of the four-poster, threatening with its rattles.

Instead of emotional stasis, the birth of a son stimulated wanderlust, a dream of frontiers. His newspaper was full of longwinded concern about the empty spaces to the north, a region ripe with possibility. There were arguments in the house in Birchgrove, and a Pontius Pilate washing of the hands at Balmain. For three years Cornelius grumbled and agitated and finally managed to persuade

Jessica Olive, her will weakened by two miscarriages, that city life was bad for them all.

Victorious, he swept his family onto the steamship *Florence Irving* and watched them vomit their seasickness all the way from Sydney to Cooktown.

"It's a state of mind," he said.

"What is?"

"Vomiting." And intoned, gloriously Irish, "Oh this wine-dark sea." There were lots of Byron, Nana recalled at those moments she was inclined to look on the funny side of things, and snatches of brogue-ridden Ovid.

"They need newsmen up there," he had reasoned. "Correspondents. Journals. Exciting times, my dear, and we must be there to catch the excitement." He thought about Bowen and put the thought quickly aside. "And there are other things. We'll make our fortunes." And he waltzed her skittishly between their reeking bunks.

"It's the gold," Nana had accused. "Nothing but that. Haring off, Cornelius, like any mad boy. And with two young children. What about their schooling?"

"Now there's a touch of nagging, my dear," Cornelius cautioned. "This trip alone is a liberal education. And you're wrong about the gold. Can you see me digging, *mavourneen*, can you? No, we'll find our own gold through honest enterprise."

Oh God, Nana had complained to her four-year-old listener, God in heaven he was such a dreamer.

It had taken them half an hour to fight their way off the *Florence Irving*, for it was being stormed by longfaced diggers busting to escape failed El Dorados. Clutching the children, jostled by shoving and tussling bodies in a heat beyond belief, Jessica Olive hoped briefly and disloyally that they might be swept back on board and this nonsense for better, for definitely worse, would be over. The township she had glimpsed from the rocking deck was nothing more than a canvas slum of hundreds of tents packed along the waterfront. Then Cornelius, overhearty with adventure, shouldered George, and there was no escape as he thrust his dressy stomach down the gangplank. For ten placatory yards a seaman trundled their cabin bags along the road and then forgot about them. In all this broiler heat boats jostled for anchorage space, men elbowed and punched through a racket of voices, while at one side of the mud road oppressed coolies were being counted out like parcels by Chinese merchants.

"What colour!" Cornelius whispered admiringly. "What atmosphere!"

Jessica Olive dabbed at sweat.

Three thousand diggers were camping in Charlotte Street and along the temporary back roads from the river, and there was Jessica Olive picking her way delicately through slush past makeshift pubs, brothels, stores and rachitic shanties after the worst season of the year. The children whined and were bitten by flies but Cornelius was inclined to swagger under the jaunty skies, furtively easing the sweat-scarf about his throat, panama tilted rakishly back from his curls. The sky was no bluer than his eyes.

For a month they lodged at the Empire Hotel, and while Jessica Olive was obsessed with George's yowls and Nadine's whimpers, Cornelius was busily investigating the possibilities of yet another broadsheet in a township that already had two newspapers made for riots and politics, for workers, whingers and bludgers, for purple-prosed dogmatism and morsels of social snobbery for the better-class people who were already settling the slopes of Grassy Hill. In the end Cornelius charmed his way onto the *Charco Herald* with permission to act as a stringer for a Sydney daily.

He cut a dash. He drank at French Charley's. There were more than a score of grog shops in town and in his tireless pursuit of copy he drank at them too. Jessica Olive brooded. He interviewed returned packers from Maytown, ships' masters, survivors from the Palmer Road and skirmishes at the Gates. He had a way of fixing his subjects with a richly interested eye, and discovered that generosity with liquor loosened their tongues and liberated fables. Jessica Olive closed her lips tight.

His silk hat had been abandoned in Sydney. He had three white linen suits, a panama, and a pith helmet. ("There won't be lions!" Jessica Olive suggested. "Always do it properly, my dear," Cornelius said, ignoring smiles.) He wrote mood pieces for the *Queenslander* in velvet prose. Under the skulls of Coongoon and Janell-ganell, whose rocky scarps cast no shadow on his day, he throve as a personality in a

town packed with characters. There were parties of unspeakable refinement at the wealthier settlers' homes, where he strutted doggily
while Jessica Olive winced. "Do sing for us, Mr. Laffey," heatworn
hostesses pleaded, unknowingly twinning the requests of the frolick-
ing girls of Charlotte Street, who loved him as much for his good
looks, his fruitily slanted vowels, his jokes, and his fatuous habit of
quotation as for his stupidity with money. "Give us a song, love. Go
on, there's a dear."

"'Trip no farther, pretty sweetings, Journeys end in lovers' meetings,'" his rum-moist lips might misquote in some waterfront shanty
towards the close of day.

The girls marvelled under sweat-lank curls.

"Just a trifle, my dears, a little trifle. 'In delay there lies no plenty,
Then come kiss me, sweet and twenty . . .'"

"Oh Mr. Laffey! Naughty!"

"And you're naughty gals," he would cry, delighted. "But terrible
pretty, God love us!"

It was impossible for Jessica Olive not to discover.

Yet unremittingly he courted her too. That failed smile was a
challenge. "'What is love? 'tis not hereafter,'" he would offer her
stubborn accusing mouth. And when that failed he would subside into
his most succulent brogue. "'O western wind, when wilt thou blow,
That the small rain down can rain? Christ, that my love were in my
arms . . .'" The words might have had him weeping as well, but—

"Go back," Jessica Olive would suggest angrily from the far side of
the bed. "Go back to Charlotte Street."

She persevered through another sopping summer while Nadine and
George lugged schoolbags to the new two-room building in the middle
of town. She learnt to snub the smiling ladies of Charlotte Street when
they waited together at trading store counters. She was waiting for
something *other*—she was not sure what.

Poor Cornelius. He was never actually unfaithful to Jessica Olive,
not in the physical sense. He was simply a verbal philanderer whom
the prostitutes fleeced as if they felt lending an ear to be of as much
value as any other part of their bodies. Looking for redemption from
drudgery, poverty, family responsibility, he'd try any diversion, any.
Under the prod of his own bonhomie!

"Try something else," Jessica Olive kept nagging. "Journalism isn't the only thing."

"I'm not a digger, dear," Cornelius insisted over the children's nodding heads. "Not."

They were living by now in a box of a house on one of the back streets of Charco. In temperatures of ninety degrees, the rudimentary qualities of wood stove and water-drip canvas safe absorbed much of Jessica Olive's good nature. Her prettiness was being startled into something else.

"You might be," she said ambiguously.

In her restless bed two hundred miles south of Jessica Olive's purgatory Connie is coughing out her amused despair. She calls to sounds in the kitchen, calls her anxiety about Reever, about Will. Or thinks she is calling.

No one comes. The afternoon emptiness of the house intensifies and settles behind the pad of feet running down the back steps. Her body is crippled with memory.

That's the packer's dray outside the Sovereign Hotel, just on the point of leaving for the Palmer.

Overdressed as usual, an adventuring dandy, Cornelius is leaning against the dray. His wife stands under the awning of the Sovereign, a parasol up against morning sun slashing in across the river. Nadine sulks somewhere at the back of the dray, trying to catch the eye, while pretending not, of Toddy the packer, a flashy chap in snowy mole-skins, a scarlet silk shirt and a wide-brimmed Yankee. She's obsessed by the Colt revolver at his hip. If she looked more closely, she could catch the glint of a Snider rifle packed carelessly behind the driving seat. Her brother is so excited his nose has blocked with snuffles. One of the men on the upstairs veranda of the Sovereign waves and tosses him a little packet.

"What's that, George?" Cornelius asks, backing off from the dray where he has rammed Jessica Olive's all-purpose bag.

George unwraps the newspaper. Inside there's a lump of washed, gold-flecked quartz.

"That's what you're after, mate!" the man on the veranda yells down.

Cornelius touches his panama in a gallant way. "My gold's in my pen, sir."

Jessica Olive quails, lowering her parasol till it cuts off her face from her husband's.

"He's so stupid," Nadine mutters sulkily, coming up beside. "Always showing off. Why show off here in this awful town?"

"It helps, I suppose," her mother says, unexpectedly benign. Perhaps it is the thought of leaving.

Poor Cornelius. Poor Jessica Olive.

Maytown will be worse.

Terrified, of course, when night came on, and by day wriggling bored on his mother's lap with the flies stinging, the sun clouting, the dray lurching and bumping vilely.

It was manly scenery.

His sister, Nadine, sat alert on two pillows watching the scrub lumber past as the horses staggered and slipped on the slate of the track, the packer yelling at them, while Jessica Olive, her mouth drooping open to receive the dews of profanity, undid her own sweating neckline and, despite the grey line of diggers traipsing alongside, their packs, rifles and shouldered picks all ashy with winter dust, hitched her skirts up to the knees for a little air in a world full of air that seemed airless. That, and a hachured vision of spears driving into their grazing horses that first early evening and the whole mob of them, the males in the party, don't count Cornelius, careering out with their Sniders, blazing away at everything black that moved, men, women, children, seeking, pursuing, then shooting as if the whole hillside was a target, leaving them there.

Nadine sobbed and sobbed. George hid his face in his mother's unwashed blouse and heard her ask bitterly, "Was that necessary?"

"They're not human, missus," one of the diggers explained patiently. He was flushed with killing and excited. "Can't talk with them. They got to learn to leave our horses be, missus. These horses could mean the difference between life and death, eh?"

Cornelius had no rifle. He was engaged by his wife's spirit—and her hitched-up skirt.

"They looked human," she persisted. "They had all your features."

"They can't use our horses for tucker," the digger repeated stubbornly. "They got to learn."

"Perhaps," George's mother argued as Cornelius turned away his smile at her tenacity onto the middle spaces of the spiny landscape, "you miners have taken away theirs. Taken their hunting grounds. They have to eat too."

George was listening with his heart as well as his ears, still seeing the moaning bodies of two old men back at the fringe of the killing grounds. Here the rocks strode uphill right along the scarp, jutting out over the scribble of a track that diggers going, diggers returning, kept tramping and flattening, rocks striding and edging threateningly towards each other, creating impossible follies for the dray to negotiate. It laboured edgewise round the angled curves through these gateways of stone, its lumbering crawl inviting ambush.

Two days of this. More skirmishes with the Sniders cracking. A party of speared Chinese coolies lying beside the road, bloating generously in ripening sun. Two scarecrow diggers flapping their despairing rags on the way back to Charco, in boots swaddled with canvas strips. And all the time father growing grimmer behind his muttonchops, his grimy linen suit, the jolly songs dead on his lips, insisting to Jessica Olive's resentful protests that it was too late to turn back now, too late, under the tilting scrub and the impassive boulders. Too late.

And then the township when they got there was again nothing more than a tent village perched on giddy slopes above the river. The grog shanties were duplicated. A bark lockup guaranteed nothing. Every sand-pit in the river was crowded with men who scooped and shook fanatic cradles.

"The solid side of nothing," George would later describe it to Connie and Will.

They would ask what that meant, safe in fresh sheets, the bedside lamp still burning.

"You'll know when you find it," he would say. "You'll always know."

Cornelius established his family in some sort of bush-pole lean-to and spent day after day wandering along the river diggings, talking with those who could bear to waste a moment, drinking in the shanties at night with the ones who'd struck it lucky. Nana coped. In the early dawn light Cornelius wrote and wrote. Nana still coped.

"I'm a man of the people, my dear," fatuous Cornelius used to say, settling back on his packing-case chair and rereading what he had just written with obvious deight.

"Was he then?" George would ask Jessica Olive forty years on. "Was he really a man of the people or simply a good-time Charlie?"

"I can't remember much," Jessica Olive would lie. "I'm too old."

George remembered so much he ached with it.

While Nadine hung uselessly about the shack or wandered Maytown's one street turning a gauzy glance at diggers, George became his father's daytime shadow, and, when the *Charco Herald* asked Cornelius to report on a new field creating rush hysteria to the east, pestered to go.

"Well," Cornelius temporised. "Perhaps."

Finally he yielded to his son's persistence bluffing out Jessica Olive's protests. "The adventure of it, Jess. Think of that now. The sheer adventure of it. Oh, the lad's got more than a dash of the Irish, my dear. This will be a liberal education."

"You said that before," his wife said.

"Did I now? And haven't I been right? You can put away those reading primers for a few days. This will make a man of him, eh George?"

"Your sort?" Jessica Olive whispered into Nadine's ringlets as they waved farewell to the pack team.

"I'm a liberal before my time," Cornelius confided to George as they bounced uncomfortably on the dray. "I'll give that young pup editor in Charco such a report, my boy. I'll open the eyes of everyone down south to all the horrors of the promised land. I'll give them 'unbiased,' 'unemotional,' 'nonprovocative.'"

George fumbled in his pocket with the little lump of quartz the miner had given him. He took it everywhere.

Midmorning of the second day, the packer pulled up to boil the billy. While Cornelius sat jotting notes in his diary, George wandered off from the track for kindling and, stopping to relieve himself behind a hump of boulders, found there a bonefield where the half-rotted bodies of a dozen black men lay in a fly-swarming putrescence. Above his head a hand stuck up from a crevice in the rocks, bits of drying skin flapping from the outthrust fingers. Stalking plump birds screeched into a high circle and George wet his pants in his bubbling terror as he fled back down the hillside, gobbling with incoherence and pointing, pointing.

The packer went on stirring the billy with a twig of green eucalypt while Cornelius went to inspect for himself. George vomited beside the track.

"That, George," Cornelius said in a kind of footnote on his return, his face pulled awry with discovery, "is the repository of the by-products of our Christian greed."

George was only eight. He kept retching into the grass.

"They were men," Cornelius went on, "with prior rights. Here, wipe your face on this."

The stench seemed to have followed them.

"For every white man killed, we kill a score of blacks, my boy. That's the government-approved ratio. There's an imbalance of justice for you."

"Drink your tea, mate," the packer ordered, thrusting a mug at Cornelius, "and we'll be making a move, eh? You can smell the damn stink down here."

As they neared another parody of a township, George whispered to his father, "Are blacks worth less?" There was nothing left to vomit but questions.

"One would think so," Cornelius replied. Momentarily he enjoyed the angry twist to the packer's mouth. "We are trained to believe so. I hope you won't."

They stayed a week in Byerstown, trapped in the turmoil of new arrivals pouring in from the Palmer. It was the most liberal of educations. Trotting behind his father, who moved through mobs of drunks and brawlers with journalistic detachment, George witnessed the bloodiest of fistfights and a lynching. At night he was kept awake by the screams of beaten women. There seemed to be no police. And through it all he also kept seeing the half-rotted bodies of the blacks and that pleading decayed hand, whose fingers formed a white bone barrier behind which protective grille these other horrors were mini-mised.

Returning to Maytown on the packer's dray, George covered his eyes as they passed the fearful place until his own fingers became in his mind those others. The packer whistled cheerfully throughout a shuddering journey during which the small boy cowered from nightmare amid the sullen daytime scrub and coiled close to his father at night, shivering himself into sleep.

In his journal Cornelius wrote steadily a vile censure of the mores of the diggings, a grand vilification of roguery, sharp practice, brutishness and greed. Watching his son quiver as he slept, he added a further denunciation that he knew would undo him. "It's time for it," he told himself.

He was convinced of sincerity and full of guilt now about his son.

"We have invented a new word for murder up here," Cornelius added to his report for the *Charco Herald*, "dispersal. This gentle euphemism is applied to the description of appalling acts of carnage directed against the indigenous people, acts which have taken place almost monthly since the diggers began moving in their seemingly endless lines out of Charco harbour and inland across the Normanby through the forbidding granite escarpments of the Conglomerate to the gold fields of the Palmer.

"Last week I accompanied a packer to Byerstown, the latest hope-raiser in these parts, and obtained at first hand some sort of insight into the tensions and pressures which could be, in certain ways, responsible for what can only be described as an undeclared state of war between blacks and whites. A Mr. William Webb with whom I have spoken at some length in Charco said that he himself had observed needless and foolish acts of provocation and aggression on the part of the diggers, and even the quasi-official road-blazing party to Edwardstown of which he was a member had indulged in unprovoked killing of natives at the Normanby River valley.

"This callousness, which seems to be a newly developing and disturbing national characteristic, is also stupidity that can only aggravate a delicate situation.

"No attempt is made to understand the feelings or even the natural rights of the indigenous peoples along these rivers. Their fishing grounds have been disturbed. Their hunting areas are invaded. All along the Palmer and the subsidiary creeks they have been pushed off

29

by an army of diggers cradling for gold. When one considers that many of the white inhabitants of this country were transported for life for indulging in the very actions to which these native unfortunates object, one might wonder that so little sensitivity and so little attempt at understanding are brought to the relationship. Who is to say that my lord's deer parks and salmon streams are more important to him than the fishing grounds and plains of the Merkin tribesmen are to them? Tribesmen who, I might venture to say, have been in possession of their estates far longer than the landed gentry of England have of theirs. Only a few decades ago, poaching in Britain meant transportation or even hanging. Here, poaching is approved by the government, and murdering the owners of the local 'grouse,' blinked at."

Cornelius reread what he had just written and found his heart pumping a little faster. Could he survive? *Go down gloriously*, his inner man urged.

"The reason?" he wrote on. "Dear reader, the locals happen to be black. Our Christian goodwill shrivels when confronted by a skin that is any shade but white.

"The men on the diggings use as excuse for their actions a variety of arguments: The natives spear the horses; they're treacherous animals who attack by stealth. (Who indeed would not attempt to defend his food source?) Yet the punitive reprisals against these poor wretches who are, in fact, merely defending their property with the same zeal with which the landed gentry of Britain defended their estates against horse-stealers and poachers, the sort of zealotry we call patriotism and whose name we invoke to impress armies, are ruthlessly savage.

"For every digger speared or killed along the mudsoaked track to the Palmer, there would be ten or more natives butchered. Many of the butchered are women and children. Blacks are now being shot on sight as if they were some pernicious vermin, and the outraged righteousness of one of our sub-inspectors of police has given sanction to the indiscriminate slaughter of these dispossessed people.

"The spear cannot argue with the Snider."

"You shouldn't send this," Jessica Olive commented when she had read it. "But I hope you will."

Cornelius came down with an attack of the "skates" after he consigned his article to the mailman. His irrevocable step hauled him by the guts.

"It's not that," Jessica Olive said. "It's the shanties. God knows what you pick up."

"It's conscience," Cornelius replied between spasms.

One of the doctors on the field, a handsome dog with a lot of bully authority, examined and prodded.

"It's the water," he said. "Take a teaspoon of this three times a day."

The doctor's deepset eyes almost vanished. His sportsman physique was daunting, as well as his reputation of beating up defaulting patients. In his tent hospital on the south bank of the river, he both nursed and cooked for his patients at an exorbitant weekly rate. Failure to pay brought them back to his hospital with clobbered skulls.

Cornelius produced his money purse instantly and was still impudent enough to request a few comments for the *Charco Herald*.

"I'm glad you asked that," the doctor replied making use of a phrase that became the foundation of a successful political career a few years away when he tired of treating fevers and patching up spear wounds and brawl-cracked limbs.

"I must ask," Cornelius pursued misguidedly, "do you treat blacks or Chinese?"

"Well, that was a foolish question," Jessica Olive commented, watching the doctor's unspeaking back.

"I'm getting tired of tact. And charm, you'll be glad to hear." Cornelius lay back and played invalid to the full. "Tired."

The editor of the *Charco Herald* rejected Cornelius's article.

Then he sacked him.

The *Queenslander* rejected it as well.

So did the southern papers.

They went back to Charco to their old house and Cornelius shot through with an irresponsible sense of bridges burnt, sang jauntily about the place.

"As I expected, my dear. As I expected. What a what a what a country! One tiny piece of home truth and the souls of our colonial founding fathers are all a-ruffle."

Jessica Olive wanted to know if perhaps they could return to Sydney.

"My dear!" Cornelius reprimanded, and he reprimanded in his most thrilling brogue, to whose sonorities his wife had not yet built up an immunity.

"There's no future here. Not for you. Not for the children." She didn't like to mention herself.

"Admit failure!" Cornelius protested. "I'm a man of stratagems." He tapped a thoughtful pipe. "Journalism isn't the only means of survival, though I admit it's the only thing I know. You know, Jess, darlin', what I always believed I admired about British institutions and the much vaunted notion of British justice was that these things gave us the right to talk freely. At least, I thought, one could always *talk*. We mightn't get justice under the bloody system and it certainly wouldn't be, isn't, democratic. But at least we could talk about it. Now we can't even do that."

"I don't care about democracy at the moment," Jessica Olive said. "I'm concerned about George."

For weeks now the boy had pestered with obsessive interest about the few old Kokobothan tribesmen who, yielding to circumstances, hung round the limits of Charco hoping for greasy blankets. For weeks he kept examining his hands, holding sunburnt digits to his face and peering at and through. They were so like and unlike the pronged rakes he had seen sticking out from the rocks on the way to Byerstown.

"My bones," he had announced one morning at breakfast, "are the same colour as Kokoba's."

Kokoba was a derelict black so debilitated by age and white settlement that he was more or less accepted, loitering dismally on the outer edges of the township with his two old wives, indifferent alike to the outraged roars of drinkers, the playful pistol shots at his feet, the fastidious withdrawal squeaks of Grassy Hill wives. Stubbornly he kept making little campfires on the riverbank until the police, tired of hustling him on, shoved him bound on a packer's dray and dumped him and his wives beyond Battle Camp.

Nadine had argued, "They have black bones, stupid. Black."

"They're not. I've seen them." George's eyes began to widen. "They're white."

"Where," Jessica Olive demanded, coming in from the kitchen lean-to, "have you seen them?"

George told.

The enormousness of the row that night between his parents staggered him. Huddled under the sheet he listened to hisses. There were sobs. Then cries of anger. Jessica Olive, who never raised her voice, began to shriek terrible resentment at Cornelius's late-home head.

"Seeing those things," George heard. "You should never have taken him."

His father's voice, flavoured with rum, became lilting and placatory, arguing that it was something that had to be seen, should be talked about. Why bring the boy up, George heard, believing the world was full of love when it was patent that everywhere was monstrosity?

George stumbled out in his nightwear and stood in the doorway of the tiny parlour. Softened by lamplight it looked almost tender: the photographs of Mama's father, the old white house at Balmain, a picture of the Virgin and the two good easy chairs only visitors sat in. His father was leaning on one of them now, his fair skin red not only with sun-scald but also a glutting of irritation. Mama's pretty face was jutting. She looked different. He could see the drive of her jaw.

His body shook with their rage, the union of hostility and love. Steered by an unexplainable impulse he crept out to the kitchen lean-to in the dark and, rubbing his hands over the now-cold stove, smeared his face all over with stove-black. That and tears. He daubed his palms. Then he crept back along the tiny passage to the parlour, heart kicking at what he was doing, and walked right in through the terrible wall made by their recriminations. Just stood there, black-streaked and shaking.

They turned and looked at him and George held out his hands, kept his eyes steady and looked back.

Connie's eyes steady, too, on the four o'clock curtain flap as the nor'easter hits her house.

Wrenched from Charco to now, she tries one foot and then the other and finds the floor firm, the fragility of light unmoving on her face, on walls, bed, floor.

Offstage there are kitchen comfort-sounds again and her son's voice returned to earth.

Sixty-three, she accuses herself, as if age is its own folly, and still witless.

GETTING
TO KNOW
THEM

This hill, scrub against blue, belongs Doldawarra and Kokowarra people.

They hear from the Kokobothan tribe on the coast near Charco harbour that strange men keep moving along the shores, building queer wurlies, killing kangaroo, taking fish, frightening birds.

Nothing stops them. They have great animals with them, big four-legged creatures with curved hairy necks. Not dog. Not possum. Not wallaby. Some of the Kokowarra men spear one to examine it and also for food and the white men run at them with sticks that shout.

This hill, grey scrub against blue, the long grasses dry before the big rains, is where Bidiggi Tandawarra crouches with his father and uncles and brothers and all the men of the tribe. The Merkins, farther upstream, had been shunted off their fishing grounds by white men making a wild magic along the sandy beaches of the river. These men held shallow dishes that they filled with water and sand and as if they were making ritual in totem dance shook and swilled and emptied again. The men of the tribe had rested their spears against trees to show they came in peace but a white man on one of the big four-legged animals had led a charge into them where they stood defence-less, arms dangling, hands empty.

This morning in the predawn dark, his eyes accustomed to darkness, Bidiggi could see the white men's own totemic circle of saddles and packs stacked to make a *bora* ring. Behind that little wall he knew, and his father and uncles and brothers knew, the white man lay in wait.

There was not a whisper in the lank grass as his own tribe lay waiting for the elder to give the signal. Behind, before, and around him, the smell of family, the smell of the tall men with the copper skin.

The softest of clickclicks. The signal.

Suddenly Bidiggi was screeching with the others, parrot cries bucking in his throat as he raced forward with his spear. Pounding and pounding over late summer grass. The darkness hanging ragged. Then the shouting sticks began to bark and fire pocked swirling air in front of him. As he ran he glimpsed his brother, running beside him, drop suddenly. Bidiggi hesitated. There were other dark shapes on the dark grass. He bent over his brother, puzzled, and shook him.

Why wouldn't he move?

There was no spear.

He shook him again, urgently. Still his brother wouldn't move.

Then Bidiggi seized his brother's arms and hauled him up, trying to make him stand, trying to set his feet in motion. His brother crumpled like a broken tree.

Bidiggi's mind whimpered. No spear. No death. He tried again while the sticks shouted all round him and his brother, still warm, dropped forward and fell flat on the ground. Once more he dragged him upright and, edging to the front of him, pushing and propping, saw the hole gaping in his brother's chest. *Burra*, he breathed. *Burra*. He tore up handfuls of grass and wadded it into the bleeding cavity, pushing and packing, his fingers dripping. "Walk!" he kept pleading and ordering in the language, "Walk, brother. Fight!"

He took his hands away from the cooling shoulders and his brother fell forward.

Terrified of this magic and the unending shouting of the sticks, he could see as the dark thinned that more and more of his tribe had fallen. He slid down into the grass and slithered back to the narrow gully from which they had all crept. He shook with fear and the grass around him shook too. He had seen his father fall, his brother and three of his uncles.

The remnants of the tribe were in flight. The men reached the little bank where he crouched, and he could feel the wind of their passing as they sped towards the trees, leaping the creek like wallaby, running and running while the big animals with four legs thudded after them. Bidiggi broke into a run too, dodging the horses, putting boulders and trees at his back, heading to where the lagoon's red disc would be glimmering in dawn light. The world was a madness of shouts and the drumming of the animals, the screams of the running men.

He found those who remained desolate in the scrub north of the lagoon. Two old men who had been left behind, and their wives. The other women had been shot as they fled. The old women wailed and were silenced. The sun came through and warmed their despair, making it hard to believe in death without cause. Bidiggi believed he carried the stench of blood with him and squatted apart, knowing the magic was too great.

Bidiggi was only twelve, and although he didn't measure by white time but by black, he knew he was a man. There had been the ceremony. His father was dead. His brother. His uncles. He moved even farther away from the group and sat by himself on the sandy lip of a creek that ran back to the lagoon. His head filled with pictures of the men on the big animals beating the tribe like wild pigs along the reedy rim of the water where they fished and swam. The pictures were blotted with blood and he could still hear the men screaming back when the shouting sticks spoke to them and see the running women and children trampled into the morning grass. He had dived into the lagoon and swum under water to the far bank, hiding in the water grass until there were no more shouting sticks and screaming.

Snivelling. Snotty-nosed and weeping in the scrub. He curled up in the shelter of a dense stand of paper-bark and fell asleep.

When he woke in the afternoon, he found the old men and women gone.

He began following the creek back to the lagoon but before he might reach the horror of its banks, he turned where the creek forked and sent one arm out to the river. Ideas were half-formed. His feet seemed to have their own volition. The white men had come this way and he believed if he found their source, he could bring the shouting sticks back with him.

All that night, keeping well clear of the track blazed by the intruders, he slipped, shadow into shadow, down through the heavy dark towards Charco Harbour. There'd been tribal songs and stories of white men who came from the water in a bird ship so long ago it was almost part of the Dreaming. And they had camped by the blue water of Charco with their barking sticks and had hunted kangaroo and trapped fish and then they had sailed away. There'd been other whites, strange lonely starvers found wandering on beaches where the sea had flung them like shells. There was a woman, he'd heard, and a man who had lived with the tribes so long, he became part of them.

Closer and closer he came to the new camp of the white men, walking all night, softer than shadow, and seeing now and again the flicker of their campfires to the west of him along the track. It was nearly dawn when he found himself on the upper reaches of the river before it swung out into the sea near Charco. His spear was still unused against the white men. He went down to a swampy place near the bank where trees made a dense cover and here he speared a small fish. Chewing and sucking at the sweet meat, he fell asleep.

Living alone made him quicker, sharper, more resourceful.

A few miles to the south of Charco township was an isolated beach where the scrub ran practically to the water's edge. For months he made this area his own, living well off fish and small bush rats and the berries and roots he had seen the women gather. Every few days he shifted to a new sleeping place, but the beach remained undisturbed by white men and he wandered the forest country and the shoreline freely.

He was small for his age. The white men would have thought him a child. By living so close to their township he quickly learned the signs of movement, the habits of settlers. At night sometimes he crept along the tracks leading to the scattered back houses and, lying in the grass outside tent or shack, heard the gabble of their tongue, saw their faces lit by lamps, watched them eat strange food. Once, after the family had gone to sleep, he crept through the back of a hut and stole a knife.

Security made him bolder. He knew there were other black men who were tolerated on the outskirts of the township. They were old and by the settlers' reckoning harmless. He longed to speak with someone. It was as if all the unspoken words clogged his tongue. One morning, just before daybreak, he came across the campsite of an old black man and his woman, and shook them awake to test them with words.

They understood much of what he said. What they told him made him think they had betrayed his people.

"They give you these things?" he wondered, pointing to the rag the old woman had tied around her waist, the bit of blanket the old man squatted on.

They nodded yes. The old man pulled a shiny piece of wood out from under his blanket. It was curved and had a hole at one end. "See!" he said. Then he took some crumbs of brown leaf that were screwed up in a piece of skin and pushed them into the hole. Then he took a stick from the dying fire and held the hot end to the hole in the wood, sucking in deeply.

Bidiggi knew the smell. It drifted all over Charco.

"Tobacco," he told the old man.

"Tocacco," the old man agreed.

"Here," the old man said, handing the piece of wood to the boy, "try."

"I'll get you more, old man," the boy said handing the wood back. "More."

He started coming closer to the township early in the morning or late in the afternoon. He allowed himself to be seen, spearless and harmless. At first men shouted at him and obligingly he ran. All they saw was a black child running like a rabbit. Someone took a shot at him and he looked back from the safety of the trees to see a second man push the gun aside.

He knew the word "gun" now, the name of the talking sticks.

He had forgotten he wanted one.

Late in the day a week after that, he came in from his beach and found Charco so silent he thought the town might be deserted. It was Sunday, the heat pressing down in clamps, the townsfolk maintaining the Sabbath in somnolence.

Near the first house he came to he saw a white boy, smaller than he was, fiddling with a knife and a piece of wood. The white boy looked up and saw him, then put his knife down and stared. Bidiggi allowed his nakedness to be caught by leaf-shadow and absorbed. From behind the stringy-bark he kept watching. Then a woman came out and emptied a bucket of water on the ground and from the shack came the sound of a man's voice singing. The wild chanting, unlike the tribal songs he was used to, frightened him. He moved farther back into the scrub and saw the singer come out to stand beside the small boy. The singing had stopped and the man was lifting a polished piece of wood to his own mouth while the small boy kept pointing towards the trees.

Bidiggi turned and ran.

He was drawn back to the shack as if there were magic pulling.

The big man waved to him and beckoned with his hand and said something to the small boy who came running towards the house from the water tank. The small boy turned as well. His hand waved like the man's.

For a week, ritual. The appearance, the discovery, the standing still, the wave. Bidiggi flapped his own hand as they did and saw delighted smiles crease their faces. Then one mid-Sunday afternoon with Charco snoozing, Bidiggi came closer to the shack than he had ever dared. He held a fish he had caught that still jerked silver in his fingers. The white boy was out by the water tank again, filling a bucket. Bidiggi waited until the boy put the bucket down and then took a step towards him. He held the fish up so that it showed and shone.

Slowly the white boy moved away from the shadow of the tank, moved one cautious foot after another, across the grass. Bidiggi backed away, just as slowly.

They were within smiling distance.

"Show me," the boy said.

His words meant nothing. Perhaps the tone could span.

Bidiggi stepped backwards, holding his catch, into screens of leaf and watched the small tail give a last limp flick at sunlight. The white boy followed. Sun and leaf made moving patches across his freckled face. In another moment they would be able to touch.

A white hand came forward and pointed to the fish. Then it shifted and pointed to Bidiggi. The hand shifted and pointed to the fish again. Then back to the black boy. Bidiggi understood the question. The sound of words that came meant nothing. He waved in the direction of the river and the white boy nodded and put out a finger to touch the fish. Immediately Bidiggi pulled the fish back but the finger followed, hesitated, followed. It touched.

40

"Fish," the white boy was saying. "Fish."

There the two of them were, midafternoon, temperature eighty-nine, the town dead on its feet save for snuffling dogs and the thud of mangoes dropping. Smiling. Cautious. Both fearful. Without warning the black boy turned and ran and the other watched him go until the scrub swallowed him.

That was the start of it.

Another Sunday.

Bidiggi brought two fish, still jumping in their nest of green leaves.

The white boy bent over them, grinning.

Bidiggi pointed to the fish, pointed to the white boy and uttered a word. "Tobacco," he said, struggling with the sounds.

The white boy looked up quickly. "Tobacco!" he repeated.

Bidiggi picked up a twig and mimed puffing. "Tobacco," he said again. And he thrust the green nest at the white boy.

The white boy moved his head up and down and turned and began walking back to the shack. Bidiggi hesitated and the other turned and beckoned. He followed tentatively, nursing the fish.

The boy pushed aside the canvas flap on the back door and was gone. Bidiggi stood rubbing his feet nervously against each other in the shadow of the water tank. Then the flap swung back and the boy appeared with something in his hands. It was a piece of cloth gathered into a little bag and he came over to Bidiggi and opened it up, showing the heap of tobacco in the loop.

"Tobacco," he said.

Bidiggi picked up a small piece and sniffed. He held out the green nest of fish. The other boy smiled and gave him the cloth.

Ritual. Every seven days. He waited until the boy came back from the building where all the children went. Fish for tobacco. The white boy's father, a big man with hair growing from the sides of his face, watched the barter from behind a tweaked curtain. The woman came out and spoke but he couldn't say anything in reply. "Tobacco," he said, saying his one word of the strange tongue. "Tobacco."

Their laughter frightened him and he ran away and didn't come near the shack for a week. When he did return the white man was sitting outside under a tree and making marks on a white thing with a piece of stick. "I'm writing about you," the big man said in a rush of

41

sounds that meant nothing. "I'm writing about my son's friend. My son has discovered the first principle of travelling in foreign lands, what should be the first principle of colonisers, what *is* the first principle of being human."

The gabble terrified Bidiggi. He fled.

The man's wife came out of the shack and scolded, "There. See what you've done. You've frightened him."

From the shelter of the stringy-barks, Bidiggi heard the man singing.

But he became bolder after all this. Sometimes he found a small packet of tobacco left temptingly near the tank on an upturned bucket. Once there was a round yellow object. He didn't know what to do with it. Then the boy came out of the canvas flap with another gold ball in his hand and started eating. "Like this," the boy kept saying incomprehensibly, but peeling the skin back to show. "Like this."

Bidiggi bit into the globe and juice ran down his chin.

The big man came to watch and the woman and even the young girl. He sucked on to please them and himself and all the faces smiled and looked kind. "Orange," one of them said, pointing. The word was too difficult for his tongue. But he stored the memory of the sound. Now he had two words. More would come.

Bidiggi took the white boy to fish at a secret bend of the river. He stood with the grace of a wading bird, spear poised, before the lightning stroke of the launch. The white boy dangled a line. They inspected each other's hunting tools. They exchanged them. The white boy missed every time and Bidiggi laughed and felt proud of his skills. He could say "fish" now, as well as "tobacco," and he said the words frequently, merely to taste their sound.

This afternoon the white boy kept pointing to himself, thrusting a finger into his chest and uttering something. Bidiggi could not understand. They sat side by side on the bank of the river and struggled with language. The white boy began all over, as if he were giving a lesson the way the old men did. He pointed to the fish lying on the bank in their leaf wrapping and said the word. He pointed to the shaft in Bidiggi's hand and said "spear." Then he pointed to Bidiggi and put his finger on the black skin and looked his question. Then he went through it again. And again.

The last time the black boy stopped the hand before it poked into his chest. He pointed to himself and said, "Bidiggi."

Then the white boy pointed and said "Bidiggi" and the black boy smiled and echoed him.

Then the white boy pointed to himself. A brown hand followed his. "George," he said.

CROSS
THE WIDE
MISSOURI

Nadine at fourteen—or nearly fourteen: dark, slender, practical yet useless, hardheaded and at the same time romantically yearning. Perhaps she wasn't yearning, merely bored. She was too beautiful for her own good; certainly too beautiful for Charco. Her face held a wondering "who, me?" look that was at the same time knowing.

Jessica Olive worried about her. Nadine resented this.

She resented schooling as well. Her mother tried to supplement the inadequacies of the local provisional school with some phrases of French. "There *is* a difference, my dear," she would say, "between *je veux* and *je désire*." Nadine refused to see it. Her mother should have been warned.

At thirteen she stopped attending the slab classroom with its smells of sweat, chalk, lunch-packs and ink, and stayed home to help. She learnt to sew and hated it, to cook and avoided it. "If it *were* help," her mother would comment blandly enough, recalling her own pampered girlhood and regretting Nadine's loss.

"There is no money for boarding-school," Cornelius repeated over and over. She will have to make do."

There she is, Nadine—there's a photo somewhere—idiotically dressed for Charco in a mud-sweeper skirt and white bodice, her hair caught in a tumult of ringlets around that marvellous face: Nadine and George, and Jessica Olive behind them both while Cornelius tells them all to watch for the dicky-bird. George is grinning amiably despite unfortunate knickerbockers and a floppy tie. Jessica Olive's handsome bones appear to have shifted into the realms of grimness or despair. That pretty pout her lips used to have has tightened as if she is more afraid of what she might let out than the moist parting once took in.

44

Every week in Charco diggers came and went, came and went. The golden rivers of the backcountry were running dry.

Nadine was courted by a wild bushman, all beard and songs, "Afton Water" floating in a fine high tenor as he rode down the track from the Gates immune to, even mates with, the dreaded black tribes, his saddlebags heavy with gold dust, his head crammed with stories.

Cornelius had interviewed him for an article for the *Queenslander* and then invited him home for midday dinner where he sat in the tiny makeshift parlour drinking mug after mug of rum-laced tea and inspecting Nadine as she handed scones and blushes. Later he sauntered with Nadine and George along Charlotte Street, chaperoned by the raking direct sunlight of three o'clock. They peered in stores, the Chinese shops bursting with crockery and bolts of silk, with gimcrack toys and spices and cooking ware. The dress length he bought Nadine she managed to hide under her mattress and when at last Jessica Olive found it, he had ridden off with his voice and billies a-jingle, searching for a track to the tablelands from the south.

After he returned he was persuasive with Jessica Olive as well and became a frequent caller. He would tweak the ribbons parting Nadine's passionate hair and he would tweak them for another fortnight until his vision of her as conspicuously female stopped the tweaking altogether as he leaned his body heavily against watching doorframes or caught up with her unexpectedly at a clothesline strung between stringy wattles.

Nadine was unable to resist the knowledge in his distant eyes.

"Where?"

"Borrow my other horse."

A mile or so south of the river he persistently instructed her.

She swelled with knowledge. Her smile, her petulant full mouth kissed stupid all those weeks, her sideways eyes.

"Will you marry me?"

It was her question.

"I don't plan on it." He stretched naked beneath the trees, flexing umber skin in the checkered play of sun and leaf. "I'm too old for you."

Nadine laughed.

"Perhaps you are. But if this goes on you'll age me quickly."

45

"I'll drink to that," he said.

He was gone before she realized it, leaving her to drop salty tears that stained the secret shimmer of cherry silk; but unexpectedly returned within the month and sat for hours drinking in the front room with the only sporadically employed Cornelius. He had stories of Chinese coolies trapped by blacks at the Gates. There were fights between the various tongs. Scores of them were ambushed. He admitted he hated the Chinese.

"You helped kill them?" Nadine would ask later, trapped in his killer arms in the long grass.

"Someone killed them."

"It was you. You trapped them. You caused it."

"Be quiet now," he would plead, "and let me get on with it."

When she was certain she was pregnant, she was fatalistic about it. He had been gone two months: some said to the Gulf; some said on one of the fishing trawlers that plied out of Charco Harbour; some said overlanding to Sydney. She knew she would never see him again but she saw his image in the crumpled curly boy she bore seven months later.

Jessica Olive had long since passed beyond shock.

"Keep him, for God's sake keep him!" Father was irritable with poverty. "What's another bastard more or less in these parts? Half the town's in the flesh trade. Half the town doesn't know its own father."

"I know the father." Nadine had been ready for sex but not motherhood. The baby bored her.

"By god you do!"

"What shall we tell George?" Nadine asked uninterestedly. "Later, I mean."

"You'll think of something," her father said. "A blasé young woman like you, so stubborn about it, and so damn indifferent. Do you plan on passing it off as your mother's then?"

"No lies," Jessica Olive said firmly, crushing the baby against her. "There'll be no muddling the boy with false biology."

"I'll horsewhip that bastard when he next comes through," Cornelius said savagely. Making an effort at outraged fatherdom.

"A waste of good leather and energy." Jessica Olive smiled steadily and lovingly into the baby's face. "He won't be back."

But Cornelius found something to do.

One September morning when the baby's howling was more than he could bear, he slipped quietly from the house and boarded the *Arawatta* bound for Brisbane, leaving Jessica Olive and the children mooning over breakfast dishes, and was not heard of again for forty years.

A week after that George came roaring into his mother's room and woke her with reports of another emptied bed.

There was a fevered search along Charlotte Street, a search that brought Jessica Olive, battered by early rains, to the steaming doorstep of one of the more notorious shanties.

There were horrifying words.

The redhead ogled Jessica Olive with some amusement.

"You can look all you like, lady. She's not here."

Jessica Olive envisaged rooms turgid with tumbling and writhing bodies. The noxious ordinariness of the establishment took her by surprise and she grew pale and then red with anger, and perspiration seemed to peel her skin away from those ever-sharpening bones. Rain pellets bit into her. Her hat brim ran with water and drooped.

"She's underage, I tell you. Underage. This will be a police matter. I know she's here."

"Listen," the other woman advised, "any age is the right age if the girl's agreeable. You'd better keep that in mind."

"Not according to the law," Jessica Olive kept shouting.

"And don't threaten me, see," the redhead went on, ignoring her. "The police know all about us. They patronize us. Does that surprise you? Time you grew up, lady. But I'll tell you, seeing you're taking it so bad. All this fuss right here in the street will give my house a bad name. Yes. She was here, but she went this morning on the *Louisa*. If you want your daughter—and she's a sulky piece to want back, let me tell you—you'd better try Reeftown."

"Then she *was* here last night. What was she doing?"

"Working her passage," the redhead said with ferocious relish.

Jessica Olive fell flat in the muddy wash of Charlotte Street.

It was half-true. Nadine had thrown in her lot with a singing good-time girl who was moving to the new settlement down the coast.

"Dear God," Jessica Olive said later, half to herself, half to George

47

and the baby, "there the damned girl goes, floating upstream so I hear, two hundred miles from here on a barge with this singing whore. She'll get herself fat again on men."

In the house at the landing, Nadine inspected beneath drooping eyelashes the other young women working for Kitty.

It was a year since she had come down from Charco and then up this sprawling muddy tidal river by paddleboat to the new settlement. Kitty, who had been a café singer in the dubious inner streets of Melbourne and had come north on the froth of the rush, sang through rain, sang defiance at weather and convention. *I'll confess*, she had admitted to Nadine, *there were things I did much better than sing*.

Committed to uncertainty, Nadine had often wondered through that first year if she had made a mistake. The endless procession of hurried and unskilled lovers sickened her. The freedom was spurious. Kitty was a strict taskmaster. Occasionally she thought of her child, now a year old, and small tendrils of remorse twined and clung. She felt there was no turning back.

The two other girls were unlikely types for frontier towns. Pale-faced Lizzie, an Irish girl, had fled the rough-pawed attentions of the selector to whose property she had been assigned as housemaid. "I thought I might as well get paid for it," she said, "as be bullied into it." She'd had a little weep at the memory. "Threatened me with no meals and locked me in the horse shed. The sisters back home would never understand. Never."

"Saint Philomena," Nadine offered with a smile, "died rather than. That's what I read, anyway. Our house was full of improving literature. Didn't the nuns tell you about her? I'm sure they would rather you'd died in the horse shed, slowly starving away."

"Well, more fool her," Lizzie said. "Saint Philomena, that is."

The third girl looked over at them and laughed. She was older, twenty or so, strong-featured, golden; she spoke in an assured and educated way that challenged Kitty and overawed the others. Her box of clothes looked expensive. She radiated indifference to her surroundings, the nature of her calling, the weather, the clients themselves. She spent most of her spare time reading. "Sylvia," she had replied when Nadine asked her name, and had burst into laughter and then began singing in a surprisingly clear, sweet voice, "'Who is Sylvia, what is she, that all our swains commend her?'" and then collapsed with laughter again. "And they do commend!" she said. "Schubert, care of Shakespeare, if you're interested."

"Why are you here?" Lizzie asked on this particularly sultry day. "You seem different from us."

Sylvia marked a passage in her book with a beautifully cared-for finger and stared hard at her questioner. Then she turned her amused eyes on Nadine.

"I like it." She laughed uproariously. "It's as simple as that. I like it."

Nadine dropped her eyes and picked at a thread on her skirt.

"And what about you? Don't you enjoy your chosen profession?"

"I don't know," Nadine said. "I think so."

"Think? You only think? If you only think, my dear, you shouldn't be here."

"There's other reasons."

"What?"

"I had a baby," Nadine said softly. "Everyone was so horrible about it. People wouldn't talk. My family would, but none of my friends."

"That's an old story," Sylvia said. "Force of moral circumstance. You should have stayed and fought them. There aren't too many who can cast the first stone."

Nadine was fighting tears.

"And you've left it? You've left your baby?" Sylvia pursued. "Well! Where's the poor little beggar now?"

"With my mother."

Sylvia was burrowing into Nadine's most private imperfections. She said at last, "Your mother must be a decent sort. My parents would have flung me out, baby and all. Into the snow, if there *were* any snow. They loved a cliché."

"There's nowhere to be flung up here," the Irish girl said. "Being here is having been flung." She laughed as well, but her mouth twisted down. "That's why I'm here. Alone, thank God, alone."

"Except for the men," Sylvia said.

"Well," Lizzie said, "well. That's still alone."

"I don't see it that way at all," Sylvia replied. She put her book down and went to stare out the window across the river into the rain forest that jungled the far bank. The water was belting down the gorge and slashing at the softened banks ready to come surging over them into the township. "My father," she went on, turning to look at the others, herself calmer and even more assured, "was a man of God. Oh what a man of God he was! Not official, mind. Not a rev. He was a banker, sanctimonious on Sunday and a swine every other day of the week. Actually, he was a swine on Sunday as well, but he kept his shouting within bounds. There are a lot of men like that. A two-faced bully of a Christian always with a hand up the maid's skirts. He made my brother's life hell. He ignored mother. It was Church twice on Sunday and bible-bashing at every meal and all the time he wallowed under the attentions of the ladies of Sydney town. One morning at breakfast I told him what I thought of him. Mother was so cowed, so dribblingly afraid, she took his part. I understood. I thought I understood. So there was nothing else to do, really. Nothing else. I simply packed a bag, took some money from his desk and got on a boat. I didn't much care where it went. It wasn't difficult. Oh that's an overstatement. It was so easy."

"But the police," Nadine said. "Weren't you frightened your parents would send them looking for you?"

"You're the one who should be worried about that," the other girl said. "I'm a lot older than you and my socially-climbing parents would be too ashamed. What a disgrace! So I left them a note saying I'd found my career at last as the whore of Babylon and that there'd always be plenty of men like father to support me. Oh, I wish I could have seen his face when he read that."

Her laughter was so boisterous it brought Kitty in from the front parlour. Her pop-eyes flashed with irritation. "I'm glad someone's happy," she said. "There won't be any business tonight, girls, not with this weather. Or the rest of the week either, by the look of it. Not unless they're prepared to swim for it."

"It might clean some of them up at that," the Irish girl said. "A bracing splash in the river. God, my last two!"

"So we're fussy, are we?" Kitty was edgy with weather and lost revenue. "You can't be too fussy in this game. Business first. Always remember that. We're in business. If you're too fussy you'll lose custom. I just charge the dirty ones more. Will you just look at that river!"

It had been raining in fierce bursts for a week and fishermen who knew the coast well talked of a cyclone. Kitty was inclined to toss the warnings off. Her house had been sturdily built by a Chinese carpenter who had given her the stoutest building in Reeftown.

"Guess she needs it," the proprietor of the Beehive commented. "All that bloody bouncing!"

Now, looking out the window at the steadily rising river, whose brown-sugar waters had developed a menacing swirl, Kitty wondered if it really were time to batten down. In the midafternoon she set the girls to hammering up wooden shutters while she went out into rain squalls, fighting her way against wind gusts to the trading store, where she ordered extra supplies of groceries and liquor. By teatime the rain stopped abruptly and a swag of canvas-coloured sky canted over the isolated settlement, the massive cliffs of forest, and the log-lively waters of the river.

With that frenzied bashing of water on iron eased, the open-throated roar of the river dominated everything. The women stood on the veranda watching the mud track down to the landing vanish as the water rose, cutting the banks. Only Nadine was frightened. She kept thinking of Jessica Olive, her baby, her brother, and frequently in that long afternoon she had recalled wistfully, and with an ache in the loins, the baby's curly singing daddy. Her body, greasy with heat, kept remembering all those other bodies, and the nibblings of compunction for a step taken in a moment of petulant sulks kept suggesting return.

How could she go back? How face the condemnation of her mother's efficient forgiveness, the lip-pursing of other young women? That was the worst, she thought, that and her mother's deadly ability to turn the other cheek. In horrible moments beneath the clumsy thrusting and hammering of drunks, she envisaged her wild bushman as bordello patron, carelessly striding into her dream where, adventurous in liquor, he would find and claim her. Once she had told this mad wish to the others.

"Rubbish!" Sylvia had said. "Oh rubbish rubbish rubbish! You do talk and think a lot of stupid nonsense. Men aren't like that at all. He'd never forgive you for this, not even if he won the trophy for the oldest longest-serving brothel client in the country. Don't you know that?" Lizzie had started to giggle. "What's good for them, my girl, is certainly not good for you and the sooner you get that little fact straight in your head, the better off you'll be. No. You're stuck with this. The only thing you can do now is endure. How do you like the sound of that? Endure till you've saved some money. And then you can head off back south. Brisbane, maybe. Sydney. Somewhere far enough for there to be no talk. Does it matter?"

"But what could I do?"

"I don't know what you could do. Keep thy foot out of brothels!" She began chanting. "'Prisons are built with stones of Law, brothels with bricks of Religion.' Blake. Perhaps you could housemaid for someone like my saintly papa. But whatever you do, don't mention this or you'll be finished. As for me, my dears, I intend owning one of these places, and after I've made my haul, I shall travel and lead the life of some fabled courtesan."

"Courtesan?" wondered Nadine.

"Same thing, dear. Nicer clientele."

They all had to giggle.

"You see," Sylvia went on, "I have the true whore mentality. The genuine A-one-at-Lloyds whoreship, inherited from my daddy no doubt. I don't even mind the term. It's a job and I like my work." Her eyes challenged Nadine. "Don't wince, silly. You don't like the word, do you, pretending what you're doing is what it isn't. We offer a service. We get paid. Sex for money. That's what it is. Poor mother. She didn't get either."

Kitty had shammed disapproval. "Clean tongues, girls. Clean tongues except with those who don't want it that way."

She looked at Nadine, shrunken on the daybed, and said, "You ought to listen to what she says, you know. Make up your mind about this before it's too late."

Nadine clenched and unclenched fingers and knew it was too late already.

It could be whimsical. Should be ironic. Should be anything but what it was: four young women housed in tough cedar cut from the very gorge that towered behind them, framed in rain and disaster.

Outside, the dirt roads, those that weren't flooded, had emptied of townsfolk. The clock hands staggered from four to six and the sky colored itself a motionless sickly chrome. The heat built steadily to bursting point, more intolerable than at midday, the air seething in the shuttered house in suddenly blunted weather. The napping land-scape ticked with warning.

Yells and fist-beats on their door snapped them into life and the urgent mug of one of the township's traders bawling alarms down the hallway. "Don't light your lamps, love," he shouted at Kitty. "Every-one's moving out if they haven't gone already. There's a cyclone on the way."

They crowded him. Kitty maintained a surface calm while she wrestled with this. She had survived last March during the big Wet when the water had boiled up through the floors. She'd given shelter to several of the townsfolk who decided to sit it out and after that the year had passed with an increased zest for business despite small brawls, a stray spearing, and a drunken packer taken by a crocodile practically at her door.

The exquisite balance sheet of purchased lust! She put it down to that as the rollicking townlet expanded.

But the man was still gabbling. Boats, he was saying, a couple of boats were trying to go down river and head for safer anchorage in the bay. Others were walking back up the gorge, seeking higher ground in the foothills. Most had left already. "You lot better get crackin'," he urged. "Otherwise you'll be swimming for it."

Kitty got the girls together in the kitchen. For one sly moment she thought incandescently of herself alone, of slipping secretly from the house after the bawler and letting the others take the cyclone as it came. The two older ones were sensible enough. It was that kid, that sulky Nadine, who worried her most, who could upset any arrange-ment with a tantrum. Underage and an amateur! There had been a policeman round not long after she'd left Charco, but even she had been forced to admire the convinced insistence of Nadine's lies as she swore she wasn't herself but an older other fresh from Melbourne.

Kitty dominantly straddled the doorway. "Listen to me," she said. "It's probably a fuss about nothing. Just another scare. It's up to you. We were safe enough last March, remember? But you can make your own choice, girls. If you want to leave it's got to be now."

Their eyes voted yes before the scramble to grab spare clothes and food, while Kitty tapped impatiently. Even as they rammed stuff into sugar bags, the wind sprang up outside with a new and snarling quality and they knew without even saying that boats were pointless in those enormous buffetings.

Outside they found the wind screaming in from the north-east. Hair leapt on their heads. Skirts ballooned about their faces. Blown onto the water-logged road almost at once as if by an impatient stage director, they glimpsed, through scrawls of water, the sky overhead, deepened to an inky bruise. Carried on the demented wind, bursts of rain whacked them like hose-jets. There seemed no consistency in the craziness of air. Trees streamed wildly in one direction, then swung and streamed in another. The world was filled with flung branches and a mad confetti of leaves and through everything, everywhere, an animal baying of water.

When they came within sight of where the landing should have been, only the tops of the handrail were visible above the munching river. The boats had left or been swept away.

The women could barely speak through mouthfuls of rain.

If Nadine was crying, no one could tell.

Faces a-stream, they gazed at a violent emptiness. The man who had come to warn them had been sucked into the landscape. Without words they turned and began pushing their way against the wind back to the house, their sodden clothes and sagging bags like drag-anchors.

In those few moments it had taken them to decide, to pack, there had been a monstrous unplugging from the high hills. Already the river had reached below the house and was sniffing at the stumps.

Kitty was practical. With lamps lit, wet clothes dumped on the veranda, bodies dried, there evolved a specious sense of safety under the racket of air. They were drawn by the idiot comfort of the kettle even as the store opposite lost its roof in one hideous crack and scream of tin and timber, the rending cries of walls devoured by wind. Their front door burst open and began hammering the wall and they rushed to jam it shut and found, looking out on the drowning road, the river lapping the third step and reaching for the fourth.

At least one was made for bravura. Sylvia began a rotund thumping on the frightened piano. "Let's sing!" she cried. "Let's go down singing!" But no one joined in and even her voice fell away when Kitty, who had been out on the wind-torn veranda inspecting raucous movement in the darkness, announced that the pub had gone. They all crowded round her, braced against the railing, and saw, in the boiling night, the great bulk of the pub rise and teeter and submit itself to the current. *Oh God*, they all kept whispering, *oh God*. Its bucking progress was halted momentarily by the trading store where the concussion slammed both buildings out into the middle of the river.

The next minute they were gone.

There was fever of panic. Lizzie began praying and Kitty fought back the impulse to slap. Instead she set out glasses and poured brandies, ignoring Nadine's puppy whimper. "The water," Nadine kept whispering, "the water. It's more than halfway up the stairs."

"I don't give a bugger if it's knocking at the door," Kitty announced, flamboyant with fear. "There's always the roof. This place is built like a fortress." She tossed her drink back, gasped, and poured another. "And if it doesn't hold, who cares?"

"I care," Lizzie said.

"Well, then, you're mad." Kitty downed her second. "Mad. It's truth time, isn't it? Truth time. Not the ideal life, is it? You really think we've had the ideal life? We've made a bit and we've had to put up with a lot. Stinking men with stinking habits whose brains are in their cocks. Maybe a couple of decent ones, now and again, but they were few and far between. So here's to survival, girls, and if we miss out, there's no one to weep for us."

About the house there was nothing now beyond its second raging wall of wind and rain. The river had lost its vigorous slapping quality of an hour ago and boomed unbrokenly along what was once the road, while above them the iron roof drummed and lifted, drummed and settled. Below, the growing tug of the rising floodwaters lurched between the house-piles with such brute strength and speed, the building shuddered and rocked.

Nadine sat shivering, whitefaced, her brandy untouched, sustained by the greasy lamplight.

"I think," Sylvia said, going back to the piano, "we should put those lamps out. If the house goes, there could be a fire. I wonder if St. Paul would have thought it better to drown than burn?"

Grudgingly Kitty doused the lamps, and they hunched in the noisy dark of the shuttered parlour, their voices and blurred shapes alien. It became increasingly hot. Only the topmost louvres were ajar, not to trap air so much as to prevent the kind of implosion an exiled cyclone could create. "Court the wind," Kitty explained as she eased the shutters apart. "It's called courting the wind. Do you like that?"

Sylvia was the only one who answered. "I do. Our way of life."

She was playing again, sadly, and her voice defeated the sound of the house straining on its chocks. Her voice flooded the room with sadness. "'Oh Shenandoah, I long to see thee, oh away, you rolling river, it's seven long years since last I see thee.'"

Nadine listened in her mind to Cornelius singing that same shanty, and after a while Cornelius's voice and Sylvia's voice became that of a curly bushman with billies a-jingle, and the words changed and the melody changed and "Afton Water" flooded her mind, so that when the first of the river came to greet them through floorboards and under doorways, she'd passed beyond terror. She had a vague vision of Kitty and the Irish girl clad only in petticoats standing above her, shaking her and shaking her and shouting that they would have to climb out on the roof.

Nadine knew that would be worse.

She found her hands stiff around the wooden armrests of her chair. Sylvia's own hands were never more relaxed as they caressed the keyboard and her voice persisted against everything: "'Oh away,'" she sang, "'I'm bound to go, cross the wide Missouri.'"

The music brought tears to Nadine's eyes, and seeking childhood prayers she glimpsed her mother conducting the family rosary with her own eyes shut against the carnal horrors of Charlotte Street. There was tumult in the room about her, the stuffed-off cries of two of them wrestling the wind at the door before their struggle for the roof gutters. *Leave them*, Kitty's voice was shrilling. *Leave them.* They were sounds, not words, and though she heard them they had no relation to herself or that continuing singing voice and the inconsolable chords.

Rejecting everything in that outer world, she found herself trying to recall the first words of the Sorrowful Mysteries but before even one penitent syllable registered, the river, lusting for the sea, gave a final rabid thrust, and she felt the house surge and lift like a boat and then begin its slow-turning waltz out to the waters of the bay.

Jessica Olive surprised herself, manageress extraordinaire, behind the bar of the Port of Call and later a force behind office desk and dining room, banked by gross bunches of potted tropic growth and pictures of southern racehorses. She didn't like to think of the in-between years, the space between Cornelius and now, the year the brothel floated out to sea.

For months, tears and more tears.

Father had rallied.

No. She wouldn't return to Sydney.

Her humiliation was too deep.

Father had rallied. Could he help financially?

Grudgingly she permitted. George was packed off to boarding school in Brisbane where Nadine's Harry, now regarded as a found-ling brother for George, would follow a few years later. Needlework and some refined housekeeping in the Grassy Hill homes where she had once been a guest sustained her until she could scrape the mud of Charco from her feet. The morning the boat sailed she looked steadily out to sea. She didn't look back.

Well, no more than anyone did.

An Irish song, a velvet touch of brogue, could undo her.

The Port of Call was now legally hers. She surveyed gleaming surfaces smug with achievement. There was even a piano in one corner of the smoking room. *Bar at the Folies Bergère*, she interpreted herself, eyeing her still handsome but never quite recovered face in the long mirror across the room, wondering how she would greet her long-vanished bumbler if he ever returned.

Not, not, she decided, courtesy of Lord Byron, *with silence and tears*. Sometimes at night she fell asleep assuaged by a glittering

58

scenario of his pleading self, of herself unapproachable in unsuitable silks, successful, occupied, independent and, by God, still resentful. Yes. Still.

How should she greet him, after these years?

I'll chew, Jessica Olive would whisper to herself, toughened by living, *his bloody ear off. Hotels have coarsened me,* she sighed. *But not George.* George, she had to admit, big gentle George, retained a private soft spot for his vanished father. He was addicted to photograph albums. *If he weren't my son,* she told herself, *generous and reliable as he is, I'd have to admit he is boring.* At twenty-three he was very nearly middle-aged.

I love you, darling, she whispered in contrition at the mirror and forcing herself to look contrite, despite.

There was no artistic volatility, she decided, repositioning poinsettia. None. Harry was the one. Potch. A cynical nickname she was trying not to use. He could demand explanations she wasn't prepared to give. "You can't call George uncle," she instructed the fourteen-year-old Harry. "It's too ridiculous. Both your parents are dead," she lied, "and you might as well regard George as an older brother. Potch, dear, I certainly think of you as a son."

"How did they die?" he would ask, only peripherally curious.

"They were drowned," Jessica Olive explained firmly. "Now let's talk no more about it."

And she didn't. Until age softened her resolve.

Nadine's genes had produced a flashy charmer who at fourteen was already flirting with every girl in Port. He had his mother's dark good looks and a double serving of rover from both Cornelius and the wandering adventurer who'd sired him. He understood to the nicest degree how to confront Jessica Olive's irritation at uncovered misdemeanour, coming up and taking her hands, both, mind you, both, to confess with stunning candor.

"You're right, nana, of course I did it. I know I shouldn't have. Don't tell George, please. He gets so, well, you know. I promise, truly, nan, I won't do it again." And he'd bend over her chair, his eyes limpid with regret, to dab a kiss on her cheek, the little devil, and she'd say, *you're your grandfather all over, so just this once young man,* and he'd reward her with a smile of such warm and pure relief she felt not like a lenient judge but aider and abettor. "God forgive me, Harry," she'd complain, "you're affecting my standards."

"Never. Couldn't do that, nan."

"But you do. You do it again and again. I'm too weak with you, lad. I don't know why I do it. I hope that school of yours takes no nonsense." Then she would shoo him off, her conscience unsalved, while he took his own on thudding gallops south of town, whooping into seawind until he wore himself out.

For the first couple of years in her business venture, Jessica Olive had handled almost everything herself: cooking, cleaning, bartending. She was splendid in the bar. Manless, she found that *grande dame* vowels and aloof turns of phrase were her best protection. The hotel was small when she bought it and could accommodate only eight travellers. She preferred regulars, bachelors employed in banks and stores. She extended the dining room and served meals to casuals. Now she had a kitchen help, a barman and a yardman. The yardman, whose services were sporadic, was a black called Bidgi Mumbler who had turned up at Port as a deckhand on a fishing trawler. Boat-obsessed George brought him home one day after running into him at the wharf. Perhaps George was looking for his own freedom and a stopgap.

Jessica Olive, seeing him, was flung back fourteen years.

"It couldn't be," she kept saying to her son. "Couldn't."

"But it is. It is. After all this time. He remembers, don't you Bidgi? Hey?"

The young black man grinned and chewed some words off for her. The fishing trawler had supplied language of a sort.

"God, George," Jessica Olive had said, "what's he saying?"

"He remembers everything. Says you were kind."

"Kind!" she said, dredging up a fourteen-year-old irony. "Kind! I was beyond kindness in those days. Or I'd never reached it."

George and the black man were exchanging smiles and excited gabble. She was frightened she might translate the past.

She bit her lip for it all. "Bring him in, George," she told her son. "It's close on tea time."

Bidgi stayed after all. He swept verandas, burnt off rubbish, swilled down the bar and smoking room, cleaned storm gutters and drains, staggered under beer barrels. He kept the dining room supplied with fish. Sometimes he went off up the coast and Jessica Olive wouldn't see him for a month. She remained tolerant. Apart from the fact that he more than earned his small wages and keep, he was a hostage to sentiment. When he returned, slipping shyly round by the kitchen door, her welcome was heartfelt.

Some of the boarders complained.

"You're too good to that nigger, missus. You'll regret it, you mark my words. Don't know what the buggers'll do next, treacherous bastards. They'll use you, pinch things. Treacherous is the word."

Hey, lady, he's a Charco boong no-good nig just-out-of-the-trees ape. He's got those rattling orbs, spread nose, shapeless mouth, well, could you call it a mouth, flannel-lipped bastard can't even talk properly, yabbering away in that lingo, skinny legs, ugly! Christ!

"Pardon me!" Jessica Olive had said. "Oh pardon me!"

She was a small straight woman who wore her still ungreying hair in a careless roll that fluffed becomingly about that well-boned face. Her cheeks—well, her cheeks, oh God, had spots of angry red on them and her eyes sparked. "I knew that nigger, as you call him, when he was a small boy. He was and is a friend of my son. Friend, do you hear? Would you like to hear, too, that his parents were murdered by some white digger as handsome as yourself? Maybe he couldn't bear flat noses, either. Do you think, maybe, that's it? Do you think that's why his daddy was shot and left rotting on the track? Well, do you?"

"Look, missus . . ."

"Don't you 'look missus' me! My name is Laffey. Kindly use it. If you don't like it here, you are perfectly free to pack up and leave—and I mean now. But the one person who does stay is Bidgi. Do I make myself clear? Just make up your mind and I'll turn your room out for the next guest."

The postal clerk shuffled about.

Even his pimples looked sullen.

"If that's the way you want it," he said finally. "My God, missus, by the time I tell everyone what sort of place you're running, you'll be turning all the rooms out."

"I'll give you five minutes," Jessica Olive said. "Five."

The postal clerk was wrong. For the next few years business was

61

never better. Harry returned from boarding school and George was freed for his brief flirtation with the sea. Then, as other towns down the coast grew and the northern mines finally failed, more and more people moved away to Reeftown.

"I wouldn't want the old scoundrel to walk in now," Jessica Olive admitted to herself in bed, those money-worried nights of the late nineties. "Perhaps I should pull out, too, while there's still some money in the bank."

She was taking things more easily. Harry's staggering energy ran the place like clockwork. And he talked about love. Or marriage. For how long? his grandmother would ask with an unbelieving curl to her mouth. How long?

Skepticism hurt Harry. He was no longer the wild boy of Port. Clytie was a force too.

"Oh go on with you then!" Jessica Olive said. "You hardly deserve her." And to George, who had worn out his love affair with blue water and had clambered back on land, she said, "You know, George, I think I like Clytie rather better than your brother, nephew, whatever. I love him. But that's a different matter."

The morning smelled of permanent summer when George told his mother that he was thinking of leaving. "It won't work," he said. "Harry and Clytie and me. I'm odd man out. I think I should be looking around for a patch of my own."

"I like you here, George," Jessica Olive said selfishly. "Don't be difficult."

"No one's being difficult. It's the situation."

He slapped his savings on an unwanted acreage near Mango, and after the first exultation wondered, as he more closely inspected the dense thickets of rain forest, what he could do with it. Half-a-dozen other settlers were struggling to clear land along that stretch and the near impossibility of it, the difficulty of the tracks in, made him groan in his dreams.

Jessica Olive insisted on an inspection. She went down to Reeftown by boat then travelled up into the hills on the new railway line. George was waiting for her as she lifted her skirts off the train.

"It's just off a piece," he admitted, handing her up into the horse-drawn cart. "I think you're going to like it."

"Heart ruling purse," his mother commented briefly when they wobbled into the makeshift track and approached the bit of a shed he'd knocked up. "What will you do with it? Coffee's failed."

There had been a black frost a few years before that had ruined acres of profitable coffee farms along the river, and cautious growers were turning to dairying. George waved vaguely at a cleared paddock some distance from the shack and a few abject animals browsing on the fringes of the scrub. From farther up the river came a sickly smell of wood burning, and lazy smoke plumes wrote failure messages across the afternoon sky.

Cut off, Jessica Olive thought, peering critically about, sniffing at woodsmoke. But when were we anything but that, she mused, in this dangerously new country? Her pursed lips wanted to scorn the romanticising of settler drudgery, the sort of rubbish that those southern jingoistic papers printed, mush doggerel by scribblers who'd barely come to terms with the day-to-day and failed to understand the tension between landscape and flesh. Only men would write it. A woman wouldn't waste the time, couldn't find time to waste.

It's these damn stupid clothes, she decided, tearing a runner of wait-a-while from the hem of her skirt as she trudged after George across his acres. They've always made it harder. Easier to be raped in. Harder to work in. She saw an unending line of women working on bare brown plains, by cow-bails, at wood coppers, at clotheslines strung between gums, at meat-safes damping down the sacking covers, sweeping tamped earth floors, tacking bits of cretonne on fruit-box dressing tables, on and on and on, thanklessly, and making sure dinner was ready on time.

She had to laugh. Old Angus Cormick's horse at Port had died in his arms. His wife never got to be that lucky.

"What's funny?" George asked.

"Nothing," she said. "Everything."

Criticism nagged. To say nothing, she thought, of those needing-to-be-pressed suits, the stinking serge the men dragged out of mothballs and mould for their formal enclaves, the priestly rites of rule over the mud-catching, leg-trapping, humbly coloured clothes of her sex, the armoured corsets, the absurd flummery of long sleeves and frills. Who had ever counted the burnt fingertips of women testing hot irons? Who?

"It would run into millions," she said to George.

"What would?"

"The fingers. Oh never mind!"

And within that long and uncomplaining line of drab workers, menstrual agonies or the stirring of the next child. My God, what nonsense, what cruelty, men inflicted on them because of their own puritan obsessions!

She'd shown more of her ankles than she should have for years in Charco and Port. Under the fashionable but secret fullness of her skirts, she omitted stays. Sometimes other women confessed they did the same. It was their husbands who protested, who found a lewd raciness in the omission.

"I don't have a husband," Jessica Olive would argue. "I have only myself to consider. It's my comfort." She said other daring things. "It's men who've invented these contraptions and chained us in them. A modern-day version of the chastity belt!" Even the word chastity implied only its antonym! "My dear, no man is going to tell me how to dress in this climate. Or any climate, for that matter."

Behind her back there had always been knowing nods and repeated rumors—also frilled. "No wonder about that girl of hers, Nadine, wasn't it? That's where Harry gets his attitudes!" For despite closed lips after the flight from Charco, Jessica Olive had never really managed to forestall the marvel of bush telegraph. It coursed, not through air, but through the drink-slackened mouths of packers, coach drivers, mailmen and diggers along half-made tracks to half-made towns whos population drifted in and out with each change of fortune.

George had been talking her blind and she hadn't heard one word.

She looked hard again across the cart-ruts, over the ungrubbed tree stumps at the indifferent cows. What really was desolate? she wondered. Behind them was a busy jungle of rain forest, river clutter and the suspected presence of blacks, no longer very hostile but insufficiently submissive to white greed. Somewhere a dog yelped endlessly. There was the distant crack of an axe, steady, rhythmic, nagging wood. Four miles away up the road was a townlet, and only that, of pubs, settlers and the beginnings of grazier snobbery.

George's shouted enthusiasms deepened her depression. He waved creator hands and established for her a low-veranda'd sprawl of a homestead farther down the slope, with a giant bamboo windbreak; he waved his hands again and fruit trees shoved up laden, close to his house walls, and the paddocks greened into a summer pasture for prodigious milkers.

She kept shaking a doubting noddle.

George was smiling at her.

"Everything takes time," he said.

"You'll need a woman to share this joy."

"In time," he said.

It all took longer than he imagined.

After he had cleared most of the property and had the beginnings of a house, three years had gone by and the townlet was already dissolving, its pulse centre at Mango another five miles along the track. He consoled himself with the thought of the railway line snaking up the appalling steepnesses that made it pause for breath within a few hundred yards of his own holding. Loggers were still going into the hills for hickory and crowding the bar at the Family Hotel, while a mile away, Mr. and Mrs. Moneybags, who had originally told George about the land release, swanned it up on their four hundred acres with paradise gardens nurtured by tamed Murris. They gave stability. In the secret centre of their Eden glowed a fifteen-room house.

The antithesis! The racking antithesis!

Dossed down between unfinished walls, George would catch the faint cries of ecstasy from parties there whose guests had been brought up by special trains from Reeftown.

Stability of a kind, he thought, awake with the mosquitoes, but too close. Reminders should never be too close.

That's what they all want, those starters.

Stability.

But there are other things.

"I'm lonely," Jessica Olive admitted one afternoon to Father Madigan. "George up there at Mango. Harry married. I feel useless. It's not as if I'm old."

Father Madigan sat at ease on the veranda of the Port of Call, his sanctified fingers curved around a worldly whisky, confidently male though celibate. Age was catching up with him, though he would be the last to admit to any slackening of religious ebullience or slowing of limb. The vastness of his parish was a cause of pride. He travelled by horse and sulky. The mystique of his calling assured him endless meals, cups of tea, donations from parishioners unable to afford it and a total acceptance of his lightest opinion. "The glory of the apostolate," he was frequently heard to say, "is the little people."

Now, benign with liquor and the leafy shade of Mrs. Laffey's veranda, he was jovially dismissive. "Now now," he said, taking another sip, "it's not like you to complain. Not at all. The Lord giveth, et cetera."

"And the Lord taketh away, you mean?" Jessica Olive had been weary of his aphorisms for years. "Don't tell me the Lord took that husband of mine off. He took himself. There've been times, I can tell you, when I've been sorely tempted to remarry."

Please God, let him argue, she prayed, the silly old fool. She glanced at the half-emptied whisky bottle resentfully.

"And lose your immortal soul!" Father Madigan rose to her remark as deliciously as a trout. "To say nothing of civil illegality. Eternal damnation for a few moments' pleasure."

"At times that seems preferable to coping with tramps and drunks. In any case, I don't know whether Cornelius is alive or not."

"Ah," Father Madigan said, sipping lovingly and running his tongue about his lips, "that is the whole point. You have no reason to believe he isn't, have you? And divorce, as you well know, is out of the question. No, no. I won't even hear the suggestion, mind you, the mere suggestion of such a thing. Even to think of it could be an occasion of sin."

"Almost everything is," Jessica Olive said softly and bitterly. "Tell me, Father, how is it that a sex which commits most of the crimes of this world also happens to be the arbiter on morals?"

"And which sex is that?" Father Madigan asked, twinkling.

"Oh God!" Jessica Olive moaned. "Oh God oh God oh God. Listen, just listen to me. All my liturgical loyalties, those reverences for the simple dogmas the poor unfortunate sisters drummed into me at the behest of a male hierarchy, have been my undoing as a human. No"—she waved her hand at him—"don't interrupt. You're too used to doing that. Hear me out. That terrified obedience you and your brothers in Christ exact is directed largely at women. Women. You've neutered us. Made us nonhuman." Did she say that? She could hardly believe her own ears. Maybe it was the heat. It was certainly a swelterer of an afternoon. Father Madigan's face looked red and lumpy. She knew he didn't think of women as human. Or perhaps too human. His attitude towards her sex was in direct line from Thomas Aquinas. When he thought of his old Irish mother, a tear in his ready sentimental eye, it was with a tribesman's horror, actually, of the fecund womb. The toothed uterus. But traditionally, saturated with Mother-of-God sermons from his own boyhood and anticipating John McCormick by a decade or two, he knew he had to pay lip and tear-duct service.

He was wriggling with anger.

"Are you finished then?" he demanded. "Are you finished? Mother of God, I never thought to hear such talk. Never! You don't know what you're saying at all. I'll try to forget you spoke to me like that, Mrs. Laffey. I'm sure you don't really mean it."

"Don't I?" Jessica Olive smiled happily. She felt unladen. "Well, perhaps you're right. You're always right, aren't you?"

"Then just be begging God's forgiveness, my dear," the thick prelate said, "and we'll say no more about it. And now—" he pushed his glass across the table in a demanding and positive way—"could you be after topping that up? It's a terrible hot day for an old body."

Jessica Olive smiled. He'd been cadging drinks from her for years, checking in at four like a wily old sundowner, watching her attendance at Mass, advising her unwarrantedly and often impertinently on the boys, and always expecting and receiving generous donations.

She looked at him sitting there, a fat-bellied Irishman, in the wrong climate for maybe the right reasons, but a narrow dominating egotistic bully as well, whose profession expected everything to come at a run.

"No," she said firmly. "I don't think so. You've had enough."

Again, was that her voice rasping out that shocking rude remark? She heard her strangled throat add "Father."

He swung a stunned puffy face.

"What?" he asked. "What was that?"

"I'm going in now," Jessica Olive said, rising. "It is time to check in the kitchen. So I'll be wishing you good afternoon."

67

"Well now! Well!" The priest puffed wind for words. "Have I said something to offend?"

"Not this afternoon. But overall."

Father Madigan could have choked. "In what way? God love us, I've never had a parishioner talk to me this way before. Never. Where's your respect, woman, where's your respect for God's anointed?"

"I'm keeping it for God," Jessica Olive rejoined with great energy. "You've just said it—that's it. That's your offence entirely." She picked up the drinks tray, challenging him to reach for his not-quite-finished whisky. The ice rattled as she removed it from reach. "You professional celibates know all the answers, don't you, to every domestic problem. I have a meal to see to, but you want to keep on sitting here as if there are no other people in the world but you. Will you cook the dinner, Father? Oh, you're specialists in a sphere you've never entered—or if you have, more disgrace to you—and about which you know nothing first-hand. Not a thing. Not the tiniest thing. You encourage men and women to breed endlessly without the faint-est understanding of the toll it takes on women, of the strain of bringing up children. You are glib about sins of the flesh. What do you know about them? If you do, you've betrayed your calling and I despise you." She watched with interest as Father Madigan's face seemed to balloon, blocking out the whole of the main street. "But your last offence, and you don't even know you've been offensive, is addressing me in that repulsive biblical patriarchal way—'woman.' You're patronising me, Father Madigan. And I won't be patronised. You're flaunting your male superiority. You're trying to belittle me. And I'll tell you this, mister, I am so tired of being condescended to by your sex and in particular by people of your calling, especially when they're witless. I am so tired."

She allowed her eyes to rest on him fully. She even felt sorry for the man. But she felt good. A thrilling energy coursed through her. She felt wonderful.

They kept staring at each other. She thought for a moment she'd cut his tongue out.

But "You are shameless," he managed finally. "Shameless. I can only pray that God will forgive you for these atrocious words."

His face was mottled with shock.

Behind his heavy black shoulders there was a heartbreaking curve of early evening water and the lilac haze of mountains across the bay. Closer in, rowing boats lay like driftwood between the marker buoys of the channel lanes. The world seemed too large and too beautiful, achingly so, to house this irritating little man.

"I'm sure He will," she said. "Even if you don't."

He stumped off to his smartly painted sulky and drove into a flurry of sunset cracking his whip hard at the unfortunate horse, flogging the debased Mrs. Laffey.

Later he was to tell many people he thought she had gone mad.

The veranda. The passageway with that peculiar leathery green light of leaves at its other end. The rooms on each side. The kitchen lean-to off the back veranda. It all happened slowly.

And just as slowly the small township along the eastern track wilted while Mango grew.

Each day George listened to the goods trains dragging their rolling-stock and supplies for the tableland a hundred yards from his western fence. Passenger trains rumbled up to Tobaccotown. Each day after hoeing, fencing, hammering, he was too exhausted for the ride into Mango's pubs. He stuck his head under the tank tap until the water ran his head clear or he'd go down to the sandspit in the river and swim the grime and muscle-strain away. He realized, and refused to see fault in the fact, that he was becoming more and more of a loner.

"You'll go queer," Jessica Olive warned. "Eccentric."

He'd laugh at her.

He had standard progress reports for her each time she visited.

"Ten milkers, one bull," he'd say. Or "Three calves this season and the mangoes have started bearing."

"Such wealth!" his mother joked nicely. Sometimes her heart broke for his solitariness.

"Keeping my head above water," he'd say.

"It's high time you were keeping two heads above water."

"I'm not ready yet."

Jessica Olive's own tendency to the eccentric had deepened as she aged. Her skirts shortened faster than fashion. She was wearing a striped cotton bag of sorts with the sleeves cut off as high as she dared. A glassy stare precluded comment. "There'll be no purgatory for us," she said, fanning ferociously as she picked a fastidious way between cowpats. "Maybe hell but certainly no purgatory."

She dumped a bag of jams and cakes on George's bachelor table and set about making tea while he watched with irritable love. A new sharpness to her jawbone, a crumpling of the fine skin about her still-determined eye made George sigh and look away. Soon the bones would speak for themselves.

He asked how the pub was going.

"That's why I'm here," she said, busily pumping the primus into action. "I'm selling. I'm afraid Harry hasn't got my touch. Business is bad."

George tried to make the right sounds of interest and distress. He was so absorbed in his own place, he couldn't have cared a bean except for the loss to his mother.

"What will you do then?"

"It's finished there," she replied, watching the kettle too closely. George suspected tears. "I'll lose on the deal but I'll lose more if I don't get out now. Harry's buying some land at Swiper's Creek. He's talking about going into sugar. As for me, my dear, as for me I'm retiring."

"Likely story," George said, unbelieving. "Here. Let me do that." He took the heavy kettle out of her grasp. "You can come up here if you like. Would you like?"

"No. No no no. That will only stop you doing what you should have done years ago, George. For God's sake get yourself a wife. And make sure she knows how to laugh. That's one thing about Clytie. She laughs. She needs to with Harry. There's been too little laughter in this family. I think your father put me off it for a while. He had an excess of jollity and look where it landed me."

For the best, George thought but didn't say. He was still in love with landscape. Even the brutality of climate.

"This is all right," he said. "We've done all right. You've done it for us."

"Cut that cake," his mother ordered. "I made it specially for you, old fool that I am."

George grinned. He told her she was a bloody great bully and impressed the words with a hug. His nearly forty years pummelled her.

"This is your mother you're speaking to," Jessica Olive mock-chided, reaching past him for the sugar. Then she winked. "You should have heard me hop into that old fool Madigan last month. What a hypocrite! At least he won't be around again bothering me. Has he been up here to report your mother's sinfulness? Honest to God, George, I never knew a parish with such boundaries. It's like the Holy Roman Empire."

George asked slyly, "Won't I be needing him if I marry? What will you do then?"

"There are other places, George. Other parishes, even if we have to travel south to find them. Make it soon, son. I can't keep on nagging you. I'm losing my strength. I'd like to think I'd handed on that chore to someone worthy of me. Or you. You soppy cautious old thing."

They were words of love.

George felt like crying, nearly forty and all.

But she checkmated him.

"George, tell me, how do you—well—how do you get on for a woman now and then?"

HEART IS
WHERE THE
HOME IS

The morning the men came, policemen, someone from the government, to take the children away from the black camp up along the river, first there was the wordless terror of heart-jump, then the wailing, the women scattering and trying to run dragging their kids, the men sullen, powerless before this new white law they'd never heard of. Even the coppers felt lousy seeing all those yowling gins. They'd have liked the boongs to show a bit of fight, really, then they could have laid about feeling justified.

But no. The buggers just took it. Took it and took it.

The passivity finally stuck in their guts.

Bidgi Mumbler's daughter-in-law grabbed her little boy and fled through the scrub patch towards the river. Her skinny legs didn't seem to move fast enough across that world of the policeman's eye. She knew what was going to happen. It had happened just the week before at a camp near Tobaccotown. Her cousin Ruthie lost a kid that way.

"We'll bring her up real good," they'd told Ruthie. "Take her away to big school and teach her proper, eh? You like your kid to grow up proper and know about Jesus?"

Ruthie had been slammed into speechlessness.

Who were they?

She didn't understand. She knew only this was her little girl. There was all them words, too many of them, and then the hands.

There had been a fearful tug-o'-war: the mother clinging to the little girl, the little girl clutching her mother's dress, and the welfare officer with the police, all pulling, the kid howling, the other mothers egg-eyed, gripping their own kids, petrified, no men around, the men tricked out of camp.

Ruthie could only whimper, but then, as the policeman started to drag her child away to the buggy, she began a screeching that opened up the sky and pulled it down on her.

She bin chase that buggy two miles till one of the police he ride back on his horse an shout at her an when she wouldn take no notice she bin run run run an he gallop after her an hit her one two, cracka cracka, with his big whip right across the face so the pain get all muddle with the cryin and she run into the trees beside the track where he couldn follow. She kep goin after that buggy, fightin her way through scrub but it wasn't no good. They too fast. An then the train it come down the line from Tobaccotown an that was the last she see her little girl, two black legs an arms, strugglin as the big white man he lift her into carriage from the sidin.

"You'll have other baby," Nelly Mumbler comforted her. "You'll have other baby." But Ruthie kept sittin, wouldn do nothin. Jus sit an rock an cry an none of the other women they couldn help, their kids gone too and the men so angry they jus drank when they could get it an their rage burn like scrub fire.

Everything gone. Land. Hunting grounds. River. Fish. Gone. New god come. Old talk still about killings. The old ones remembering the killings.

"Now they take our kids," Jackie Mumbler said to his father, Bidgi. "We make kids for whites now. Can't they make their own kids, eh? Take everythin. Land. Kids. Don't give nothin, only take."

So Nelly had known the minute she saw them whites comin down the track. The other women got scared, fixed to the spot like they grow there, all shakin and whimperin. Stuck. "You'll be trouble," they warned. "You'll be trouble."

"Don't care," she said. "They not takin my kid."

She wormed her way into the thickest part of the rain forest, following the river, well away from the track up near the packers' road. Her baby held tightly against her chest, she stumbled through vine and over root, slashed by leaves and thorns, her eyes wide with fright, the baby crying in little gulps, nuzzling in at her straining body.

There'd bin other time year before she still hear talk about. All then livin up near Tinwon. The govmin said for them all to come long train. Big surprise, eh, an they all gone thinkin tobacco, tucker, blankets. An the men, they got all the men out early that day help work haulin trees up that loggin camp and the women they all excited

waitin long that train, all the kids playin, and then them two policemen they come an start grabbin, grabbin all the kids, every kid,
and the kids they screamin an the women they all cryin an tuggin an
some, they hittin themselves with little sticks. One of the police, he
got real angry and start shovin the women back hard. He push an
push an then the train pulls out while they pushin an they can see the
kids clutchin at the windows and some big white woman inside that
train, she pull them back.

Nelly dodged through wait-a-while, stinging-bush, still hearing the
yells of the women back at the camp. Panting and gasping, she came
down to the water where a sand strip ran half way across the river. If
she crossed she would only leave tracks. There was no time to scrape
away telltale footprints. She crept back into the rain forest and stood
trembling, squeezing her baby tightly, trying to smother his howls,
but the baby wouldn't hush, so she huddled under a bush and comforted him with her nipples for a while, his round eyes staring up at
her as he sucked while she regained her breath.

Shouts wound through the forest like vines.

Wailing filtered through the canopy.

Suddenly a dog yelped, too close. She pulled herself to her feet, the
baby still suckling, and went staggering along the sandy track by the
riverbank, pushing her bony body hard, thrusting between claws of
branch and thorn, a half mile, a mile, until she knew that soon the
forest cover would finish and she'd be out on the fence-line of George
Laffey's place, the farm old Bidgi Mumbler had come up and worked
for. She'd been there too, now and then, help washin, cleanin, when
young Missus Laffey makin all them pickles an things.

For a moment she stood uncertain by the fence, then on impulse
she thrust her baby under the wire and wriggled through after him,
smelling the grass, smelling ants, dirt, all those living things, and
then she grabbed him up and stumbled through the cow paddock
down to the mango trees, down past the hen yard, the vegetable
garden, down over a lawn with flower-blaze and the felty shadows of
tulip trees, past Mister Laffey spading away, not stopping when he
looked up at her, startled, but gasping past him round the side of the
house to the back steps and the door that was always open.

Mag Laffey came to the doorway and the two young women watched
each other in a racket of insect noise. A baby was crying in a back

room and a small girl kept tugging at her mother's skirts.

The missus was talkin, soft and fast. Nelly couldn't hear nothin and then hands, they pull her in, gently, gently, but she too frightened hangin onto Charley, not lettin go till the white missus she put them hands on her shoulders and press her down onto one them kitchen chairs an hold her. "Still, now," her voice keep sayin. "Still."

So she keep real still and the pretty white missus say, "Tell me, Nelly. You tell me what's the matter."

It took a while, the telling, between the snuffles and the coaxing and the gulps and swallowed horrors.

"I see," Mag Laffey said at last. "I see," she said again, her lips tightening. "Oh I see."

She eased the baby from Nelly's arms and put him down on the floor with her own little girl, watching with a smile as the children stared then reached out to touch each other. She went over to the stove and filled the teapot and handed the black girl a cup, saying, "You drink that right up now and then we'll think of something. George will think of something."

It was half an hour before the policemen came.

They rode down the track from the railway line at an aggressive trot, coming to halt beside George as he rested on his spade.

Confronted with their questions he went blank. "Only the house-girl." And added, "And Mag and the kids."

The police kicked their horses on through his words and George slammed his spade hard into the turned soil and followed them down to where they were tethering their horses at the stair rails. He could see them boot-thumping up the steps. The house lay open as a palm.

Mag forestalled them, coming out onto the veranda. Her whole body was a challenge.

"Well," she asked, "what is it?"

The big men fidgeted. They'd had brushes with George Laffey's wife before, so deceptively young and pliable, a woman who never knew her place, always airing an idea of some sort. Not knowing George's delight with her, they felt sorry for that poor bastard of a husband who'd come rollicking home a few years back from a trip down south with a town girl with town notions.

"Government orders, missus," one said. "We have to pick up all the abo kids. All abo kids have got to be taken to special training schools. It's orders."

Mag Laffey inspected their over-earnest faces. She couldn't help smiling.

"Are you asking me, sergeant, if I have any half-caste children, or do I misunderstand?" She could hardly wait for their reaction.

The sergeant bit his lower lip and appeared to chew something before he could answer. "Not you personally, missus." *Disgusting*, he thought, *disgusting piece of goods, making suggestions like that*. "We just want to know if you have any round the place? Any belonging to that lot up at the camp?"

"Why would I do that?"

"I don't know, missus." He went stolid. "You've got a housegirl, haven't you? Your husband said."

"Yes, I do."

"Well then, has she got any kids?"

"Not that I'm aware of," Mag Laffey lied vigorously. Her eyes met theirs with amused candour.

"Maybe so. But we'd like to speak to her. You know it's breaking the law to conceal this."

"Certainly I know." George was standing behind the men at the foot of the steps, his face nodding her on. "You're wasting your time here, let me tell you. You're wasting mine as well. But that's what government's for, isn't it?"

"I don't know what you mean, missus." His persistence moved him forward a step. "Can we see that girl or not?"

Mag called over her shoulder down the hall but stood her ground at the doorway, listening to Nelly shuffle, unwilling, along the lino. When she came up to the men, she still had a dishcloth in her hands that dripped suds onto the floor. Her eyes would not meet those of the big men blocking the light.

"Where's your kid, Mary?" the sergeant asked, bullying and jocular. "You hiding your kid?"

Nelly dropped her head and shook it dumbly.

"Cat got your tongue?" the other man said. "You not wantem talk, eh? You lying?"

"She has no children," Mag Laffey interrupted coldly. "I told you that. Perhaps the cat has your ears as well. If you shout and nag and humiliate her, you'll never get an answer. Can't you understand something as basic as that? You're frightening her."

She looked past the two of them at her husband who was smiling his support.

"Listen, lady," the sergeant said, his face congested with the suppressed need to punch this cheeky sheilah right down her own hallway, "that's not what they tell me at the camp."

"What's not what they tell you?"

"She's got a kid all right. She's hiding it some place."

George's eyes, she saw, were strained with affection and concern. *Come up*, her own eyes begged him. *Come up*. "Sergeant," she said, "I have known Nelly since she was a young girl. She's helped out here for the last four years. Do you think I wouldn't know if she had a child? Do you? But you're free to search the house, if you want, and the grounds. You're thirsting for it, aren't you, warrant or not?"

The men shoved roughly past her at that, flattening Nelly Mumbler against the wall, and creaked down the hallway, into bedrooms and parlor and out into the kitchen. Cupboard doors crashed open. There was a banging of washhouse door.

George came up the steps and took his wife's arm, steering her and Nelly to the back of the house and putting them behind him as he watched the police come in from the yard.

"Satisfied?"

"No, we're not, mate," the sergeant replied nastily. "Not one bloody bit."

Their powerful bodies crowded the kitchen out. They watched contemptuously as Nelly crept back to the sink, her body tensed with fright.

"We don't believe you, missus," the sergeant said. "Not you or your hubby. There'll be real trouble for both of you when we catch you out."

Mag held herself braced against infant squawls that might expose them at any minute. She made herself busy stoking the stove.

"Righto," George said, pressing her arm and looking sharp and hard at the other men. "You've had your look. Now would you mind leaving. We've all got work to get on with."

The sergeant was sulky. He scraped his boots about and kept glancing around the kitchen and out the door into the back garden. The Laffeys' small girl was getting under his feet and pulling at his trouser legs, driving him crazy.

"All right," he agreed reluctantly. "All right." He gave one last stare at Nelly's back. "Fuckin' boongs," he said, deliberately trying to offend that stuck-up Mrs. Laffey. "More trouble than they're worth. And that's bloody nothing."

The two women remained rooted in the kitchen while George went back up the track to his spadework. The sound of the horses died away.

At the sink Nelly kept washing and washing, her eyes never leaving the suds, the dishmop, the plate she endlessly scoured. Even after the thud of hoof faded beyond the ridge, even after that. And even after Mag Laffey took a cloth and began wiping the dishes and stacking them in the cupboard, even after that.

Mag saw her husband come round the side of the house, toss his hat on an outside peg and sit on the top step to ease his earth-stuck clobbers of boots off. Nelly's stiffly curved back asked question upon question. Her long brown fingers asked. Her turned-away face asked. When her baby toddled back into the kitchen, taken down from the bedroom ceiling manhole where George had hidden him with a lolly to suck, Nelly stayed glued to that sink washing that one plate.

"Come on, Nelly," Mag said softly. "What's the matter? We've beaten them, haven't we?"

George had picked up the small black boy and his daughter and was bouncing a child on each knee, waggling his head lovingly between them both while small hands pawed his face.

Infinitely slowly, Nelly turned from the sink, her fingers dripping soap and water. She looked at George Laffey cuddling a white baby and a black but she couldn't smile. "Come nex time," she said, hopeless. "Come nex time."

George and his wife looked at her with terrible pity. They knew this as well. They knew.

"And we'll do the same next time," Mag Laffey stated. "You don't have to worry."

Then George Laffey said, "You come live here, Nelly. You come all time, eh?" His wife nodded at each word. Nodded and smiled and cried a bit. "You and Charley, eh?"

Nelly opened her mouth and wailed. *What is it?* they kept asking. *What's the matter? Wouldn't you like that?* They told her she could have the old store shed down by the river. They'd put a stove in and make it proper. Nelly kept crying, her dark eyes an unending fountain, and at last George became exasperated.

"You've got no choice, Nelly," he said, dropping the baby pidgin he had never liked anyway. "You've got no choice. If you come here we can keep an eye on Charley. If you don't, the government men will take him away. You don't want that, do you? Why don't you want to come?"

"Don't want to leave my family," she sobbed. "Don't want."

"God love us," George cried from the depths of his nonunderstanding, "God love us, they're only a mile up the river." He could feel his wife's fingers warning on his arm. "You can see them whenever you want."

"It's not same," Nelly insisted and sobbed. "Not same."

George thought he understood. He said, "You want Jackie, then. You want your husband to come along too, work in the garden maybe? Is that it?"

He put the baby into her arms and the two of them rocked somberly before him. He still hadn't understood.

The old men old women uncles aunts cousins brothers sisters tin humpies bottles dogs dirty blankets tobacco handouts fights river trees all the tribe's remnants and wretchedness, destruction and misery.

Her second skin now.

"Not same," she whispered. And she cried them centuries of tribal dream in those two words. "Not same."

"**I**t's everywhere," Harry said—chanted really. He chucked his stained work hat down on the kitchen table and a swarm of flies rose.

Harry stank of cane and sweat and a sicklier, subtler, aromatic failure.

All month and the month before that the men on the road had been going through looking for work. Their humility was stunning, corrosive. They would do anything, anything, for a few bob. He'd had to turn all of them down. After the first dozen or so, he got tired of explaining that the crop had failed that year with unseasonal rain. He got tired of telling them he was nearly through himself. He couldn't bring out the words to describe the week there'd been nothing to eat but pumpkin. Couldn't. He simply couldn't cry poor mouth when he had a roof over his head.

The men stood hopelessly before him, their eyes with that dead look peculiar to long hungers, their clothes baggy around the skinny bodies.

He simply waved his arms in an emptying gesture that took in the flattened soggy fields.

There was always a sandwich up at the house, he said. And a cuppa.

Most accepted. Some didn't. Those who followed him to the kitchen nibbled at Clytie's "doorsteps" as if the sight of food made them shy. "Thanks, missus," they mumbled, looking past her, because this beggary had reduced them below humanity. One of them had even wept.

The last one had been more insistent, a lash-thin man of forty or so, though at first Harry had thought him older, with blank puddle eyes. His swag was the thinnest Harry had ever seen, the blanket so worn, so lacking in essential fluff, the threads that composed it had the clarity of hopsack fibres. A skillet and billy and mug were tied to the outside rope and a little canvas pouch for sugar and tea.

Not that he was insistent verbally. He had merely stood there in his amazing thinness, his eyes without emotion as they looked back at Harry without seeming to absorb his refusals. He might have had no shadow and there was only the sickening heat of later afternoon walloping the landscape.

This one wouldn't get much farther, Harry decided, apart from the fact that the track up the coast petered out to a horse trail beyond the next farm. There was nothing there. Nothing. And "There's nothing there," Harry said again, dragging a forearm across his own sweaty essence. "Sorry, mate."

He began to turn away but the man went on standing as if Harry hadn't moved, standing in an abstract of himself, refusing the clichés of knock-back, his own substance left in some southern squalor when the jobs gave out, the susso law keeping him on walking and walking until he might tramp light-headedly and empty-bellied off the tip of the Cape. Months of hunger had driven him to the stage where he did not take his body very seriously at all.

So the man stood watching Harry Laffey turn away, and the small girl who had been hanging about could see her uncle didn't want to do this, that he felt uncomfortable, and she kept staring from one to the other, twisting her yellow hair about one finger; and when her uncle turned round and said sharply, *Come on, Connie. Come on!* she looked right into the man, who didn't seem to notice at all, and then Uncle Harry came back along the fence, the sun exploding in his face, and he took her hand and said to the man, "You'd better come on up, too. No sense getting sunstroke."

Clytie was putting out the tea things on the kitchen table just as usual, but when she took a look at the man wavering in the doorway, she went back to the safe and hauled out the last of the corned beef and began cutting slabs.

The man's eyes at last acknowledged surfaces, the shine on crockery, on kettle and pot, the light slicing along the bread knife, and his lips moved, struggled with thanks that couldn't come out loud enough for anyone to hear. He sat upright at the table as if plenitude frightened him.

But he couldn't eat much.

His mouth laboured with the bread and meat and he tried a smile of apology. Crumbs dropped from his lips and fell unnoticed on his lap. *He was beyond it*, Uncle Harry said later in the kids' room, *poor bugger. The poor devil needs a hospital.* And Aunt Clytie whispered quickly, *If you send this one off, Harry, I'll never forgive.* And then she shut her lips tight.

He managed the tea. He drank three big mugs of it and finally got half a sandwich down and when Harry said, forgetting, that he could take the rest of the food with him if he liked, Clytie slammed a plate on the sink top and said she didn't like to interrupt but he could doss down in one of the sheds where they kept a shakedown for casuals. The man told him his name then and young Will, who hadn't said a word all through the meal, grinned at this and said, "That's my name too."

"Hullo, mate," the man said. He heaved himself up and thanked them, pulling his face into what was meant for a smile, picked up his swag and walked slowly across the paddock to the shed.

Harry watched him go, stared after him through the kitchen window while the sound of plates being washed and put away went on behind him, the back of his mind taking in the comforting permanence of soap and hot water and Clytie's voice weaving in and out the voices of the kids. Later that evening he took a lamp across to the shed to see if the tramp wanted anything and found him lying stiff and silent on his blanket, unfocused eyes gazing out at the fireflies.

"Nothing," the man said. "Thanks."

"Where are you from?" Harry asked. "You got a family some place?"

What little energy the man had seemed to expel itself in a sigh. He turned his starved face towards Harry's and the lamplight picked out cheekbones and nose above the straggly beard and pocketed the eyes.

"I've been walking since Adelaide," the man said. His voice was soft and listless.

"God Almighty!" Harry cried. "That's a helluva way, mate. How long have you been on the track?"

"Two years," the man said. "Two whole years. It was all right for a while. In the fruit country. It was all right there."

"What about your family?"

The man was silent. His bony fingers picked at the edge of the blanket with a rasp of torn nail and fabric that set Harry's mind on edge.

"I don't know," the man said at last. "There was a wife and two kids. I tried. I tried a long time. Then I got tired of trying." There was another small sigh. "Real tired right through the bones of me. So she took the kids and went back to her people's farm. God knows how they were coping. So I just hit the road."

"I'm sorry, mate," Harry said. "There's been dozens like you through here this past year but they always turn back. There's nothing up at Charco. It's the end of the line here. Well, just about."

"I won't be turning back," the man said. He kept seeing the long hot stretch of the Hop Wah road and the Chinese gardens along the creek.

He had tried every cane farm on the way in, the dairies, the slaughter-yards, and at the end of the day a man he met on the waterfront took him back to the showground where the unemployed were camped. He hung around there for a couple of days, long enough to be driven out by police. He kept seeing the horses, hearing the shouts, feeling the crack of pick-handles and rakes turned into weapons. The man who'd helped him kept cursing through broken teeth and blood, spluttering his hate as they stumbled off in the darkness. His own face was torn open along the cheekbone but the pain became distant as he staggered away, his unrolled swag shedding most of the last few things he owned. There'd been nights on the beaches north of town and then he rode a goods train up the tablelands to Molloy and started walking again. Somewhere down the Bump road a farmer's wife gave him tea and bread. But no work.

There was never any work.

He ran one finger across the scar on his cheek. It was puckered and red like bad stitching.

"Memento of the north," he said to Harry. "Something to take with me."

"How did you get that?" Harry shifted the lamp so that the light flooded the gaunt face beneath him. The man's eyes winced from the glare and he flung an arm across them.

"The law," he said. "The law and some earnest townsfolk. They don't like beggars up this way. They don't like them much anywhere, come to that."

Harry set the lamp down. "I heard about it. Where were you? Squatting out at the showgrounds?"

"Squatting!" the man replied bitterly. "I thought this country was founded on squatting. It's all right if you squat on a bit of land big enough. They respect you then. All we had in Reeftown was tent space. A few lousy feet of tent space, less than I had on Gallipoli, somewhere to doss, and they begrudged us that."

"Gallipoli!" Harry said. "You were there too?"

The man nodded. "That's how the wife and I got the farm. Soldier settlement from a grateful government. It wouldn't grow a bean. Squat!" the man said. "They treated us like blacks in Reeftown."

"It's the same everywhere," Harry said. "People are scared."

"Scared!" the man scoffed. "I could tell them about scared." He shoved out both hands and the knobs on his wrists stood out so sharp they hurt. "Most of us were too weak to run. It was a massacre."

Harry nudged the lamp and the movement swung an oily glow on the nothing outside the shed.

"Look," he said, "it's no use going on. Charco's a closed shop. They've been coming down from there too. It's worse than here. You'd be wasting a lot of footwork. You can stay on a couple of days, rest up a bit. I can't pay you anything, mind, but we're right for tucker at the moment. What do you say, eh?"

The man closed his eyes against this effusion. Outside the thud of night animals tracked spoor across his despair.

His eyes were still closed when Connie and Will crept over to inspect him before breakfast. The sound of their whispering woke him.

His eyes had lost their muddy look, although they were still prowling feverishly the perimeter of moonscapes.

"There's eggs," the small boy said, "for breakfast."

"Is there?" the man said.

"And bacon," the girl said. "You have to have bacon with eggs."

"Christ," the man said. "Bacon and eggs. Oh Christ!"

"You're crying," Connie accused.

"I could be," the man said, "if I had any juice left."

He talked to them over the meal, telling them stories of life on the track. He ate slowly and carefully between words and was still mopping up yolk long after the others had finished. "Can't tell you, missus," he said to Clytie, "I just can't tell you what that means."

"You don't have to."

Clytie's mouth had gone all funny, Connie noticed. And then the man did something she had never seen a man do before. He got up and stacked the dishes and filled the washing-up dish with hot water from the stove and beat the water into a lather with the old wire soap-saver and started washing the plates.

Clytie sprang up as if she were outraged by trespass and then she began to laugh.

"All right," she conceded, "you can do it and thank you. It'll be the first time in twenty years I've had a man help me."

He stayed the rest of the week after that, working in the vegetable patch, splitting kindling for the stove and giving Harry a hand with the clearing of a back paddock. Every afternoon after the children rode back from school, he spent a while yarning with them and he showed the small boy how to build a gunyah out of saplings. It was finished by the end of the week and on the next morning after he had dried the dishes for Clytie and burnt off the rubbish, he said he'd best be going.

"I don't know how to say thanks," he said, standing there, his roll hitched over his shoulder, his old felt hat crammed down on his head.

"I'm the one," Clytie said, "who should say thanks. You've given me a holiday. All of us. Things have got to get better."

"They have already," the man said, and raised a laugh.

Clytie had packed him a small bag of groceries. "There's some eggs in there," she warned. "Careful how you carry them."

"I won't forget," the man said. "Not anything."

Harry walked down the track with him as far as the first gate and warned him again against turning north. "There's nothing out there. Not for the next hundred miles."

"That'll do me," the man said.

They raised hands to each other in that old bush signal of recognition, the sign that transmits arrival or departure and recognition from one being to another, and then the man hoisted his swag a little higher and trudged off along the track.

The children were waiting for him out of sight of the house where the home trail met the packway going north. Their hands gripped small newspaper parcels.

The man stopped and wrenched up a smile for them, for the girl—pretty, he'd noticed, her swag of bright hair drooping straight beside her face, but especially for the boy who reminded him so much of his own kid. The boy's eyes trod ahead of the present. The man understood that.

They pressed their small packages onto him. He could feel the weight and shape of pennies.

"Go on," the girl urged. "We want you to take them."

He stared down at them both a long time.

"There won't be any shops," he said at last. "Your uncle said."

"Why don't you stay then?" the boy asked.

"I can't do that."

"Why?" the boy persisted.

"Because," the man said, remembering the old childhood answer. "Just because." He looked at the girl and knew she understood. "I've got to keep going now."

"It's an adventure, isn't it?" the boy asked, hoping.

"I suppose it is," the man said. "A sort of adventure."

"I like adventures," the boy said. He was kicking one foot eagerly against a clump of guinea grass.

The man kept looking at them, and the space and the distances, the dark puddle looks, seemed to have come back to his eyes.

"Would you like to come with me?" he asked, looking at the boy. He heard his words and was surprised that for the time those words took he meant them. His loneliness was crashing in again, and the awful solitary crawls between towns, along with the lack of responsibility for any human except himself. He needed that most. Responsibility. Foolishly he thought their presence might stop the inevitable. Yet even as he thought that, he knew the inevitable was what he wanted.

They didn't laugh at him. They didn't shy away. He was grateful for that.

The girl treated his question with an adult seriousness.

"I'm afraid it's not possible," she said. She looked straight into his face, unsmiling in the clarity of her understanding. "We can't do that. Not yet."

"When can we?" the boy demanded. "When can we, Con?"

"Soon," she said. "One of these days."

The man was already drawing away from them down the track. He felt their terrible comprehension overtake him as he put one hand to his hat in a kind of farewell.

"I'll remember that," he said.

That winter the frangipani in the convent gardens lost all their leaves before June. There were mornings of slashing frost and then the pallid blue of the high sky. At night the world was gritty with moonlight. By midday patches of sun, warm as sawdust and as golden, sprawled against the chapel walls near the tennis courts and the rear garden trellis where the passion vines grew.

Her best friend whispered, serious behind the covers of *A Winter's Tale,* "I don't think I can stand it much longer. It's all right for you."

"Stand what?"

"This place. This *place*."

Connie felt guilty but relieved for herself. She was a five-day boarder. At the beginning of each term Uncle Harry used to drive her and Will down to Reeftown from Swiper's Creek along the new coast road, and in Reeftown she would wait for the train up to the tablelands while Will vanished behind the doors of his own boarding school. For the first year Uncle Harry made surprise midterm visits as well to each of them on the pretext of bringing a little joy into their lives, but his real reason was an excuse to get away from Clytie and saunter off to the disorderly houses in Sunbird Street, coasting the shores of the goodtime girls.

Clytie suspected. Then she knew. She arranged for the children to spend weekends at her sister's home in Reeftown and returns to Swiper's were limited to term holidays.

"Every weekend?" Sister Perpetua considered this as lingeringly as if it were some cosmic decision on morals. "It will upset your routine and ours. Does your aunt want to do this?"

Surely her aunt wouldn't want to do this! The mere suggestion spilled its outrageousness all over the glassy linoleum, splashed across framed Sacred Hearts, Holy Families, nuns on mission fields.

"I don't know, Sister,"

"It's a training in selfishness. The other girls are not permitted to be so self-indulgent. Of course, I realise yours is a rather special case, your dear parents being dead. But still."

"It's Uncle Harry," Connie explained, her eyes suitably lowered. "He's not very well."

"Is he not?" Sister Perpetua looked hard at the closed face across the desk. "Frankly, I cannot see the relevance but I suppose your aunt has her reasons. I could consider this only as long as these—these interruptions—do not interfere with your schoolwork, your obligations to school activities and so on. Do you understand?"

"Yes, Sister."

"What do you understand?"

Giggle. Shame. The laughter spluttered out uncontrollably. Then she lowered her head and began a little weep. Three terms had taught her the usefulness of mollification.

Every Friday, avoiding stocking-mending followed by basketball practice, the slow rattle-trip over the tablelands, the walk in the eight o'clock dark with Will who met her at the station, through streets smelling of sea and the despair of the unemployed, to the waterfront. How describe the intensity and amplitude of those Saturday mornings when, her brother hauled back to school for football practice, Connie, the hated uniform dangling crooked in the wardrobe, pulled on her best summer frock and sauntered into town to nose along the musty shelves of the School of Arts; to trail later with unsuitable reading matter to a patch of grass along the front under the figs, still snuffling from library dust but prepared to drown in words and ultramarine.

Saturday. All Saturday. Limitless.

At night they slept in sagging veranda beds listening to the sea while the mosquito netting twisted in the wind through the wooden louvres. In the dark, she and Will threw words to each other softly across the splintered boards.

There she goes, every Saturday, walking through an older Connie's dreams, strolling the waterfront, taking deep breaths of mangrove stink and salt and the personal odours of the town. Her eyes gulped in as much. Blacks slept beneath trees, women shoved their shopping home in recycled prams, carts dragged up side roads, tethered horses dropped dung pads, men propped up pub verandas and sometimes a car rattled past through a halo of dust. By nine the heat clawed at flesh. Horses went limp in sulky shafts and the morning shoppers headed for the purple shadows of awnings. It was then that Connie turned her back on the sea and, facing the high ranges where the convent hid itself in memory and trees, walked a block to the School of Arts, up the stairs and into the long book-filled room with the deep verandas off it from which, again, the bay, the sizzling blue, the hyphen of an island.

The world caught her by the throat.

Every Saturday morning.

She would run lightly with some electric urge up the stairs, hand patting rail, patting rail, the satin polish of the wood slipping under her fingers. She ran into expectancy.

Every Saturday morning.

And every Saturday morning, as if he expected her, or they expected each other, he would be there.

She had noticed him the very first Saturday.

She had looked up from the magazine rack where she was selecting something for Aunt Tess and had become conscious of a large broad-brimmed hat dipping over a deepness—was it brownness?—of eyes, of skin. Was it a sombreness of mouth? There was a morose attraction. He was forty or fifty, she judged, some vast age her years could not guess at, but the thickset and gloomily pervasive stance filled her with unanalysable fear and delight. There was a heavy and clumsily curved imprecision of body, and the more unmoving he stood, the more the nature of this force reached out to her.

And then the two of them, the only borrowers in the long dust-scented room, revolved from rack to rack, shelf to shelf, baiting each other with occasional unsmiling glances of pure gravity in a kind of slow ballet.

It made her sharply aware of her own face and body, of the nakedness of arms and legs, of the slim unformed quality of bone and flesh, and she could sense, across musty histories of the region, the rows of local memoirs, the shelves of classic and popular fiction and piles of damp-mould newspapers, his own grave interest.

Every Saturday.

Silence. The books. Silence. The slow pavane. The desk-clerk writing quietly, uninterested, at the far end of the room. Just the two of them. And then she would look up, suddenly solemn in the juvenile section *(Remember, I am only a schoolgirl!)*, hand paused on a tattered spine, turning, her shoulders describing an unhurried arc of the most impure innocence, to find that he was watching.

Sometimes she took a book out to one of the deck chairs on the veranda, and, sitting there confronted by unread pages and the sea, felt his presence in the room behind. Once he came out to the veranda as well and looking at her, looking at her, sat in a chair one away. Then she became too frightened to look across at him though she sensed a spiritual branding taking place. As she walked home later with the books she grabbed up without choice, her excitement shook her and persisted throughout the tumid morning.

There was no one to tell. She did not want to tell. The words she tossed Will in the dark told nothing. It was as if for that briefest of longest hours every Saturday morning, she executed a privately adult mime.

So it went on through May and June. The expectation, the steady exchange of glances, the agreeable sensation of delight and terror. Something prevented her smiling. Was she too frightened to smile? A smile could be the ultimate disclosure of her self. She was not yet ready to smile. On two occasions when other borrowers came early to the library, she noticed that he went directly to the veranda and sat there reading, severed from her by the page, and she would choose her books quickly and leave with a sense of something unfinished.

That winter, too, she developed chilblains on every finger.

At night in the dormitory, the envelope of heat beneath the blankets made them itch unbearably and she scratched and tore at the inflamed flesh until the skin burst and ripped like a rag and her hands became banded with scab and pus.

She couldn't conceal them during class and after a week Sister Boniface turned from the blackboard in the middle of an algebra demonstration and said curtly, "Do something about those fingers, will you, Constance? Doesn't your aunt know? They're quite disgusting."

Humiliation came easily at convents. It was good, someone must believe, for the soul. Passion, resentment, the beginnings of diffident cries of protest, even overt anger, would meet a contemptuous "Control yourself." Contemptuous? Not quite that. Distaste, perhaps. A sort of well-bred fury and disgust that one could be so—well, so human. Control yourself. They all lived by that dictum. At porridge time, at bread-and-butter time, at stew time, in class and out, in chapel, in study, at prayers, tennis, basketball. *Constance*, a voice would ring out over the bitter grass at the edge of the courts, *don't throw your body about like that. Show some control!* The other girls playing had stared at her as if she were committing an obscene physical display. She felt she had perpetrated a loathsome impurity. Her bottom? Had she shown her bottom? Her breasts? Had they bounced? They were barely there. Had she flashed her gangling thirteen-year-old legs with the sensual motions of a stripper? Had she? She knew about strippers. Her best friend had seen a film in Brisbane and the black-and-white frames recalled in the darkened dormitory still shot guiltily across her mind.

For the rest of that game her services flopped down the court like patted dough lumps. She minced to return balls with her knees jammed together. Should she even part her feet? *(May I walk, Sister Boniface? May I have permission to walk, to part my legs so I may get from here to there?)* She was resentful. Her efforts to avoid immodesty and display the utmost control became tinged with the ironic. For one silly week, she flattened her gently erupting breasts with a broad ribbon band tied under her school blouse lest they offend.

Do something, Constance, about your legs, your breasts, your disgusting, disgusting fingers.

After the last class that afternoon, she excused herself from sport, taking delight in displaying the suppurating reasons to Sister Regulus, and went back to her desk in the classroom where she kept a tin Aunt Clytie had packed with an elementary first aid kit: gauze, cotton wool, a pair of nail scissors, iodine and sticking plaster.

From the chapel came the voices of the school choir practising a Latin Mass. *Agnus dei*, they sang in four heavenly parts, *qui tollis peccata mundi, miserere nobis*. What was the Latin for chilblains, she wondered. And began to giggle. Lamb of God who takest away the chilblains of the world, have mercy on us.

The gauze unrolled across the desk. Through the open doors of the school hall she saw the frostbitten lawns roll to the treeline; above the trees soared a cutting blue. She snipped off a length of bandage and began wrapping the worst of her fingers.

Dona nobis pacem, sang the choir.

It was harder binding her right hand. She felt like a juggler. *Sanctus, sanctus, sanctus*, the choir intoned. Angelic. Angelic. Cut off in mid-polyphony by the pistol crack of ruler on harmonium top and a cry of musical affront from Sister Alphonse, a cry that rang down the chapel corridor, across the winter trees and into the hall. Holding one bifurcate bandage end between her teeth, Connie looped and tugged the other with her free hand. Twist, tug, knot. Furiously she sang, but softly, *qui tollis all chilblains mundi*, over and over. The choir had commenced singing again with the demanded delicacy, and the *attacca* and diminuendo of the repeated syllables brought tears to her eyes.

She started on her thumb.

Then a greyness darkened the already greying air of the hall and a swish of robes, a rattle of beads, particular warnings she carried long into adulthood, sounded behind her.

Angrily Connie kept wrapping, refusing to acknowledge the sounds.

Sister Perpetua's voice spun silkily over her shoulder.

"Well, Constance? Well? Look at me child, when I address you. What are you doing?"

Sister Perpetua stood with her head to one side, angled to match her smile.

Connie held out the still unbandaged fingers. They looked disgusting, just as she had been told.

"Wrapping my fingers."

"Wrapping? Your fingers?"

The gentle educated voice quivered with disbelief.

"Can't you endure a little pain?"

"Sister Boniface told me to wrap them."

Sister Perpetua picked at the rosary dangling from her belt, let it slide easily between her fingers, then rattled prayers like pebbles. "You're soft," she said. "Soft. Already we indulge you. Think of Christ on the Cross."

Connie looked up. Fold upon fold of choral music wrapped round her as the choir spent its adolescent energies on a *jubilate*. The injustice of those words. Rejoice! Rejoice!

"Christ cured the sick," she argued, stung by inequity. "You taught us that." She could feel a shaking in her chest, her heart thumping at her daring, and watching Perpetua's calm mad face, she became terrified at her blurted words. The nun's features seemed to do a little dance. It was as if they had all microscopically changed position.

Sister Perpetua leaned back from her, took a step away and supported her rage on a desk.

"You put yourself above Christ," she gasped. "You put yourself above the Church. You interpret!"

Connie could not reply to these charges. They bore the monolith horror from remembered studies of the Inquisitionary Courts. Grand heresy became a nimbus, the dark around the body.

A blob of yellow matter disengaged itself from the right thumb and plopped to the floor. Her eyes followed it. Sister Perpetua's mouth twisted briefly and from outside the hall a bell rang the end of another division in the day.

"Self self self," the voice was going on, through the bell's clangor, through the distant noises of feet surging from the chapel and voices that would shortly find them here. "You think only of yourself. A truly self-involved young woman with no capacity for endurance, for submission to the divine will." Sister Perpetua thought about the divine will for a few seconds. Her eyes rolled up reverently as if seeking and her lids closed. Connie was embarrassed at witnessing this private ecstasy. "If it's God's will you have chilblains, then it is His will. Do you understand me? And it is your part to endure, to offer them up as an act of submission to that divine will, to one who did so much for you" —her voice cracked at this point—"He laid down His life."

The classroom had filled with girls whose voices fluttered into silence as they saw the stage set, the persecutor, the victim. Faces, horrified, delighted, curious, became smug with there-but-for-the-grace-of-God looks. Sister Perpetua ignored them. The extras tiptoed virtuously around the two to their desks, took out textbooks, and bent their heads in frightful assiduity.

Ready for catharsis.

Sister Perpetua stretched her moment of silence to breaking point like an old stager, on, on, on, so that her final words would crack like rocks.

"May God forgive you," she said, spacing each word monstrously, "for your unpardonable selfishness. You will come to a sticky end."

Her hand began to shake wooden prayers from her waist once more. She held her head so far sideways as she examined her victim, she created a problem in balance.

"You're mad," Connie replied loudly and flatly.

Did she say it?

She hoped she had said it. She wishes she could have. No, she will remember long afterwards, she didn't say it.

The cold air following the opening doors at the end of the hall blew between their voices, carried between the two of them other voices and laughter from the playing fields, the rapturous indifference of latecomers to study, and a smell of drying leaves.

Perhaps she had dropped her eyes submissively, hidden her disfigured hands behind her back while the bandages unwound slowly and she agreed humbly from her shrunken and humiliated self, "Yes, Sister, yes."

She saw Sister Perpetua swing away to the senior section of the study block while she stood there, tears of anger and mortification swelling in her eyes but not running over. She sat down and under cover of her desk lid examined her hands and her hatred. Then, slowly and systematically, she proceeded to bandage the last sores.

Her solitariness was underscored by furtive glances. There were smells of sandshoes and sports-smocks, of chilling sweat and the breathy stifled energy of the latecomers. She stared at her Latin grammar and thought of nothing at all. *Nihil nihil nihil*. Automatically she copied a vocabulary list into a notebook, saying the words *nihil nihil nihil* over and over while her mind fled for refuge to the grounds outside, sped over the lawns to the wrought-iron gates and banged them behind, fled down through the hilly township to the railway station, and clattered off along the track through smudged sunsets to the coast, the old house on the front, the sea-bitten veranda, to Tess and Will and Saturday morning.

Next Saturday, she decided. Next Saturday.

He would be there and her private world would become the real one. The convent would shrink like a pip.

Her best friend was nudging her, her hand sticky with caramel.

The gesture was too late. She refused the nudge, rejected the sticky hand, wouldn't look across. *Prohibeo*, she wrote, dutifully and resentfully concentrating, *prohibere, prohibui, prohibitum*.

Next Saturday.

He would be there, the link to otherness, his eyes assessing across the long dusty room.

She knew this and she nourished half-formed notions of mouths and hands and Rochester-like passions springing to life between the dead and dying volumes on walls and tables.

As she wrote she shuddered at the peril of it for she knew what she would do this time.

Then she laid down her pen and touched her burning fingers together beneath the desk. She closed her eyes and saw Saturday behind her lids, ignoring the whispered urgencies of her friend. Too late, she thought. Too late. Beyond this stuffy room she was interesting. She was loved. And she knew what she would do, unsure of what her action might produce, but committing herself to it.

She would absorb his sombre eyes totally. She would float on their desperate lakes until she was beyond reach of shore, beyond.

She would open her lips and smile.

Yes. Turning from whatever book-clutter had trapped her, at that salient moment, moving slowly, immeasurably slowly, she would look into him fully at last.

She would smile.

THE KISS,
THE FADE-OUT,
THE CREDITS

He can't stop himself. He's not sure why he does it.

If perhaps one were to say, *It's that Nadine coming out*, he would reply vaguely, *Who? Who was that? Do you mean mother?*

I'm part of the established Australian social structure, he would say, *and I can't help it*.

> *mate*
> *horse*
> *dog*
> *missus*
> *wog*
> *poof*
> *boong*
> *that's*
> *the*
> *pecking*
> *order*.

See, he would say, *a poem, a kind of poem of structure. And as many girls as you can get on the side*.

Do they count? someone might ask.

You're kidding, he would say.

Each new woman was the starting point of a line he drew between boredom and repletion. She became the ultimate moment, the goal that must be charged into. His interest-span was brief. There was that obsession with new flesh, new features, the release between his thighs and then, within the month, even the week, he was sated, a homebody swilling thankful tea between bouts in the paddocks, relaxing in the stern but somehow assuaging presence of his wife.

How could he tell her that even at the moment, *that* moment, one bored foot was feeling around over the edge of the bed for its boot?

She always knew.

He knew she knew.

He knew she knew he knew she knew.

That had a certain rhythm to it that shaped itself into a kind of absolutionary aspiration in his mind, a wee ballad he sang while he worked along the cane-rows at burn-off.

At fifty-seven, give or take a year, he was, in his grizzled way, better looking than at twenty. There was something splendid about that well-tenanted face with the lines the Depression left, and too much sex. He still had a mass of hair, pewter grey, and his nose had settled into patrician assurance. It was the mouth. That unnerving plumpness of the lower lip still appropriately juicy, with corners that appeared to smile even when he felt least like smiling.

He drove his new Ford truck along the coast road, the sun not quite reaching him inside the cabin. The tray was loaded with an adulterous dispensation, a wife-pardon, Clytie's old treadle sewing machine buggered, thank God, and in need of vitals he knew nothing about. "There's a bloke down in Reeftown," he had assured her, "who's making a specialty of these old models. Fix it in no time. Or give you a trade-in. Let me get you," he pleaded, his eyes genuinely moist with affection, "a new one."

And this time he knew she didn't know.

Later, of course, she'd smell it on his skin, she'd sniff out his stained old soul.

Back before tea, he'd threatened. Promised. *Back then*.

Clytie had gone on smacking dough.

You'll forget, Clytie said.

Not me, love. God, of course I won't.

His kiss had flattened a small area of her cheek. *I love you*, he said unexpectedly, even to himself.

She hadn't even turned her head.

God, he murmured to the rattles of the truck, *god god god god god*. *Oh she knows that I know that she knows that I know*. He sang the words, roared them out as his hands fondled the steering wheel. After a while his mouth was clutching a real smile.

You could take all that blueness, he thought, consuming the slipping sea from the crests of small hills and at thigh-like curves in the road, and still not have enough. Never enough. Its rippled silk stretched into the tight blue sky-skin and formed a parachute of blue. He was wallowing in yellow and blue. The tremendous arc curved its delicacy between him and the love-object, the too-imaginable delights of that waiting new skin.

Always too easy. Charm, as Jessica Olive used to say with a remembering and bitter downturn of the lips, plus the bit of gallantry—how could he miss?

At sixteen he had been beautiful. That was his trouble. He still felt sixteen. Singing *he knows that she knows that he knows that she knows* he flicks the words to *I feel that I am oh I feel that I am*, not missing a beat, cuddling his vanity with all the confidence that had come early to him—the athlete's body, evenly tanned skin, and a smile. He smiled now between phrases. He even thought kindly of Clytie as she was when she first came teaching at the small school at Swiper's Creek, a dasher in tight-waisted skirts, curls tumbling, eyes ready to laugh. He had proposed marriage before he realised what was happening.

For a while: bliss. She miscarried that first year and during the second. Their first child died of pneumonia in its second year.

The fourth time Clytie conceived, a muddled operation left her childless and made further pregnancies impossible.

Harry felt his masculinity assaulted.

At the outbreak of World War I Clytie returned to teaching. Harry tried to enlist and was turned down with flat feet.

Again he felt assaulted.

They tottered their strained relationship around the farm with an ageing Jessica Olive watching cynically from the wings. Harry groaned aloud over his acres of Cheribon and Badilla, worked alongside the hired help during the cutting season, and in a desperate way began a career of Don Juanism.

At first he kept his forays in the environs of Tobaccotown whenever he made the long haul up the Bump Road for supplies. Sheer laziness drew him closer and closer to his own nest. *Oh the girls of Port*, he'd sigh as he grubbed his way along the unending lines of sugar-grass.

His best friend, a cane farmer from five miles in, invited Harry to be best man at his wedding. The bride was new-chum blonde with eyes stricken by the appalling quality of life in the north, but fervent for what she saw as married freedom. Her daddy was a bank manager in Port. Parents fussed, organised receptions and teas. Clytie made herself a new dress as matron-of-honour while the groom, who had quietly enlisted at Reeftown ready to pull out within days of the ceremony, eager to fight for his country, was to marry in khaki.

Picture it.

There they all were at the long trestle tables in the Port of Call, banked by masses of flowers Jessica Olive had bullied into submission. Women had been baking for days. There were two hundred guests, the officiating Anglican minister, a frightful pianist and an army of waitresses.

The groom rose to respond to the toasts.

His face was thin and nervous.

His bride was half-hidden by virginal frills. There was a great deal of orange blossom.

The groom's speech was brief.

I want to thank everyone, he said, his voice shaking a little with the emotion of the occasion, *for this reception, and I especially want to thank my best man, Harry Laffey, for fucking my wife last Thursday afternoon behind the cordial factory.*

Then he stepped neatly behind his chair, left the room and was never seen again.

During the bride's hysterical screams, Harry was conscious that Clytie would never forgive him.

Well, that's that, he decided. *Sheep as lamb* became his philosophy. *Sheep as lamb.*

In divorceless days they lived celibate. Clytie taught till she dropped. Then his brother died and after that George's children created purpose in their days, re-fused some kind of union as Clytie made a religion of parenting and housekeeping that threatened mud-clogged boots, discarded overalls, tracked lino, smoky ceilings.

A new softness, however, took her by surprise. She loved the children as if they were her own. Harry bought a small patch of land near the Cape and built a shack there for summer holidays. In time, he and Clytie would ease out the last of their days above the beach listening to the thud of dropping mangoes.

There'll be time to sit back a little, he had said to Clytie.

I would hope. She couldn't avoid ambivalence.

He survived the Depression. He extended the house. He became a model of domestic concern as he and the children aged.

In time the children went to boarding school and the house, emptied of their daily needs, rang hollow. Harry was left alone with the cane and Clytie. Once she went to his bed in a kind of anguish for lost loving.

I can't, love, he said to her, apologising. *I just can't. It's been too long, can't you see? It doesn't mean I don't love you.*

Her humiliated weeping made it worse. He began driving fortnightly to Reeftown, using the children as excuse.

While they're with Tess for the weekend, he would say, *I'll take them out for some fun.*

Why don't you come too? he would add, not meaning it.

You'll have more fun without me, Clytie always answered. *We both know that.*

So he sang. He had left the sea behind but its delight remained. The love-object was unaware of his approach and that made the situation more exquisite. She worked as a typist for his lawyer and he thought of this, regretting that distance, age and the smallness of Reeftown aborted the courting process while heightening the excitement. He had written her a little note suggesting lunch but not specifying a day. *How can he take her to lunch? Everyone will know. He knows they will know. She's twenty-four and bored. Her family lives in Townsville. At least they won't know. He hopes they won't know.*

It was easier, after all, than he could have imagined. Young Mr. Galipo dealt smartly with his business and Harry, keeping his bright eyes shuttered as he was being farewelled, heard the typist complain of a sick headache. "Take the afternoon off, my dear," Mr. Galipo said generously and patted Harry on the arm. "We're not too busy."

"May I drive her home?" Harry asked politely, sticking to the safe anonymity of the third person pronoun and looking across as if he had never seen her before. *Why the pat on the arm?* "It's getting hotter outside. I think we're in for a storm." He regarded the sluggish ceiling fan.

"Why thank you, Mr. Laffey," the alert girl said. "It's only to my boarding house. I would be so grateful," she said.

They drove several miles out, on roads lifeless with siesta.

Why the pat on the arm?

Lunch? the girl mentioned.

Harry was dubious. "There is nowhere," he said, "nowhere where we . . ."

He drove on another mile and pulled up at a roadside store. He bought sandwiches and fruit and was ripe with apologies. *This isn't what,* he said. *Not this way,* he said. *I wouldn't have it like this but what are we to do?* His hand on her knee, apologetic, seemed a natural accompaniment to the words. He remembered the pat on his arm. His eyes were abject with sincerity.

They found a picnic spot near one of the creeks in a glade almost braceleted by trees. Only a dirt road wandered past.

Harry had brought a rug.

She was appropriately reluctant, but after a while he overcame this and she too became absorbed. His eyes, his beautifully worn face, his plump lower lip with that suggestion of youthful gloss, his smile!

Every now and then they had to readjust the rug and spread it comfortably. The midday sun swung into midafternoon and twenty yards away and above them Arch Malloy, linesman and current beau of Connie, perched on his power-pole and moaned with frustration.

Ten miles north of Reeftown, Harry remembered the sewing machine in the back of the truck. He remembered the parcel for Will. He groaned, too. He didn't know that by now Arch Malloy was being treated for sunstroke and would later spread the reasons for it through three Reeftown bars.

Whimpering, Harry backed and filled the truck and swung back to town.

He was late reaching Swiper's township. The glister had peeled off his day to reveal the mud-coloured shape of cheap trinketry. *Why?* he kept asking himself, bumping his truck along the road to the ferry. *Why?*

He had missed the last ferry.

He drove over to the ferryman's house, prepared to plead.

The ferryman's wife had just finished putting the tea things away.

"Sorry," she said. "He's gone to Lodge. First thing in the morning, though."

"Well, that's not much use, love, is it?"

Harry was too exhausted for charm.

"I don't suppose it is."

She looked at him as if she knew. Could she know? Christ, they all know, have always known.

Wearily he climbed back into the truck and headed into Swiper's and the Swiper's Arms. Already the memory of breasts thighs mouth was becoming so dim he could not associate the morning's urgency with the evening's depletion. The mauve cube of a room in which he lay drained him. There was no battery recharge of the spirit. None. *Bloody fool*, he accused himself, pounding a sleepless pillow. *It was never worth it*. He lay awake smoking and thinking of young Will.

Will had been pleased to see him even though it was just on dinner-time. Boys crowding past to the refectory had glanced slyly at them as they stood talking there at the rear of the college. Each had a reputation.

Last year Will had run away from school and had been picked up by the police on the Sunlander somewhere between Townsville and Giru.

"Is he a troublemaker?" an annoyed Harry had asked the head brother.

Brother Clement looked bland. "Far from it. A quiet boy. A studious boy. We thought perhaps there had been some trouble at home."

Brother Clement and Harry Laffey studied each other for a moment.

"He's not very keen on football, though," the brother continued. He was a large man who'd moved easily from the ruck to the mission field. A front-row man for God, he liked to describe himself modestly. Not afraid of the tackle.

"Good God!" Harry had cried in mock horror. "Not keen on football!" He'd indulged in shaking motions of the head intended to express marvelling disbelief at such abnormality.

The head brother shrugged rugger shoulders and tried to like Harry Laffey.

"Of course he had a couple of nasty accidents last season as you know. First his collarbone and then a dislocated shoulder. Painful thing, that. However, those things didn't worry him at all. Nor should they any manly chap."

"Naturally, naturally," Harry lied, recalling Clytie's distress. "Make a man of him."

"That's what we endeavour to do with all our boys, Mr. Laffey," the head brother said with formidable virtue. "Make men out of them. Learning has its place, of course, but in the real world . . ." He paused to allow his predicate of scrumdowns and last-minute goals in business mergers to suggest itself. "No. It was after he broke his fingers in that end-of-term match that he began to be—well—difficult. Not that he actually broke them, as it were. One of the boys got a little overwrought and bent them back and snapped them. Most unfortunate, but these things do happen in the boyish enthusiasm and heat of the game. Of course he couldn't play for some weeks, but when matron thought it time, when we *all* thought it time, for him to get back out there on the playing fields, well, he refused."

"Refused?"

"Oh yes. He was polite enough about it. But he refused, adamantly, to play again. I wondered if perhaps the boy was a coward." Brother Clement waited to let the insult take effect. "He wouldn't say why, just that his fingers meant more to him than he cared to discuss. Well, of course we understand about his interest in the violin and so on, but it was his bowing hand and violin playing won't do much for him. Not out there. I think a lot of the lads regard it as a rather effeminate interest."

Harry Laffey nodded and nodded.

"Now you must see, you must understand, Mr. Laffey, that we are running a school here and we cannot, we simply cannot tolerate direct disobedience. If a lad is told to play sport, then play he must. If every boy were allowed to go his own way there would be chaos. You can see that, can't you?"

Mr. Laffey agreed that he could.

"Rough and tumble with the team, you understand. Team being the important word. Rough and tumble there equates with the rough and tumble of life."

Oh Christ, you bore me, Harry wanted to say. Instead, pricked by the slow-working insult several quibbles back, he said, "He's not unmanly. Not by my standards."

"And what are your standards, Mr. Laffey?" the head brother asked gently.

He knew. Harry knew he knew. And the head brother knew he knew he knew.

"He can ride any sort of horse. Muster cattle. Wire a fence. Handle a cane knife. They're reasonably manly things, aren't they?"

Brother Clement put down the fountain pen he had been fiddling with.

"That is all beside the point. It is a matter of school rules, and your nephew is infringing school rules. You cannot expect an organization of this nature to make exceptions. If we did it for one, we would be expected to do it for everybody."

"Then you won't take him back?"

"I cannot see how we can. Not unless Will gives a firm undertaking that he will conform. It seems a great shame. He is one of our best students and until last term one of our best footballers."

"But you'd rather lose a good student than retain one who won't play football?" Harry found himself scowling.

"Regretfully, I'm afraid so."

"Then there's nothing else for it, is there."

Harry rose, grappled with the brim of his hat which he seemed to be crushing rather than adjusting. "You can return the fees. I'm not inclined to make a donation."

The head brother stared up at Harry coolly before deciding to rise also. His mouth was vanishing behind skin. "It seems a pity," he was saying. "A great pity."

But Harry was already out of the room and striding down the gravel path, his feet skidding on small stones, to where Will was waiting in the front seat of the truck. He got in without a word and drove furiously along the dirt road to the esplanade.

"Bloody bully." He snarled from one side of his mouth. "And those hackneyed old theories. Listen, son, another year there and you'd be philosophically retarded. I've been through it. I know. Now, I don't give a tinker's cuss what your aunt says. You can finish your last couple of years off at High. You can stay with Tess. She'll be glad to have a man about the place and you can get up to Swiper's most weekends."

Will plaited his long, knuckly fingers and stared out at the water, acid-blue in midmorning. The hills to the south curved like enclosing gates. "Sorry," was all he could say. "Sorry about this. You know, I really liked that place."

"Hell," his uncle said. "Hell, boy, then why did you run away?"

"I wanted to make a point."

"You certainly did that. Was it really about the football?"

Later that evening Will attempted to tell. He could only echo his father's story of the bones, the hands beseeching sky, the sprawl of colonially administered death by the side of a bush track. "I can't help it," the boy kept saying. "I'd never really forgotten the story but I didn't think about it much either. Then when my fingers were snapped it all came back. Nightmares. The lot. I couldn't stop dreaming about it."

"That George," Harry said. "He had no business telling a kid stuff like that. No business at all. It's all past, now, son. You've got to live for the day. Take it as it comes."

"It was their day too," Will had argued stubbornly. "And they took it as it came."

"Well!" Harry said. "Well! Out of the mouths of babes and all that. So now, lad, tell me what I do, eh?"

Clytie solved it. A generous donation to the building fund and a long and private session with Brother Clement, pleas bolstered by medical certificates, made the rough places plain.

"You underestimate me, Harry," Clytie said after everything was resolved. "You've never given me credit."

"I've never underestimated you," Harry said. "Never."

Clytie knew. Already she knew.

Harry rolled his truck onto the ferry next morning and then slogged it up the track between the heavy scrub. He'd bought her some flowers in Swiper's and they were dying already on the front seat. But they were nicely wrapped. He clung to that. Nicely wrapped.

At the home gate he was hit by the stillness around the place. There was no smoke from the kitchen chimney, no sound of radio, no sight of Charley Mumbler dodging about the vegetable garden.

He parked the truck near the top shed, grabbed the flowers and walked back to the house.

"Clytie!" he yelled. "Hey, Clytie!"

Nothing.

The back door was ajar and he could see right down the hall to the front veranda. The air was printed with leaves. A salty wind off the sea blew emptily through the house.

"Clytie?"

The kitchen was dead. The back spare room. The kids' rooms. The front sitting-room. Their own bedroom looked as if it had never been lived in.

He went out to the veranda where the deck chairs had rejected last imprints of bodies. The little wind blew more strongly here.

He roared his wife's name again, swore and went back to the kitchen to shove the flowers in a jug. Nothing would revive them, but he dropped an aspirin in the water as he had seen her do and swallowed three himself.

Oh God, he said aloud. *It isn't worth it.*

There'd be no questions, no arguments, no tears, recriminations or promises. All that had stopped years ago. He could have coped with that. *Ah shit*, he thought. *Shit.*

He made himself tea and sat there smoking. Then, against his will, forced out by all the silence of the small sounds of the emptied house, he headed out down the track again to the little beach where he knew he would find her. Lawyer vine caught his clothes. He tripped on tree roots and cursed. This, and then that! God! But the beach was empty, too, when he stumbled onto the sand and looked north and south along its gentle golden curve.

When he got back to the house Clytie was sitting in one of the deck chairs reading as if she had been there for ever.

The jug of flowers was on the table beside her.

She looked up from her book and they stared at each other.

"You know I have nothing to say, Harry," she said at last. "Not a word."

"I wish you had," he said. "God, I wish you had."

Clytie closed her book and put it down carefully on the table. Then she heaved herself out of the deck chair, took the jug of dying flowers, saying, "Aspirin won't help. They're too far gone," and pitched the lot into the garden.

Connie wrote:

Will dear, this is sad news but Harry died last week.

Actually, he was killed by the doctor on the operating table in the Canecutters Community Hospital.

Or he committed sideways.

A lot of people commit sideways up here, Malloy says. (Yes, Malloy's still around. We are resigned to each other.) It's something about the place. Fourteen percent of deaths are due to unnatural causes. Perhaps it's the heat. Or nothing to do. Or read. Last time I went to the newsagent's in Swiper's, there were only three paperbacks and they were all called Take Love Easy. *That cut right across freedom of choice, didn't it? No wonder there's all this sidestepping.*

Will, it should never have happened the way it did. Appendectomies are the simplest operations. The anaesthetist working with young Maxie Tripp is well known in these parts for his neurotic and dangerous fear of overdoing it with the ether ever since that mishap three years ago with the Carascatti kid. Remember? He stints on the anaesthetic and patients are always half coming round mid-op and catching the appalled eye of the attendant nurse.

There they were probing Harry's stomach and in the middle of it all, he sat up and said, "What the hell's going on?"

He never did find out. Dr. Tripp was in shock for days and Clytie is convinced that either he killed Harry or Harry flung himself on the scalpel. I don't mean to make this sound funny, but it is, now I'm over the first of it. Clytie's doing outrageous things. She's inserted a notice in the Reeftown Courier. *Died violently, it says, and with the spleen of forty years of marriage to fire her, she's added, Harold Patrick Laffey of Swiper's Creek Homestead, husband of Clytie Rose- anne, mourned by Lucy Compers, Martha Zweig, Etta Pan- ici, Jeannie Wilters, Kath Shannon, Annabel Partridge, Betsy Trimble and others too numerous to mention.*

After that you can imagine the horrible interest I've been contending with. Then to top it off she fought her way past hospital authorities and had the body brought out here on the old Chev truck. Don't ask me how she did it. It hap- pened. And then with Charley Mumbler assisting, she buried Harry in a kind of emperor-sized garbage bag down by the second paddock.

I think you'd better get up here, Will, as the health au- thorities have been making a tremendous fuss. Clytie refuses to assist in any way and all Malloy, guide philosopher and friend, can do is laugh. She's planted a large durian over the grave and honest to God if it weren't that I saw it done I wouldn't have any idea where the burial place was either. Clytie's sworn me to silence and I feel I should humour the poor old girl. Certainly the health authorities are baffled and now she's taken to her bed and refuses to budge. You know, Will, she really did love . . .

Connie put her pen down with a crack on the table top.

This is crazy, she thought. How could she send Will a letter like this? She tore the pages off the pad and crumpled them as she went out to the phone. Even there, hand raised to dial, she was confronted by absurdity. The whole house creaked with Harry's presence and absence, a presence that made her want to ask him what she should do. Standing at the doorway to her aunt's room she began to protest "Listen!" but the grieving wafer beneath rumpled sheets was asleep at last and not even the throbbing summer heat disturbed her.

Connie had been brought up thinking that God had this enormous interest in her. A direct line to the Lord. Tap in. Tap in. Listening to Sunday primetime ravers on radio, mercifully thwarted by distance and bad reception, she marvelled that so far her personal life had spared her Clytie's final frenzy. In a way, those frost-filled convent mornings had bred a spiritual selfishness so vast that when she recalled the pathetically shrunken form of her aunt sucked off into slumber, after a week of angry grief, she was ashamed to discover she was still filled with self. Not even her son Reever could make demands beyond a certain point.

After her twenty-seven years of total self-concern—discount mothering duties, niecely attentions, sisterly obligations—it was still all self.

There had been tears for Harry. But only tears. Yet one Friday she had looked at elderly gnome-shaped Mr. Carascatti, run into as she was filling the old Chev with petrol at Swiper's Creek service station, and, observing that gentleman's carved aristocratic face honed out of peasant frame, she knew that he too believed he had a direct line to the Lord and was unpleasantly and selfishly shocked to think of God's diversification of interest. Not only her! but Mr. Carascatti as well and perhaps garage owner Stubbles and Malloy, bumabout on his trawler, and all the little Stubbles and the Carascatti grandchildren scampering in long lines through the sugar lanes of the north.

She picked up the phone receiver and began to dial long distance.

War had parted them.

Will thought back to those prewar highjink times when Connie had lugged him, pliable younger brother, to school hops and later into foot-stumbling dance halls with the whine of sax-tortured foxtrots and two-steps. There'd been raw-voiced girls who'd made him shrink into supper rooms or side porches where other bumpkins hid, or simply walk away, right away into darkness with the sexual smells of dew and leaf and cane tearing at him. And she would come pelting after him, wobbling on new high heels. "Will! Will! It's okay. We'll go if you can't stand it. We'll go."

"But what about Malloy, sis? He's your partner, isn't he?"

"Oh, Malloy! Malloy won't mind."

Yes, war had parted them. Not that he wanted to fight for king and country. It simply seemed, like so much else in this life, inevitable. There were government lies and evasions, officially blessed. The north knew more about the air raids on Darwin when they came than the newspapers admitted. There were a hundred killed. Two hundred.

Reeftown knew. The folk at Swiper's Creek knew. His uncle Harry watched the panic move south with curled lip. "Can't leave," he announced to Clytie. "No matter how hard they try to persuade us. I've a crop to look after. By the way, did you know there were ten blokes on the wharves up there killed when they were having their morning cuppa?"

"Well, that's a good enough reason for enlisting," Will said. "Buggering a man's cuppa!" He regretted his irony almost at once.

At twenty he found himself with the 9th Battalion somewhere north of Torokina on the Numa Numa Trail in a platoon led by a commercial traveller, engaged in what seemed pointless leap-frog exercises to take a knoll called Little George. He was nauseated by the idiocy of officers, the injustices of the army class system, the lousy food. The world became a green pavilion of leech, stench, rot, sniper and spilled guts and he disloyally found himself not caring which side won or lost. It was the football ethic all over again and the folly, the pointlessness appalled. His only pal, a stretcher-bearer, was blasted to pieces five feet from him. After that, taking over from his dead friend, he stalked uncaring into impossible places to drag wounded men to safety.

He was decorated for bravery.

"That's a laugh," he told Con later. And when she asked to see the medal he told her he'd dropped it into a trash bin in Queen Street. "I ran the wrong way by mistake," he said. "Or through fear. This bastard Corker kept screaming at me to get him out. He was stuck in a thicket under sniper fire with half his arm blown off."

"But you did it."

"He frightened me. I was too scared not to. Officer. If he'd been rank and file there never would have been a medal. No gong, you can bet on it. I just hated his guts. Funny, I don't know what an officer was doing so far forward. He must have made a mistake somewhere along the line. But then most of the officers were cretins."

Demobbed.

His civvy clothes had hung on him like dusters. Shaking over the telegram forms in the Brisbane GPO, yellow with atebrine, his handwriting palsied as an old man's, he'd let them know. *Back in the land of the living. Get that kettle on.* Connie's reply came next morning, poste restante. *Milk and two sugars as usual question mark*. He burst out sobbing on the greasy timber counter and when officialdom became too concernedly intrusive took the telegram out into the city sun and read it again and again, touching the words lightly with his fingers, pausing at Connie's name.

He was too shaken and ill to absorb the ambiguities of the future. Tropical ulcers on legs and arms were giving him hell. Before he caught the train north that night, he spent the morning riding the Edward Street ferry backwards and forwards, finding the chug-chug of the ferry's motor a soothing constant like the shabby sunburnt houses on the southern bank, the city skyline and the park on the other. "Nowhere to go, mate?" the ferryman asked him on the fourth trip. Will dragged up a grin. "I'm just enjoying not being shot at." The ferry kept filling with kids with tennis rackets and students from the university and technical college. They had less reality than Japanese soldiers, dying men, dirty-mouthed sergeants.

On the train north Will slept in restless spasmodic pieces, shaking with fever against the sooty leather. The carriage was packed with other demobbed men sprawled on seats and corridor floors. The train seemed to crawl. The men in his compartment talked horses and grog and women for hundreds of miles and were irritated by his sick yellow face bleak against the headrest, aloof from their yabber. "What's up, mate?" they kept asking. "You missing it? You want to be back there?"

He blinked awake on the second morning into sticky light as the train dragged through canefields into Reeftown. The air was heavy with smells too much like those of the Pacific islands to stir him with the sentiments of homecoming. The sky stood off hard and blue even at this hour.

He hauled his pack off the rack and leaned out into the sugary air, feeling the heat grab him, solid and damp. Crowds were on the platform cheering as the train limped to a halt. Bunting over the tearooms. A banner that said "Bless our Boys." But not seeing Con. Not seeing. Shoving his way out through the gates past kissers and huggers and squealers, not seeing, out into the street, hunkering down on his bloody pack as the sun straight in from the sea smote him, not seeing, his nead in his arms, suddenly howling oh shit oh shit shit shit, howling into the unrecognised recognised marvel of Con's voice above him, closing in and down on him, her clutching warmly and bossily him bonily weeping and rubbing her brown smiling face against his.

"Hey!" she kept saying. "Hey! What's all this? God, Will, you look exactly like old Ah Fong from the store squinted up like that."

Then he rocked with relieved mad laughter as she held him at arm's length, pushed up the corners of his eyes for her, and jabbered stupidly and burst out crying again.

"There," Connie soothed. "There. It's all right now, chaps. It's okay. Hey, you're here."

There. There.

The comfort words.

After submission, he wanted to pick away their stickiness.

The farm had been doing well since the start of the war, and despite a labour shortage, Harry had got by at first with drifters, draft-dodgers. But they were tiring, Harry and Clytie. Age was writing little warning messages about their eyes. Harry talked seriously to Will that first morning back. "It's your turn, now, son," Harry said. "Your aunt and I are getting too old for this game. It's all here waiting for you. Clytie and I are moving up to the beach shack at the Cape. We've extended the place and it's time we gave all this away."

Will found his face going blank. He wasn't ready for it. Wasn't adjusted. Those ravenous green acres gaped for attention. All morning he walked around the property trying to think himself back into it, but that afternoon he confessed to Connie, as she sat nursing her baby at the shady end of the veranda, "I don't think I want this, Con. I'm nearly twenty-four and all I know is that this isn't what I want. Not yet. You've got something. You've got Reever. I can't see myself, not yet, anyhow, accepting the sort of existence that contents you."

"How do you know it contents me?"

"It does. I can see it."

"But I'm off in a couple of months. There are grandparents somewhere in Washington who want to inspect this little chap."

"That's it then, isn't it? You'll stay. They'll persuade you to stay."

Connie's face flushed slowly with annoyance. "This is home," she said. "Don't ever, don't ever, Will, suggest I'd run out on this. When I come back, and I will come back, I'll move up to the Cape with Clytie and Harry. They can lease the farm."

He'd gone back south after a month and found himself a clerical job in the public service. He hated it. Brisbane was frayed about the edges in the aftermath of war. He was lonely. *So what's different,* he asked himself. *You've always been lonely.* He lived in a boarding house in West End and found the other boarders a patchy lot involved with weekend races and bingo evenings. Weekends he spent mooning around the Art Gallery or catching a train down the bay to sketch, a windblown lonely figure on the cliffs above Sandgate. Malaria had weakened him, and in the first months of what was called spring, he was hit by a return bout of fever. The public service was unsympathetic. "The war's over now," his section head said indifferently. "You returned blokes can't keep poling on the system. You have to face a return to reality sometime."

"Get stuffed," Will said pleasantly, holding his wavering body upright between his desk and that of the poor devil next to him. He slung his jacket over his shoulder and walked out.

Rage and illness kept him in bed in his depressing West End room for a week. Then one night someone he got talking to in a pub bar in the Valley offered him work in the records library of a commercial radio station. It wasn't, he discovered, so very different from public service clerking. A heavy dividing line was drawn between personalities of the air and desk hacks. Officers and men, Will told himself. Outraged by the shallowness of the whole business, he salvaged sanity by enrolling for art classes two nights a week. He agreed equally with his instructor that he hadn't much talent. "I want to daub my resentment," he said. "Well, that's a sophisticated enough reason," the instructor admitted. "But you could paint yourself dry."

"That's what I want."

He spent more and more time with his noisy atrocious paintings that were still silent enough to please the rest of the boarding house, but resonant enough to exhaust him. He found unbridgeable gaps between himself and the young students at art class and the office workers at the radio station. One of the announcers ("Star stuff," Will told himself amusedly), an older man who had spent the war years in

115

air raids over Europe, came up to him as he left the studio one afternoon and suggested a drink.

Will hesitated. It was the last class night of the term. He'd spent most of his last week's pay on paint that seemed, these days, to rush excitedly from his brushes. His obsession had the drag of love. He was writing something this way—journal? confession?

Cassidy was persuasive. Yet, cuddled by malt-stink in a pub somewhere near Petrie's Bight, hedged in by drinkers' roar and the rattle of trams in the street outside, Will found himself with nothing to say. The other man's age and sophistication left him floundering. He shifted uncomfortably in his chair while he watched Cassidy return to the bar for drinks. *Cheers*, Cassidy suggested, toasting with his refill on return, and then a profound silence dropped between them.

Will inspected Cassidy's angular face. He was a tall, gangly man without either moustache or verbal affectations that had seemed standard equipment for RAAF types. His voice was rich and cultivated. He'd been a rear gunner and had developed a proper respect for all the stabilities of living. He looked over the rim of his glass at Will and smiled and said, "I just wanted the chance to tell you we're all bored with the job, you know. I could see you felt that way. Totally and unutterably bored. After all that." The backwards jerk of his head brought into focus the whole arena of World War II. "It's hard to tell anyone who wasn't there how meaningless all this stuff seems."

Will nodded. He gulped more beer quickly and found himself thinking of his missed class.

"But you seem more out of it at the studio than I do. You're pretty lonely, aren't you?"

Will's yellow skin reddened.

"I was. It's okay now." He hesitated to admit to an interest in painting. He dreaded pretentiousness.

"Are you getting any enjoyment at all out of the job? With the records, I mean?"

"It's fair enough," Will replied cautiously. Was Cassidy a staff spy? Was he an accessory to managerial ear? "The collection is pretty bitsy."

"It's a new industry, you know. And the war's given it a hammering. You know something about it?"

116

"Not a lot. But some. My sister's pretty musical. We both learnt an instrument as kids. I'm afraid I'm at sea with the popular stuff."

"What did you play?"

"Violin."

"And have you kept it up?"

"Hardly." Will found himself laughing and the laughter kicked at his tonsils. "The army claimed me. Not much time for practising my vibrato in Bougainville. Except when I wanted to scream," he added defiantly.

"So you were scared?"

"There's got to be another word for it."

"Well, so was I. So was I, my God, scared enough to stink out my pants every time I went up."

"God," Will said, looking down into his beer-glass, embarrassed for both of them, "that's pretty good to know. There were times I thought I was the only one."

"Don't you believe it," Cassidy said. He leaned forward and looked warmly into Will's face. "Don't you bloody believe it. Why the hell do you think my lot went on with all that verbal crap—piece of cake, bit of a dust-up, all that swagger facade of gallantry, eh? They had to keep their bloody spirits up with any sort of pretence. The meiosis of bravery. Like a game. Like a bloody kids' game. I hated the whole damn business as much as you. I hated what we were sent up to do and I hated even more what the other side was going to do to me if it could."

Even inside the noisy bar, the two of them could hear explosions on the jolley poles of the trams as they cracked off from dust on the overhead wires.

"That," Cassidy said, nodding towards Queen Street and the open doorway, "that's the friendliest detonation I've heard in years. I love it."

Will felt something inside him unknot.

After that conversation moved more easily, and when the bar filled up and worked to its six o'clock frenzy, Cassidy suggested they have a bite to eat, and it seemed pleasant enough to sit over a piece of fish in a Greek café near Roma Street and push words around a little longer.

Cassidy admitted to marriage. Conservative Will wondered about the meal out, the lack of interest in departure. "It's over. A Yank," Cassidy said without rancour. "Great fucks. Great dressers. Snappy lines. I think she's somewhere in Philadelphia now. Who knows? I don't. I can only confess to a vast relief. It was a mistake from the start. Her parents were always over-eager."

After that evening, Will found work at the radio station not less boring but somehow eased over. Cassidy would drop into his cubicle to have a yarn, "slumming it," as Will commented once, lounging gracefully against filing cabinets. Jaunts for one became jaunts for two. There were concerts, films. Cassidy got lots of free tickets. "A natural deadhead," he said. "Natural." They drove down to the bay in Cassidy's small sports car, hiked out to Samson Vale and one weekend went down the coast and stayed at an old boarding house in Surfers.

It was a patchwork day of abrading sun and water, the hot grate of sandhills, the lashing bodies of swimmers, the tanginess of salt, melting ice creams, gut-achers of drinks gulped in hotel bars. Throwaway stuff, the pith of all seaside holiday.

But that night, in the wind-worried room fronting the water, Cassidy crossed, he crossed the narrow space between their sagging stretchers and, sitting bonily haunched on the wooden frame of Will's bed, took his hand and held it, warm and hard.

Will let his own lie like a rag.

Then Cassidy's other hand was moving towards his pillow, was stroking his salt-sticky hair and the protests that came bubbling up thickened around his tongue like the gaseous drinks he had swallowed earlier that day and he could only hawk out sounds that meant nothing at all.

Could they mean nothing? Could the other man not understand?

When Cassidy's mouth began planting dry and papery kisses on his face, Will struggled upright, pushing that skinny sunburnt body back. "I can't," he whispered. "I can't."

Cassidy's hands paused. His mouth drew away and Will saw in the shadowed face a mixture of shock and disbelief. Outside the sea hacked at the coast without tenderness, slammed in by a rising wind. Along the corridor a radio crackled. There was the sound of the Inkspots asking *Why tell them all the old tales?*

"What do you mean?"

Who kissed there long ago. Jesus!

"What I said. I can't."

"But haven't you ever—well—I, mean, I'm not usually wrong. I thought . . ."

"Yes," Will admitted. "I have." *Whispering grass, the trees don't have* . . . God, that bloody radio! "But it was different."

Was it? he wondered. *Was it so different?*

"Then what's wrong?"

"Nothing's wrong. Nothing, Cass. It's just . . . hell, I don't know what it is."

"Oh God," the other man said. "Please."

Will threw the sheet back and got out of bed. The watery light from sea and star caught his thin body as he crossed to the window, not knowing what to do, to say, hating to give hurt. Yet it was different somehow and he hated the excitement in his flesh. Stubbornly he stared out at the seesaw water.

Christ, he thought, oh Christ! Am I really one of those? The canteen and locker-room jokes? The sly nods? The passing insults from louts? There'd been other men in his unit he'd heard talked about, but he'd always regarded their activities as a rough substitute for heterosexual needs. He understood. He really thought he understood. But Cassidy was crying now behind him, a muffled sort of frightful sniffling, and there were words between the sniffles as he apologised, saying over and over, "I'm so bloody lonely, so lonely, mate."

"I'm sorry." Will threw the words backward but wouldn't look. "I'm sorry."

Cassidy began dragging on clothes. His voice, sweater-muffled as he pulled the garment over his head, came out with drying tears and an ache of bravado. "Just going out for a walk. Okay? I'll just take a turn along the front."

Will kept his back turned as he heard the door open. Briefly the Inkspots entered and vibrated through the room, then the door closed and Will listened to Cassidy's footsteps until they faded at the foot of the stairs. Below him in the dark the front door opened and shut and he went back and lay on his stretcher listening to the radio fight the complaints of the sea. Despite everything, he fell asleep and didn't wake until sun sliced under the holland blind and reached for his feet. The bed across the room was empty and Cassidy's clothing and bag were gone.

For months after that at work they avoided each other. Cassidy resigned suddenly and Will shrank from social contact. As the year tottered to a close, one of the jollier typists pursued him with such avid attention his first amusement became outrage. He applied for other jobs but always missed out. Brisbane was hotter and dustier than he liked. He was tiring of its dismal geography.

When Connie's phone call came he took half a minute to decide the next move.

Will flew home on the night plane that brought the southern papers.

Connie watched his lone figure striding out across Reeftown's tarmac and clutched her small son's hand tightly.

"Who's that?" Reever asked.

"You know who. Uncle Will. Don't you remember?"

"I was too young," Reever said distantly. "Let go my hand."

He climbed out of the car and stood with sturdy legs apart, clutching the door-handle and looking at the man getting closer. His mother was waving and smiling and calling. Then there were skinny arms round the two of them and a smell of tiredness and tobacco and Con felt her heart open as it had never really opened for any other man, not with this assurance of familiarity and warmth and touch.

"I still don't remember you," Reever was saying, and the grown-ups weren't listening and he kept shouting it louder and louder through his mother's half-crying laughter, firing his shouts at the skinny man's grin. And then Connie tugged Reever hard in against her, and pulling an excuse-this face looked wryly over his head at her brother, and the kid gave in and said, "Well, I do a bit. But only a bit."

"That's better than no bit," Will said, rumpling Reever's fair hair. He slung his canvas bag in the boot. "Can I drive? Sentimental homecoming."

Connie said, "Oh God, it's so good to see you, Will, you can crash the damn thing if you want."

"That's silly," Reever said.

Connie agreed it was silly. She leaned back against the car door, rubbing the nape of her son's neck, and stared at Will over Reever's untidy thatch.

"It's nearly two years, Will. Nearly two. Please stay on for a bit. Please."

He stopped smiling. "I've resigned. Thrown the job in. Just like that. Finished. Kaput. A promising career sorting plastic discs cut short at its outset."

That stopped her. Her eyes widened. "You mean you're coming back up here?"

"It looks like it, doesn't it, sis? The heart is where the home is."

She appeared humbled by the suddenness of it. "What will you do, then?" she asked. "You know Harry sold Swiper's just before he died. Just after I got back from the States. But there's plenty to do up at the Cape."

He was vague with excitement. This and that, he said. This and that. Something would turn up.

"I'm going to school soon," Reever interrupted.

Will edged behind the steering wheel and looked over his shoulder at the small boy.

"Are you, mate?" he said. "You'll be able to teach me, then."

That night, with the house asleep behind them, they scrambled down the track to the beach and sat on the sand smoking and watching the sea. It rippled in thick black silk between the headlands, its surface alive with the faintest skin of moonshine. Will built a small fire on the sand to keep mosquitoes and midges away, damping the dry twigs with an armful of seaweed. Sand clung to their bare skins like sugar.

He dragged deeply on his cigarette and looked along the white rind of beach.

"There was lots of this stuff where I was in the war, Con. I never thought I'd get to hate it."

"Do you?"

"At the moment. But it was never like this. Silent. Secure." He shook his head with a nervous movement. "Despite spending half my time here as a kid, this feels, well, virginal."

"Virginal?"

"Like me." He gave a sort of laugh.

"And are you?" Connie asked, drawing something in the sand with one finger.

"Just about. Your way, anyhow."

"What do you mean my way?"

Will stubbed out his cigarette and tossed the butt on the fire. He lay back on the sand, his arms behind his head. Something was driving him to say this but he couldn't face her. He had to keep his eyes away. Perhaps the antitheses of beaches, of army life and Brisbane life and the house-stored memories of Swiper's and the Cape were squeezing admissions.

"I've never had a girl, Con."

There was the slightest emphasis on the word "girl." The word floated on a breath.

Connie lay on one side, propped on an elbow, and stared at him by the twitchy light of the fire. He looked like an overgrown boy, still with the beauty and pathos of adolescence: the over-long legs, the too-young face, still rounded despite the war and what it had done to him, with an almost prepubescent softness.

"What have you had?"

He understood he could tell her. She was the only one he felt truly safe with. They'd shared bed and bath as small children. In summer holidays they'd skinny-dipped in water-holes in the gorge. Her body was as familiar to him as his own all through his school years, and, because of her mothering, even more dear.

"He was in my unit. A bit younger. He was scared shitless up in the islands, like me. Both of us scared out of our minds. He was a stretcher-bearer." Will stopped speaking and felt around for his cigarette pack, seeing Mike racing and shuddering through undergrowth. "It just happened. I can't tell you how. Maybe we just meant to comfort each other. He was killed not long after. That's all."

He sat up and lit another cigarette from the fire.

"There'll be girls," Connie said, looking at him and looking at him.

"Will there? I don't care much. Not too much. Not at the moment. I'm back. I've survived. That's enough for the present, coping with survival, wondering what I do with it. And I've got you, Con, haven't I?"

Connie's face was patched with doubt, with pain. "Of course." She watched her big toes digging away at sand, cascading waterfalls of silver in the starlight. Then she dragged her legs back and knelt up.

"You're making me sad, Will," she said. "I don't want to feel sad when you've just come back to stay. Let's go for a swim. It's so long since we've done that together."

She stood up and walked away from him a little and pulled off her shorts and shirt until she stood stripped, her body pale against the black moving sea-canvas.

Then she walked back to her brother and stood over him.

Will looked up and smiled.

"God, Con," he said, "I even like your stretch marks." And he ran one finger gently along the faded puckering at the crease of her thigh.

She kept smiling at him, a fluid smile that rose and found her eyes and sank and found her heart, and she tugged at his hand and pulled him up and in a moment he had stripped and they were racing like old times to the water together, splashing in and swimming out and out before turning, parallel to the shoreline, moving with the purposefulness of sharks to the far end of the little bay, turning and swimming back.

The water was soft as milk. Their fire glittered at them from the beach. They trod water, gasping and laughing and splashing each other, re-learning childhood ritual, and then Will dived and pulled her under, wrestling her close to him until lack of air forced them to a spluttering surface. Automatically they turned towards the beach and began swimming until their feet touched shingle. They hadn't spoken one word.

Connie ran ahead of him towards the fire and stood with her back to the rain forest, her arms opened and welcoming. The ritual was changing. Will walked slowly up to her and she drew him with her, back beyond the fire, back to the softer sand, holding and pulling until they were lying together, her arms around him rocking and rocking the sudden horrible sobs of one man's war, while he clung closer and closer until the warmth of her body absorbed his.

The little fire on the beach had gone out. There were only ashes and glints from the ashes. Mosquitoes droned in.

They dressed in silence, looking away from each other.

There'd be the morning after this and the next and the next and the next week and the next month and "I don't care," Connie said finally and stubbornly. She kicked a fire-blackened stick away with a deliberate toe. "I really don't care."

"Don't be silly," he said. "We both care."

She was silent.

"I can't stay," he said. "Not now. Not here."

"Oh rubbish. Of course you can stay."

"Be realistic, Con." He shivered in the cooling air. "You know it's impossible."

Con began to weep roughly and angrily. "Oh it's guilt." She excused herself. "Guilt. Don't worry about me, about that. We both know why. Don't let's talk about it. Will, we need you, Clytie and me, now Harry's gone. We're cut off up here."

"You'll find a man, Con. How couldn't you?" He looked at her face shadowed by starlight and felt like howling. "But it can't be me. There's Malloy, isn't there?"

Connie stared straight past him at the bay. "There's no passion in it," she said. "Not what I'd call passion. I'm nearly thirty. Do you think I have a right to passion still? Sometimes when I looked at Harry and Clytie and saw them crimping the edges of their quarrels after forty years of wedlock I wondered what was best. I still wonder. They were united by the vitality of loathing."

The vitality of loathing. It was one of those phrases that had stuck with her like the first lines of poems learned by rote or the propositions of certain theorems.

"You'll marry, Will," she went on. "You'll find yourself a girl."

He looked at her sideways out of his strangely flecked eyes, and his mouth shrugged at the corners.

"I think I'm one of nature's grand neuters. I need no one. Not yet."

"You could be wrong," she said. "Don't go back."

He dragged ideas from the air. "There's still the old place up at Mango dad left. That way we'll still be close."

Her smile had the grave arc of some painted Florentine martyr's. It held the hint of secret knowledge.

They walked back to the house parted by what had happened. There should have been horror somewhere but there wasn't quite that. Will felt as if something had entered his life and then drained it.

He was still incomplete.

He wasn't one of your Hi-there born-agains with a king size bedroom voice deep and comfily American, a personality that stroked conscience and wallet into instant release. Chant would trumpet *God loves you loves you loves you* so forcefully and fiercely convinced, the listener trembled at such divine interest.

"This world," the prophet man in the angle of the Swiper's Arms veranda was racketing, "has its sickening limitations." He demonstrated limitations with his hands. "Worldly goods!"—he dismissed them with a pudgy wave. "Power and fame!"—a snap of finger and thumb. "What we are seeking," he shouted, "is the extraterrestrial infinity, the infinity of the miracle."

"Bullshit," Reever thought, watching the speaker and the acolyte mob that had moved beer glasses closer to revelation. *Bullshit*.

All the same, he edged a little closer as well to take soundings of this watery piece of humanity togged up in a cobalt sheet. The face didn't match the words—or the voice for that matter. There was no congruence between utterer and that which was uttered, for when the voice began unrolling its thesis, there were both stridencies and a rich gravy-like quality that battled together. Even drinkers lounging under the mango trees by the fence had turned to stare when the prophet first spoke.

But the face was a florid turnip with a small pouting mouth that anticipated high pitch, and beneath that a submissive chin alien to the dogmatism of the tongue. The hair was a sandy thinning flat-cap on that football skull and the eyes, yes, Reever could just make out the eyes, might have been small excisions from the toga.

"Miracles all about us," the voice went on, "we have only to look. If you know how. If you know the secret of looking. The world is its own miracle. And you. You are your own miracle, you yourself your own miracle." The voice dropped a perfect third. "Think of that."

Reever couldn't help glancing then at a couple of Murris collapsed drunken by the outhouses and found himself whispering "Yeah, think of it. Think of it, Garfield, you're your own miracle, mate, and we've helped you be that way. You too, Chocka!"

The inky voice of the speaker was processing all the permutations of the banal, but the crowd of listeners, instead of fidgeting, of growing restless, was riveted on the pulpy face and goldfish mouth through which these plangent nothings pumped. Reever tried catching the eye of one after another of his friends to tip them the full slow ironic wink but they wouldn't, couldn't look. Maybe that was a miracle in itself.

"Prayer," the blue turnip was pronouncing, his exhortations vertiginously out of place in the humid blue of the afternoon, "prayer" *(here it comes,* thought Reever) "the greatest miracle of all because it is your direct—yes, I repeat that—direct line" *(oh a comic! a swinger! a with-it techno!)* "to God, can work further miracles for you. For you personally." *(What about impersonally?)* "Palpable miracles" *(Palpable, eh?)* "that can only extend your further belief in prayer."

Out on the lawn one of the abos began a noisy retching.

But the prophet didn't falter. He didn't turn to give aid, either.

"My group," he told them all averting their faces from the monstrous sight on the grass, "my dear friends and followers, through the power of Mary, Mother of the Lord, and through her intercession on your behalf, on all our behalves, can perform any miracle at all. Any. You need only believe."

His voice ceased and he resumed his seat. There was uncertain applause. The slow hot afternoon grew perilous. From the bar came the spatter of radio, and pop music underscored the silence in this corner of the veranda. The sick abo hawked himself to a standstill and over the gun-cracks of the expanding tin roof, a leather bird's song shrilled, violently sweet.

"What's that blue for?" someone asked. The followers were wearing blue cloaks, blue headbands, blue sashes.

"It's Mary's colour. Traditionally Mary's colour."

"They're making a mock," some other voice said. "Stupid bastards."

126

Then yet another offered to buy turnip a drink and this broke the mood even though the offer was declined. Reever heard talk of meeting places and times and saw two of them rise from disciple haunches where they had been squatting on the veranda railing and begin to move among the listeners handing out leaflets.

Soon one of them approached Reever.

She had taken off her cloak because of the heat and was wearing some kind of white cotton sack hauled in by a blue sash that trailed from her thin waist. Why, Reever thought, there is so little of her I could blow her over. But his words didn't.

"No collection?" he asked derisively. Her pointed wan face, powdered with an ancient grief, regarded him directly with an expression he could not quite gauge.

"That comes later," she told him, handed him a leaflet, and moved on into the bar without another glance. Behind him, laughter.

Reever had dropped out. After completing a science degree with a major in biology, he had worked for three years in a government laboratory until he had been hauled hair-wise backwards and arrested by a Brisbane policeman during an anti-Vietnam protest. Reever, in a headlock, his feet projecting at impossible angles as they manhandled him into a paddy wagon, was viewed by half of Swiper's Creek until the jerking bands of the television image whacked the screen into oblivion.

"That's it, man," Reever had announced when Will flew south and bailed him out. "That is positively it. You can shove your nine-to-five security. This government's evil."

Reason had not prevailed. He vanished that afternoon with two other bailees and reported in at Swiper's Creek months later. Skin-alert. Body-careful.

They were all doing it, Connie consoled herself. The north was crawling with middle-class dropouts just too late to synchronise with Haight-Ashbury. Still . . . "My God, it's just like the thirties," she'd say, watching, from the front veranda of her house at the Cape, the straggles of cheesecloth clad women and be-jeaned men drifting past on the track to the Roads. "Except," she added, looking sideways at her son, "these ones aren't *looking* for work. They're—"

"Don't say it," Reever warned. "Just don't say it."

He'd been working on Malloy's trawler for the last three months and had returned to Swiper's solvent and with a longing for solid earth under foot. Malloy came up to him, still laughing. The texture of prayer, prophecy and miracle was somehow altered by beery goodwill.

"Just another wind-artist," Malloy said. "Boy, do we get them up here!"

"It's called political mouth. Infectious. Should be notifiable." Reever's inspecting eye was unpassionate. "What," he asked the air, "would a girl like that be doing with a con like him?"

He was to discover within the week.

Chant—they all called him that—and his group of the enlightened prolonged their stay in the area by ingratiating themselves with a commune a few miles up the coast. Friends at the beach snuggery told Reever of revivalist meetings in hot moonlight, of the laying on of hands, ("I'll bet!" said Reever), of candlelit pray-ins on milky sand strips.

Reever talked about it with Connie, who was exhausted these swollen days of the build-up. She lay back on her lounger watching the passion vines blow ragged in the nor'-easter.

"I know about them, dear. I know. One of their dodgers was pinned up on the library notice board. They can't spell 'divine'."

Reever giggled. "Think they're fakes?"

"How would I know, my dear? I've been a sucker for fakes all my life. They could be. Then they could also be genuine suffering utterly bored truth-seekers, those obsessional god-searchers who believe implicitly in every word they utter. We've had a lot of them up this way. That doesn't make them fakes. It doesn't make them good spellers, either." She closed her eyes. "How your great-granddaddy would have loved them. He adored originals of every kind."

"How would you know?"

"My dear, I *am* your great-granddaddy. I refer, of course, to the Canadian side, not the American. I'm all of them. Jessica Olive, Nadine, George. Especially Nadine. *Manquée*, by the way. They run through my blood. And into you. You're all of them. Can't you see that? How the world repeats itself!"

"It's the weather," Reever said to her, and he patted her hand. "You always do get sentimental during the build-up."

At the beach commune, Bo, a large and gentle hippie with mind-fog from five years' pot-smoking, admitted to enthusiasm and conviction as he told of the next meeting.

It was, he said, to be held in an old banana shed on the Carascatti's allotment. Willing hands had patched the building, swept it and decorated the walls with heraldic scrolls of blue-and-white sheeting. A marquee had been pitched nearby. *A miracle*, Chant commented on this house built without hands. *A miracle*, he said, as furbishings that hadn't cost a penny appeared overnight. *Miracles*! he would cry joyfully when, after the ceremonial of homily, after prayers and invocation, refreshments appeared in plastic mugs, a libation of soursop and mango.

Reever was hunting the dodger-handler.

The self he had suspected might lie glistening behind that outer earnestness was not there. Not there to him. She was simplicity itself.

"See." She made him inspect her left hand. She drew back a bangle of blue celluloid. The riotous red lines of a fearful injury still showed across palm and fingers and as she revolved her arm he saw that the bracelet of wounded tissue extended completely around the base of her hand. "A machine where I worked." Reever was silent before this blatant exposure. "My hand was useless. All the doctors said it would be useless. All the movement was gone. Tendons, nerves, all severed."

The sea-coloured shallows of the girl's eyes reflected no pain and no memory of pain.

"Then I met someone who told me about him. About Chant." Surprisingly she raised the injured hand impertinently close to Reever's face and snapped each finger against a contemptuous thumb—snap snap snap snap—right under his nose. "Wouldn't you believe?"

"Oh God," the girl said. "But it was instantaneous. Just like that. Just—like—that. One minute I'm at the meeting, my hand dangling like some dead thing, and then Chant comes up, he comes right up as if he's singled me out from everyone there, I mean everyone, and he picks up my hand and presses it between both of his own for half a minute maybe. Presses and presses and I can feel the warmth, this tremendous warmth as if my hand is in some thick glove. And then he takes his hands away and says, 'There. Now you go round and hand

129

these out for me. Use that hand.' And I do. I do. Just like that."

Then she smiled, and Reever, who might have been going to ask "And when did he lay you, baby?" felt ashamed in the face of such fundamental conviction.

At thirty-one, -two, whatever he was, he would have believed himself beyond the seduction of easy impressions, the quick dipstick into somebody else's magic—look, water sloshed everywhere, and look, the colours coming up on the page, though in this case there was nothing but blue. There had been magic enough in the extraordinariness of the world, of the people he encountered, the quirks of latitudes: beach hermits, crazy ferals, tin scratchers, yacht freaks, madmen still fossicking for gold in tableland backwaters, dole gurus in Mango's hills, southern sharpies declared bankrupt there but mysteriously solvent here, junkies and dope dealers all under the protection of police and government provided they were big enough, unexplained visaless Yanks, Germans, Canadians making out on isolated river stretches and in forest clearings with all mod cons and no visible means of support—an army of workers, scroungers, pseudo-saints and the real thing. A kind of human confetti.

Chant? Chant?

Reever wanted to probe further.

You see, he might have heard his mother saying, *that's your great-granddaddy coming out—investigative journalism!*

Bum, he would say.

He still wanted to probe further.

He attended another meeting. And another. There was a dubious sameness.

Nevertheless.

He followed the group, or girl, as Chant went proselytising up past Mango into tin country; down into Reeftown markets and a small waterfront park where the police moved them on; at a rival scam-merchant's health farm near Tobaccotown.

That December, every day, flaunted the cerulean of Chant's obsession. A confluence between two abstractions: sky and creed. Each made the other valid.

Reever began to wonder if, for all his years, he had the desiccated qualities of settled bachelorhood. He thought of Uncle Will. He loved him. He tried not to think of him. He thought of Chant. He thought of Con's amused scoffing. He thought of Chant, examining the prophet for chicanery or cash zealotry. His examination did more to reveal Reever to Reever. It showed nothing of Chant.

At eighteen, twenty, twenty-plus, there'd been ideals in plenty. There'd been sex. Once there'd been love. Time for each separately and together. He'd lived with a dedicated fruit-eater for a year, testing the limits of his mother's endurance when the two of them moved north from Brisbane after his arrest and built a shack on the seaward boundary of the farmlet at the Cape.

"She's shy," Reever explained to Connie. "She doesn't say much." Reever was inclined to apologise for his girlfriend.

"I guess she's too weak," his mother said.

"Now don't start that," Reever complained. "Don't start that three-meals-a-day shit. I don't want a lecture on vitamins."

"I've no intention. Since when have I ever?"

Connie had banged her way to the piano and began bashing out some Brahms with a lot of technical flair.

Reever went after her and plucked his mother's hands from the keys.

"Listen! Listen!" he was shouting. "Listen, for God's sake!"

"Pretty rude," Connie commented, not resisting but looking speculatively at her son. She wanted badly to laugh.

"I like this girl," Reever said. "Flute means a lot to me. She's intelligent. She's kind. What more do you want? And she sings prettily, quite prettily. You ought to like that."

"She sings moderately," Connie said musingly. "Don't get carried away. But is she really kind? Really? That's very nice if she is. Very nice. But she's terribly underweight. Her kindness has made her terribly underweight."

"Oh Christ!"

Reever had sulked back to his shack on the treadway of resumed Brahms. He was extra nice to Flute, who didn't notice or care. He believed he was in love. Within a month she had left him and hitched her way to a commune farther up the coast, and after the initial pride-jolt, Reever had to admit to himself that he was relieved. There'd been too much vegetable-chopping. He enjoyed being on his own in

131

the shack. He enjoyed once more the freedom of unaccountability. He began to practise trumpet again.

"I know we're a musical family, dear," Connie would say. "Cornelius sang, you know, and Jessica Olive probably didn't play as well as I do, but still. And Will, of course. There is nothing nicer than that fabulous ripping sound of chromatics early in the morning. If it doesn't attract nosey bastards, Reeve, then at least it might keep our patch clear of intruders. Do you miss Flute?"

"I think," he said to her, grinning, "you're unkind to my talent. As to the other, maybe I'm a natural bachelor. Like Uncle Will."

"Ah," Connie said, looking at him, looking away, looking down to the beach. "Will. Well, that's another story."

Connie and Reever rubbed along harmoniously enough in their separate houses. She had worked for years supporting the little family by nursing at the Canecutters Hospital. When Reever came home she retired from Canecutters and amused herself by taking piano pupils, teaching in a studio she rented in Swiper's township. "I need to be busy," she said to Reever. "I need the interest." Jobs took Reever away for months at a time and the elastic of his absence stretched unendingly. Their affection was given in passing, as it were, but was still a factor of permanence.

"When you come back," Connie would say to him, "I want to be told about it. I mean *told*. Every funny sordid pernicious wonderful detail. Sometimes I feel like Jane Austen stuck in Bath. You can find me a miracle, too, if you would."

Reever looked slyly at her. "What sort?"

"Oh not that sort, Reeve. I only have to watch you. No." She propped her chin on laced fingers and stared through louvres and leaves at the tantalising aquamarine of sea. "Not travel. I'm a stopper now after that great binge when you were small. Not that. A change of government maybe. Or government heart. I can't stand living in a dictatorship that poses as a democracy. Thank God we're away from the source up here. True charity in the churches? How does that sound? Some really impossible thing like that. No sports broadcasts for a year. Something."

"This is Oz, mother," Reever said patiently. "Life in the golden pineapple."

Chant?

Examine Chant. Examine Chant apart from those obvious attributes and failings. He sings, leading full-voiced, Adam's apple wobbling in Marian hymns. Ignore that. He preaches—gutfuls of hokum—fulsomely. Ignore. Because the very emphases breed a verbal phoniness, the listener tends to suspect content as well. His ferocious commitment makes him, publicly at least, suave with hippies, straights, junkies and prosperous farmers. He's been seen chatting kindly with old smelly people. Any categories omitted? Politicians? He's lunched with the Member for Cannabis, a pot-hater of distinction who has ruthlessly pursued small-time growers along the beaches while failing to take even the slightest interest in those plantations discovered on his own vast acreage. Does Chant hope for a conversion?

At the meetings there were testimonies, scores of them. It was like watching a film award junket: *an' I wanna thank my producer an' costars an' the director Marty Ravelshed an' all those lovely people the props boys an' sis who put me through acting school by working the game an* . . . Sorry, Chant. Sorry. That's to belittle. But it ran a parallel course of cured neuralgia and myopia and unspecified lumps and they all thanked Chant who'd led them to Miracleland as if it were some Gold Coast Wonderworld and they forgot, the joy was so stupendous, to thank God at all. And then Chant interposed nods and becks and wreathed smiles and if they cared, but only if they cared, to make a donation towards the good work, well, that would be . . . and they did . . . and it was . . . received.

At first Reever thought the hype too electric, too theatric. He noted that the group now drove around the mission field in two brand-new Toyota ranch wagons. Yet he found he had merely to listen to Sister Seawater (*My name is Frances,* the thin girl had reproved, *Frances!*) and he rejected suspicion, rejected at last even the notion of duplicity.

"Tell me," Connie bullied when he next went back home from work in the field, "tell me. Are there orgies?"

Father Rassini, who was visiting, choked on his brandy and dry. (*No ice, Connie, for God's sake, if not mine!*) He was indulging in the socialising he permitted himself with those of his far-flung flock whose worldly bank accounts were more solid than their spiritual. There was method in this. Connie understood: he suspected her of wealth. His sleek Volvo parked in the driveway was as black as sin and had the satisfied gleam that comes from having rendered unto both Caesar and God.

"You should come along. Both of you." Reever went back into his mother's chaotic kitchen to fetch a beer.

When he returned to the veranda, Father Rassini, without preamble, began unsubtly to damn Chant and all his works.

"The Church," he pronounced, "can have no truck with the manifestations of hysteria."

"Hysteria?"

"Hysteria." Firmness was all. "Groups like this tread a perilous edge between heresy and genuine faith. The gullible can be seduced. The unwary, trapped. No, Connie—yes, my dear, a little more—no, Reever: this man is not even a minor prophet and he can do incalculable harm to those who pay spiritual tribute to the Mother of God."

"But he does. They do." Reever settled down in beastly torpor in a deck chair and gulped half his beer. He could see his mother trying not to laugh.

"Do what?"

"Pay tribute to the Mother of God. There's a daily rosary."

Sipping elegantly, Father Rassini reached for an olive, nibbled it thoroughly and then deposited the stone neatly beside six others. Having achieved this dramatic pause—they all stared at the ranked olive pips—he laughed lightly and dismissively.

"But of course. Of course. What else would you expect? My point, Reever—and for a bright young man you do seem to keep missing it—is that this group of miracle hunters or whatever they are does not have His Holiness's blessing. It is not sanctioned by the Church. There is no ordained authority in charge to lead or guide, to help them avoid the pitfalls of wild belief. And he's probably"—another sip—"a racketeer."

Reever, to Father Rassini's irritation, refused the bait and practised his own dramatic silence.

His mother smiled between both men as if she were bemused by continuing words.

The silence kept extending.

"Well," Father Rassini said at last, prodded by discomfort and rising to an inspiring height while he dabbed his fingers on a beautifully laundered handkerchief, "you have been cautioned. Connie, I must be going now. By the way, did I speak to you about the new assembly hall for the—"

Connie heaved herself right through his blandnesses to the living room and came back with a sealed envelope she placed without comment in his unsurprised hand.

"God bless you," Father Rassini said. "You may be less caring than you should, my dear, with regard to your spiritual obligations, but your heart is certainly in the right place. By the way, that was an excellent brandy."

He raised one smooth hand, said as an afterthought, "Goodbye, Reever" and went down the steps to his car.

Reever watched the expensive machine lurch down the ungraded track to the road with satisfaction. "God, Con," he said, "how can you stand that patronising bore?"

Connie smiled. The repetitiveness of the world amused her but did not surprise. How many weeks was it since she had insisted on her family identity? I am Cornelius, she had said. I am Jessica Olive and Nadine and George. The world made its statements over and over and she remembered Clytie defining Father Rassini as the ghostly clone of a Father Madigan who'd been the parish priest so many years before. Her smile widened.

"No money this time, but the very nicest card wishing his project well. I've always believed God likes a good laugh. Now tell me, son, *were* there orgies?"

Reever invited Chant and his followers to the shack for a weekend.

"The pursuit of truth is tireless," he told Connie.

"Must you?" she asked.

"Too late. They'll be here tomorrow."

"I feel you'll regret it. We'll regret it."

"You won't have to do a thing. Not a thing. Not even come to the orgy."

"I have no intention of doing a thing, even *at* the orgy. I grew up in

135

retreat revivalism and I'm far too old for those larks now. People like that exhaust me."

"You haven't met him."

"I'm a prejudiced old lady and I don't want to."

"Oh go on," Reever coaxed. "I'll invite you down. For the Joyful Mysteries."

"Don't."

But he did. And she went, outrageous in the shabbiest gardening trousers she could find, her hair plaited and carelessly finished with bows of string. Her feet were wallopers in ranch boots. Her still-enchanting features glowered above a fourex t-shirt and under a stained digger's hat.

"My mother," Reever said.

"Dear lady," said Chant.

There was a glut of blue. Chant was persistently gracious and attentive to Connie's fury. Sister Seawater doled out blood-cooling fruit juices while Connie sat, her mouth opened in a social smile of the utmost cynicism, smoking between smiles and spilling things with party-pooping zest. She dropped her fruit juice as she groped for salad, her salad as she reached for tea and towards the end of the alfresco smorgasbord unloaded a whole tray of lumpy sandwiches and organically grown carrot spears.

"Jesus, mother," Reever whispered, "do you have to? You've made your point."

"Well, it's a bit dull, isn't it, dear? They don't seem to have any small talk."

After an hour Connie's restlessness set her pacing the perimeters of the crowd. Her audacious grubbiness seemed not to matter to these blue-and-white missionaries. She suggested liquor. The sun was already sliding down the sky towards the hills. She suggested it again, loudly, lusting after the *frisson* of disapproval, but Reever was already hauling six-packs out of his refrigerator and stacking them on trestle tables under the bean trees.

Everywhere blue grew limp with sweat. At the back of the shack the generator thumped unendingly.

Chant had disappeared inside his cobalt burnous.

Was he meditating? Connie wondered.

Glass-chink recalled him. People redisposed themselves on

136

Reever's secondhand divans, on his canvas deck-chairs and along the veranda rail. Others lay beneath the trees. Someone proposed a toast.

"To the Order!"

"I'll drink to order," Connie said.

"*The* Order," Sister Seawater corrected.

"Didn't I say that? Drink up, everyone. It's a drinking afternoon. When Reever's stock runs out you must allow me. I'm going to perform the miracle of Cana. Me personally. I myself."

"Your mother," Chant said to Reever, "is such a character."

The group became noisier. The tape deck was whacking out hot gospel numbers. Connie trudged back up the hill followed by "Oh Lord, didn't it rain," and reappeared shoving a wheelbarrow load of assorted bottles. "Father Rassini's cellar," she commented cryptically, and became the life of the party, slapping up a punch of tremendous alcoholic proportions over a mulch of bruised pineapple. "Drinkies!" she cried. "Drinkies! Miracle punch!"

"Now, now," Chant admonished with a liquor-varnished smile—corners up, eyes crinkling, voice richer—"don't make fun. You created this with love. We'll drink it with love, with a sense of brotherhood."

"I bet you will, buster," Connie said, and started ladling.

In that sulky heat, ice melted as it dropped in the bowl. Chant seized the expectant moment to launch an exhortation to disciples suitably befuddled as they clutched their tilting glasses. A fog of prayer began to enclose the two small rooms of the shack and seep out towards the veranda and garden. He called on everyone to link minds and hearts in a thanksgiving goblet. "Well, that's one way of describing it," Connie said to no one in particular, and, as Chant began to bray "Stand up and be counted," "They can't count," she whispered to Reever. "Not these days."

"Stand up!" Chant cried again, in the decibels of soul-throb. "Stand up for Mary and the Lord and the age of miracles!"

"Any moment," Connie commented to Reever, who was trying to disown her, "there'll be a storm of alleluias, sweet Jesus and a hippo-mouthed collection bag."

"Wrong," he said. "And anyway you don't have to stay."

After the prose-rhythms, singing. And after that Reever started playing chords on his guitar. A flop-haired young man from the beach commune produced a harmonica and something nice began to happen, an intricate coiling of plaintive reeds in and out, the notes strung like a vine through the sturdy trellis of sound Reever was constructing. Fragile, lovely, the green harmonies grew across the room to the veranda in the early night air. The punch lay neglected and warming. Glasses paused on veranda railings and Reever and the harmonica player became the sole carvers and creators of what was left of the meeting. Others from the commune had drifted up from the beach and the air thickened with the sickly sweet smell of dope while the two players, as if inspired by each other, created further and further tendrils of music that writhed around the one central motif to which their lips and fingers kept referring.

Reever looked up for a moment and saw Chant lean against the darkening air. Who can explain the stillness that had overtaken them all in that broiler of a jungle clearing?

Aural amity expanded through the body's every cell.

Was Chant stirred by something wilder than the stock platitudes of his professional religiosity? From the eastern horizon, still streaked with reflected light from the sea, massive clouds, black-bellied and with lightning in their guts, swung ponderously across the skyscape. A medieval gouache. An illustration of the day of judgement.

The air suddenly lost light and, chiming with plucked strings, the first drops of the Wet, isolated and large, smacked onto the tin roof, onto banana leaves, onto Chant's upturned face.

Later, stimulated by alcohol and the overpowering force of unuttered prayer craving utterance, most of them wandered down to the beach where forest crowded the water. Rain crashed through leaves, pocked sand, bit skin. No one cared. They rollicked, singing and calling in the release of rain, right down the beach to its northern end.

There, encapsulated by water and darkness, they chorused as one. Vainly Chant tried to insert a religious tone into their rain-gulping mouths but was drowned out by the beach commune, who insisted idiotically that raindrops kept falling on their heads. They made clumsy dancing steps. They solo'd and sashayed backwards and forwards, pelting their words to glory. Chant's pleas were flattened. His sonorous baritone tracked a lone and desperate path through the

"Salve Regina" as if he were dealing with rebellion.

Then one of them, wandering from the outer fringe of dancers, pointed along the sand to a deeper shadow, a patch of raised darkness lumped on the beach.

"What's that?"

The question was wiped out as if by a sponge. The singing went on.

Bo asked again. He shrugged aside their indifference and ambled soggily away, up the beach to the high-tide line and along to the sprawled shape.

A man lay there face down, body awry, clothes a muddle of shingle and weed. Bo knelt and gently turned the man's face towards him. His terrified and curious fingers touched stilled flesh. He thought, but he could have been mistaken, that an eyelid flickered. The rain, he thought. Small shells and grit blocked the nostrils and delicately he picked the debris away and then pressed his ear close to the man's chest. Nothing. Nothing. Yet there was the faintest warmth lingering in the skin as if this fire were not quite doused.

He straightened up and began to yell, but his cries were baffled by weather. So he stumbled back through sand and rain to the singers. He grabbed arms and shook.

"Listen, hell, listen! There's a bloke back there. A young bloke. I think he's drowned."

Chant was arrested mid-vibrato. The singing dribbled away. No one was prepared for this intrusion of the real world.

Where, they kept asking. *Where?*

Bo's pointing hand made their rain-addled heads turn. He led the way back, ploughing through driftwood and sea-trash. Reever galloped past all of them and by the time the singers had gathered about this piece of jetsam was already straddling the body and beginning a steady, urgent pressure on the man's chest, bending, pressing, breathing into the gaping mouth. He gasped between breaths, "Fetch Connie, someone. She's good at this. Fetch her."

From under his soaking toga Chant produced a flashlight whose beam cut the beating rain into shreds of silver. It shone on Reever locked into the concentration of rescue. He didn't even speculate on how the man had got there. He didn't think at all, merely surrendering to crisis in a down-up, down-up, even and firm.

All around a kind of febrile uselessness.

"Pray," Chant was ordering. "Pray. Pray now for a miracle." He began intoning, and as the troopers gradually joined their voices to Chant's, Reever, previously aware only of the urgency of hands and breath, was surprised by a waspish sting of irritation. Although a mouthful of water and sand had dribbled from the parted lips, the body was showing no response. The sky made for a second drowning unless they moved him. Rain was whipping the air with lashing force, plugging his own eyes and mouth, yet all the time he could sense that feeble warmth he was afraid to stop the pressure.

It had seemed there could be no more rain to fall, but terraces of cloud collapsed suddenly in great waterslides that suffocated as they hit, shouting their way into the forest. God, Reever prayed, bending and breathing, God.

Then there was Connie's voice, and glancing sideways Reever saw she was lugging a groundsheet and mackintosh. Her plaits ran like down-pipes and as she came into the eye of the torch, he saw the rain washing across her face like flawed glass.

She was full of orders, full of practicality.

When Bo and Reever lifted the body, the drowned man's mouth gushed seawater and mucous, spilling in a sad puddle on the sand. Torchlight wavered across beach, sky and trees, and the party scattered ahead of the stretcher-bearers, who were moving at a jog.

Inside the shack thoughts cleared, needs clarified. The man was hoisted onto a divan, stripped and covered with a blanket. Connie knelt beside him, and, looking up, was hooked by Chant's fanatic eye.

"You see," he nagged, wringing water from his cloak all over the floor, "you do see that prayer is the first and last, the ultimate resort?"

She feigned deafness, bending her face to the waxy one below her, lowering her head until her mouth fitted over the greenish lips of the young man. She breathed into him. In. Pause. Lift. In. Pause. Lift.

"Pray," Chant kept saying against the racket on the roof and trying to rub himself dry at the same time. "Pray, all of you. Pray."

Between breaths Connie fumbled for the young man's wrist, felt for a drunken pulse, never breaking the rhythm of her movements, while the old kitchen clock above Reever's stove ticked with her, timing, racing, timing.

Inwardly, she was praying too, but she decided, thinking impatiently of Chant, that it was to a different end, somehow, or a different God. Fifteen minutes went by. The disciples had worked their voices into a compulsive refrain of supplication. When Reever offered to take over, she shook a stubborn head, denying him. Around her the praying became a soft and regular litany. One of the women began heating coffee, and Reever slipped into the crashing dark and beat his way uphill to the big house to ring for help from Canecutters. The weather fought him like a wrestler as he slushed his way up the streaming track.

He shook with tension when he picked up the receiver. There was no dial tone. He slapped the instrument angrily. Nothing. Obstinately he dialled again and was rewarded finally with a high and loathsome hum.

"There's nothing," he urged the stragglers back at his shack, "that you can do. Nothing. The line's down and if Con can't bring him round in another few minutes we'll have to try to drive down to Swiper's."

They were useless words. Every creek would be impassable by now. The ferry across the river would have stopped running an hour ago.

Chant was still praying or mumbling. For a while since Reever had returned the only sound in the room had been his fruity appeals for heavenly aid, until Connie indicated that his prayer rhythms clogged hers. But his lips moved insistently in a low rumble behind the clock's impersonal click. The followers stood uselessly around, eyes up or down as they sipped their coffee. Then the electricity wavered and finally died to a last thunk from the generator. "Oh fuck," Reever swore softly. "Fuck it. Fuck it." He blundered about hunting for candles, set two of them in bottles on a shelf near the divan, and lit a kerosene lamp. The unbroken battering of rain swallowed every thought. Through the windows could be seen palisades of water.

Forty minutes. Forty hours. Forty days and nights.

It was only minutes.

There came an unexpected spasm in the man's right arm that jerked the watchers as well. Connie shovelled air into the drowned mouth as if she would empty the world. A hand twitched. In a minute they all heard the gulp as the mouth below hers guzzled greedily before a gasping explosion of coughing and choking. The head convulsed on the mattress and began to struggle against her pressure and she levered him over on his side while he threw up more water and phlegm and gasped and strained. Then the head dropped back and, while she knelt watching, while the others watched from across the room, hearing those syncopated wheezings, the eyes opened, red from salt, and lost.

Connie rammed a pillow behind his shoulders and eased him up. His eyes, blinkless, remained staring beyond her into this golden shadowy room where now even prayer was silenced. Suddenly another spasm of retching convulsed him, and, swaying uncontrollably towards Connie, the man emptied his belly over her and the floor in a mass of watery bile until, drained, he collapsed against the pillow and closed his eyes.

Connie hauled her cramped body upright. She was as drained as the man who had suckled air from her, so depleted of passion she would leave it to others to give water, brandy.

Chant was silent as she went across the room and flopped into a chair, but Reever came up behind and put both hands like words on his mother's shoulders. The italics of pressure.

"Nice," he said softly. "Nice."

The man lay easily now, breathing steadily, evenly, eyes still closed to the world. Someone adjusted the blanket and Sister Seawater held a tender glass to his lips but the drowned man's hand pushed hers away, not impatiently but wearily. His stillness impressed the room into tentative movements, lowered voices, wariness. It was as if his passivity were a controlling force.

Then Chant's phoenix voice began a public and prolix gratitude that began to bubble, challenging the rain.

"Don't do that," Reever begged softly across his mother's exhausted head. One of her plaits dripped vomit. Her blouse and trousers stank with the filth of it. "Please. Don't do that."

Chant was deaf. His voice rose describing parabolas of thanksgiving that curved from wall to wall.

Reever jumped with fury. He bounded across to Chant and began shaking him, smacking out the words, *Stop it! Stop it! Maniac!*"

Violence dragged Chant earthwards. He glared at Reever, flushed and indignant. "Not offer thanks?" His voice couldn't believe it. "Not offer thanks to heaven for a miracle of this magnitude?"

"It wasn't your miracle," Reever argued inflexibly. "It was Con's. Con's."

The turnip face went mushy. "It was Mary's miracle," he shouted. "Your mother the agent. How can you be so unbelieving?"

"Bugger you," Reever said coldly. He glimpsed Sister Seawater's shocked eyes. "Prayer isn't simply words. Con's been praying nonstop for exactly forty-eight minutes, do you hear? That's what I call prayer."

He looked past Chant to the divan and found the man's eyes were open, travelling the room and the watchers, finding the world again. He could see the lips moving, hear the voice struggling to come out. There were half sounds that riveted them all.

They watched this castaway as he lay limply there, staring at and beyond. His eyes squeezed shut again and they could see, even by the fluttering lamplight, that he was crying. The sea wept out of him. *Thank God.* Reever prayed. *Thank God.*

He moved over to the man and leant closer to catch his words.

They came out whispered and terrible.

"Thanks for nothing," the man was gasping, eyes shuttered to everything. "For nothing. Nothing."

This country eats up towns.

Not those temporary Xanadus gummed lightly to the seaboard, but the wind-shot, bush-pole scrubbers tied into settler hearts and nailed down with the excitement of vision.

Funny, that, Will thinks. *And yet we're still here. Still part of it.* Part of the sun-wizened flutter-skins of those towns that now, as he gets older and finds decades like so many bites at a—well, guava, say—seem to be closer, quite ripely present for him still, with all that solvency of spirit that went on in them.

Past has become now.

Bo can't see that. Bo's twenty-five, -six, some remarkable youthfulness. Bo regards the year Will was born as a time so distant its veracity is in doubt. Did Hannibal really exist? Scipio? Peter the Great? Marco Polo? Did he? And the energies Will's father used to limn of those first years in Charco are prehistory to Bo, mythic as Rameses or Aristotle.

"But they lived, they lived!"

"It doesn't impinge."

Bo's crotch-rot jeans and tight umber skin impinge, too, on the very frame of the boy as he stands easy with his chipping-hoe taking a breather from the veranda path weeds. Bo takes a lot of breathers. He is taking a breather now, he says, from a postgraduate degree in political agronomy, odd-jobbing about the country and postponing his confrontation with the conservative strictures of the work force until . . . well, until.

Are we so different?

Were the madmen of 1873 so different in the bum-rush hysteria with which they abandoned homes, families, jobs, and headed into lost

144

*country behind the Palmer? They worked, if father was right, with animal intent, but the reason was—*Will hated to say avarice but might as well—*gold-hunger. Bo says money bores him. He prefers to sit drinking endlessly at coffee or wander in the softened edges of twilight down the track to the river where he'll sit till mosquitoes and sand flies drive him back through the drenching dark. He does odd jobs around the town but,* Will hears, *there's a small stack of pay envelopes in his room, still unopened.* The tale refreshes him.

Bo's skin shines butterscotch in the three o'clock sun.

"My skin used to be like that," Will says to the polite but faintly incredulous smile. "And my father's. Does age worry you?"

"What's that?" Bo asks. He stretches his arms above his head like a lovely lazy animal and the hair in his armpits, luxuriant and black, sparkles with sweat.

Will can't tell him either. His yesterdays stand bolt upright for him, muscle-hard, pulsing with blood and closer now than they have ever been. Across the grass-stitched track from the railway line he looks past the rusting rolling-stock abandoned at the siding and then away from there to the river where scrub and bamboo have grown back thick among the wild mangoes. George Laffey strides up over the lip towards him, dead now more than fifty years, but still bulky in his flannel shirt and moleskins, mud-streaked from the creek, his pants tucked neatly into snake-boots, his hat brim down against the sun.

God, Will says. *God, you look well, dad!*

And the figure keeps smiling and striding, smiling and striding until it strides on into him.

Can't remember mother, though, Will thinks, *except as a picture of artistic grain Connie keeps on the dressing table at the Cape behind the cologne bottles, the little boxes of pressed powder she never uses. Can't remember except as a story dropped here or there, accidental additions to what the family strenuously preserved.*

Her name? Ah well, it was Mag.

Is that a name?

Jessica Olive and Clytie only used to smile at his small-boy questions, remembering the impossible handsomeness, the self-willed audacity.

It's time to push back his past-present.

145

Will opens and closes his hands with a nervous movement as he looks across the paradise gardens of his patch. Arthritis is making sorties at his knees, his finger joints, his hips. He looks at the green sward and sighs. It is neverending, this cutting business.

When he had first moved back—more than thirty Wets ago now—to his once-home, the newness of it all raced through his veins with a lust to hoe, slash, plant. Apart from the paddocks he set aside for fruit and milkers, he planned, in a grandiose manner, a few acres of park-like lawns that would unroll their enchantment to the boundaries. The previous tenant had used all of the holding for dairy pasture and the house his father had built was neglected and shabby. For five years Will divided his days into reclearing and planting or tearing out dry-rotted timbers and replacing panels of rusted roofing iron.

At forty he had still managed these things with ease. At fifty, if in the early evening, sitting back on his veranda and gloating over the vibrancy of croton and poinciana fire, he felt, perhaps, a crawling doubt about his ability to maintain the nirvana he had created, he beat those thoughts back. God, it's so beautiful, he thought. So beautiful. The house shone white against drooping swags of bougainvillea. A deeper green shade lay under the canopies of cascara trees and flamboyants. His greatest pleasure came after each fresh mowing when the razored lawns swung richly away towards his eastern and western fences under the overpowering fragrance of cut grass, under the sociable groupings of shrub and tree, leading the greedy eyes on to further groves.

His tapedeck played Delius. A daily celebration.

But at fifty his body began to protest. The neglected fruit-trees were attacked by mould and fly. In his seedling house everything grew. Dying trees were rooted out and replaced. He groaned with the effort. In a garden stillness ripped apart only by bird-cry, he mowed and spaded as if conclusions were discoverable beyond the labour. He groaned further. It was as if the fecundity missing in his personal life transferred itself to the luxuriance of his park.

Connie laughed at him, at the extravagance of his passion.

There they were, two middle-aged potterers in cart-wheel shade-hats, ambling midweek away in his paradise gardens. In high summer, slapping at March flies.

Connie urged him to go commercial, make his nursery a money-spinner.

"I like to give."

"That's all very well. You must need the money."

"I get by," he said amiably.

"I'll help," Connie nagged. "I'll help. If the business side of it appalls you, Will dear, I'll help."

"And so will I," Reever said, coming on them suddenly from a bamboo thicket. "Let me put my uselessness to work. It will please mother no end."

Despite a preference for privacy over people, Will found the various encounters made with customers envigoured him. The small income meant less than the bartering of words, of discussing his obsession. Customers came to view the grounds as much as to buy and their delight became an emotion to be sustained. But after some years of it and after almost three decades of unending physical labour, he found himself dreading what had begun as an act of love.

Grass filled his dreams, grew into swinging oceans that rolled into breakers of impossible cutting height. Seed spume became that of salt. He could drown in it. There never seemed to be pause from mowing. He went to sleep thinking about the next section to be done and woke up dreading it as the heat racked humidly over and his creaking joints moaned. His dreams became nightmares. During dinner he swore he could hear the hiss of blades spearing up through the river flats. It greened the Delius. It swarded his mind.

He complained to Connie one Sunday when she had driven up from Swiper's Creek. He swore he would sell off the place.

"Anno domini," he said. "It's too much for me."

Reever forestalled him. "You need a break. Go south for a bit during the build-up. I'll lawn-sit."

Yet even in the middle of concerts, sipping coffee on the harbour front outside the Sydney opera house, standing solitary in packed theatre foyers, he found himself wondering how the lawns were going, if the pleasure-grounds still stretched their seductive green beneath the great umbrellas of the trees. Almost, he was sick with a foolish nostalgia.

Fifty. Plus.

Take a grip, he kept telling himself. There's more to life than husbandry. The Capability Brown of latitude fifteen, he self-mocked. His body morally ached for the yoke. There's more than mowing, he argued, watching Harbour lights, taking ferry trips, drifting through arcades. More. He spent hours in book and record shops. The Harbour waters became bleak. He felt his bones chill. There must be more. He took lonely train rides into the mountains, sat lonely in film houses, outcast even from the raincoat brigade, fidgeted during plays of breathtaking superficiality, found himself a-snooze during a Strauss opera, and admitted finally that his whole being ached for endless sun and heat.

He had to buy another bag to accommodate the records and books.

Connie picked him up at the airport and drove him back to Mango.

"The story of our lives, isn't it," she commented on seeing his drawn, unrested face, "partings and meetings. The place looks superb. Reever has mowed himself silly."

That inexplicable sense of homecoming assailed him as they turned into the dirt road out of Mango. He might have been away years instead of a month as he took in hungrily the familiar dispositions of road-curve and tree, the swerving planes of paddock and segmented hill. All these things gripped his heart, squeezed it like a fist, and he found his eyes moist.

"Crazy, isn't it, Con?" He looked away, pulling his mouth down in a self-critical curve. "Simply crazy. I should be beyond the age of sentiment."

He remembers those words now, watching Bo.

Reever was at the gate to meet them, shoulders blazing with sunburn. Everywhere was the pungent smell of cut grass and over that the ammoniac stench of woodsmoke. Reever acted chipper. He rubbed his hands down his cut-off jeans, leant through the truck window to slam a kiss on his mother's cheek, reached across and pumped Will's hand ("Nunks!" he says ironically) and, all grins and with a thumb's-up sign, hopped on the truck tray and rode back with them to the house.

The garden had been designed so that the drive in failed to reveal the homestead until the last surprising moment: tracks wandered about absent-mindedly between palm clumps and banana groves, skirting a dam whose banks were plastered with rock and fern. Then the main drive plunged towards the river before swooping up again under poincianas to the turning circle in front of the veranda.

The intensity of his delight stunned Will. The place moved him as love might have. He dumped his bags inside the hallway and went back to stand gazing out through a series of shaved glades at the greens and yellows and scarlets of his garden. Compresses of leaves. He found himself shaking his head in the emotion of this homecoming. The smell of grass overcame him like a drug, persisted and followed him into the house, nuzzled walls and timber ceilings, swooned on beds, floated out onto the riverside veranda and created a green haze in his mind.

He looked at Connie and Reever as the three of them sat drinking tea.

"Why don't you stay," he begged, "just for the night at least. Lay the ghosts of my absence."

But although they stayed and although he slept deeply for the first half of the night, grass reentered his dreams and he found himself shuddering awake, ant-size in a forest of natal, of fescue, of guinea. Floundering and beating through the jungle-scape of nightmare, he swept back arm after arm of grass, his body a living scythe working upwards towards blue air he knew must lie beyond.

There was nothing but green, months and years of grass drowning him, through which he thrust to wake yelling.

Reever caught him as he stumbled across the living-room floor.

"Okay now. Steady. You're okay."

They sat over a brandy in the kitchen listening to the river hit the rapids just beyond the house.

Will was incapable of explanation. Was it a failure of his humanity that all the time he sat sipping his brandy, he was aware of the innate wildness in the tamed lawns outside? Rain spat on the roof and developed as the clock wore down the night into a steady thrumming that exploded scents of earth and grass to expand more pungently into the receptive white flower of the house.

Reever watched him patiently. When finally a watery dawn light began streaking the rain forest canopy, Will gave himself up to admission, to passing off his horror as an aberration made for laughs.

Reever joked too. "Classic neurosis, man!" Then he added thoughtfully, "I can stay on it for a bit if you like. Or I can find someone who'll help out round the place."

Reever's existence was golden and undemanding. He odd-jobbed with flair, making most of his money on prawn boats during the season. When that finished he messed about. "I've found myself, Con," he said.

"Where were you?" his mother asked nicely.

"Oh come on!" he'd protested. "No one else in this family seems to want the nine-to-five. Why me?"

"Why indeed!" Con had agreed for the sake of peace.

For friends Reever mowed, slashed, built rock walls, slung railway sleepers around, created large ponds, did artistic bulldozing, raided back-country forest and replanted protected trees with zest in the gardens of dropouts. "Horticultural sculpture," he said. "Think of me as an artist, Con." He mixed it with coastal and hill ferals. He knew every hippie bum between Swiper's and the Roads. He looked carefully at Will in the green light of the kitchen and said gently, "I can help. You'll lose some privacy, but it's the best thing I can think of. And it won't cost you. Anyway, Will, maybe that's always been your problem, eh? An excess of privacy."

His uncle's face, grey in the dawn, turned sleep-lost eyes on Reever. If you could stand it, Reever was pursuing, the intrusion that is, he knew a couple of people, well, a few anyhow, who were looking for a place to live. They wanted to lease a patch and get, hum hum, their act together. Even Will managed a laugh. "Not get it together, surely," he said. "Isn't getting it apart what it's all about?"

"Whatever." Reever looked offended. "They haven't much money, but if you'd let them shove up a couple of shacks, you could do a deal. How about it?"

Will thought about it. A few days after Connie went back to the Cape and Reever had kicked his motorbike into life and vanished in a cloud of petrol fumes, he made up his mind.

Reever brought his friends up within the next fortnight and after seeing them as far as the turning circle politically vanished.

Will should have been prepared for the assorted four who spilled out of a decaying Kombi van and stood about making the ecstasy noises of youth, their eyes skimming the gardens with unfocused pleasure. The spokesman for the group was called Bo, a big gentle caftan'd bumbler so hairy only a minimum of feature showed. "And this is Flute," he said, introducing a sharp-chinned young woman with a drag of red hair looped through a circlet of shells.

"Flute," repeated Will, bemused.

"And this is Shark," Bo said, minding his manners and smiling at an absurdly pretty girl with trailing hair the colour of wet sand. Her mouth had the old-fashioned pout of jazz-age beauties who once advertised Pears soap or were caught by the camera under beach parasols in the lopsided costumes of the twenties. "And Groper."

Groper, a lean, cleanshaven character in John Lennon specs, was devouring house and garden with intense blue eyes.

He nodded and regarded Will assessingly. His glance was too direct. Will sensed challenge.

"I was thinking of a lease," Will ventured. *(Shark! My God!)* "For—well—say, five years. Longer or less depending on how we get on. But very cheap."

"How cheap?" Groper asked. The accent was American.

Will blinked. "Ten dollars."

"Ten dollars a what?"

"A year."

"Wow!" Bo said. "Oh man, that's great! That's really great!"

Will dredged up a smile. "I want to be fair," he said. "There's a catch. I hoped Reever might have explained." He felt them tense for it. "I'll let you have a couple of acres of riverfront down there." He waved an arm towards the river. "Up from that bamboo grove. See?" They all turned to see. "But in return there's one thing I want done. I want the garden—my garden, that is—mown, looked after."

Bo and Groper looked at each other. That damn Reever couldn't have explained. The thought of physical labour seemed to give them pause. There's a whole new generation out there, Will thought as he examined this lacuna in proceedings, who seem to achieve peak physical condition by merely sitting around.

"You've got a lot of garden," Bo said gently.

"Quite a lot."

"How—uh—big exactly is it?"

"Well, the garden area, that's the part I'm concerned with, is about six acres."

"Uh huh," Bo said.

"And there's a couple of other things. Well, three, actually. The fruit trees in the orchard paddocks need looking after. And I'm afraid I'd want you to sign a lease—a properly drawn up lease, you understand. It would protect your rights as much as mine. And I'm afraid, too, there's a numbers limit."

"Numbers?" They all looked innocently baffled.

"Yes. Six of you at the most."

"Uh huh."

They went into a sort of huddle. Will caught the word "heavy" several times. That's the trouble with the north, Will thought. Time warp. They're still thinking and talking like dropouts in the seventies. He moved away, giving them space, but his mildness was dissipated by sudden biting exasperation. How much, just how much, did this generation want for virtually nothing? Did the little buggers want him to make the land over to them by deed of gift, for God's sake? Couldn't they face getting off their butts? Did they want to move in half the parasites of the north?

Bo called out, "Mind if we look round a bit?"

Will wanted to ask bitterly could they walk that far but instead suggested they hop in his panel van and he'd show them the piece of land he had in mind and then he'd leave them free to wander round the gardens and talk it over. "No pressure," he said, talking their talk, smiling their smile.

The paddock he took them to was thickly treed but there were cleared pockets and one particularly lovely plateau above the river, too close, he mentally noted, to his own house, a plateau which looked down over a spit of white river sand. Beyond that spit the river swung into a wide reach before curving away to the next set of rapids. Across the river on the other bank, the land heaved up sharply into thick rain forest.

There was movement, Will observed, behind the hair on Bo's face. Did he detect enthusiasm? The others were equally engaged.

Groper asked unexpectedly, "You wouldn't sell?"

"No. I wouldn't. Sorry. Only a lease."

The four of them continued to stare lustfully and silently at the silver bracket of the river, the beach shallows, the dense green.

Then Flute said, "Like, I mean, well, is that really fair? What about any house we build? It's not really ours, is it? I mean it's like on your land. That doesn't seem cool."

"Doesn't it?" Will said mildly. "Well, I'm sorry about that. If you were renting a house, say, it wouldn't be yours either. But I take your point about, like, building." Nastily entering into the spirit of it! "Yes. You're always free to remove whatever you build, you know. You weren't thinking in terms of double brick triple front were you, with terra cotta tiles and *en suite?* Look, it's really a campsite I'm offering, but I'm making it a period long enough for you to settle, if settle is what you want. We can even extend the period. That's up to you. But it can only be lease. This place doesn't belong only to me. My sister's involved as well. In any case," he added, irritability spilling over, "both parties have to be happy with each other."

He was angry that his words echoed pleading. Stuff them, he thought. Stuff their precious little alternative life-style wheeling and dealing. If they're not interested, they're not interested.

"That old shed," Shark said softly, (her drawl was American too), "the one over there behind the black bean tree. Could we use that, maybe, for starters?"

She smiled prettily.

Will stared and shook his head. It seemed to him absurd she should want to live under lawyer-vine and bamboo. But there she was with Groper, her thin, intense mate, and the very antithesis that her appearance offered to her nickname made a whimsical irony. Dropouts were heavily into irony, Will knew. It gave point to activities that might otherwise be regarded as artistic bludging. Call her "Shark" and she would respond with such delicate compliance, her head turning sweetly and neatly on its charmer of a stalk, contradiction would overcome you. It was as if Dante had addressed Beatrice as "Scarface" or Romeo called Juliet "Fang." Will tried to repress misgivings.

"If you want."

He envisaged ethnic slums.

"If you want to use the timber in it to build something else, that's fine. It used to be a drying shed for coffee and then just a barn. My father built it. It's still not in bad shape, considering."

He swung away from them back to the van. "I'll leave you to think about it. Take a look around the grounds when you're ready. I'll be back at the house."

He fixed himself a drink and took it out onto the veranda, worrying already if he'd done the right thing. They seemed so stupid and at the same time so conniving. Their raised voices floated up and over the trees, sliced by the bamboos into indistinguishable syllables. Now and again he heard one of the girls laugh.

Speculating on them he realised, surprised, that it was an hour, a good hour, since he had really given thought to the tyranny of grass. Perhaps he would be getting the better of the deal, two huskies like beard and steel-rims who could knock the mowing over in a day or so if they put their minds to it. Well, three days, maybe. Three days every fortnight in the summer and maybe once a month in the dry. He drained his glass. No. It was a gift, a gift either way.

It was another half hour before he saw the four of them sauntering—sauntering was the exact word—down under the poinciana trees. Already they moved possessively as if they'd come home and they strolled up to his veranda with the casual and relaxed confidence of owners.

In this afternoon breeze off the river.

A ruffling of beard and Indian gear.

The bodies looked cool and assured.

When Bo spoke he was first hesitant, somehow shy.

Good Christ, Will thought. Diffidence!

"It's a great place. We'd like to go ahead if that's cool."

Will nodded. He'd always found silence useful.

"There's one thing—uh—" Foot shuffling, hair groped back from face, eyes peering through thickets. Just a lovable old Rousseau tiger!

Will maintained his silence.

"The—uh—mowing. Um—do you supply the mowers and petrol and stuff?"

Will smiled. Gently. Gently. "I do." He took a sip at his drink. "There are three mowers all in good working order. But you'll have to keep them that way. Check the oil, clean out the filters and so on."

Was this too much for them?

"No sweat," Groper said with a half yawn. "No sweat, man."

"Then it's settled, then? You don't want to go away and think it over for a few days?" Will decided against offering them a drink. He was not yet ready for mateship. The intrusion had bitten off enough of his day.

"One thing more," Bo ventured. "I've got to ask. Hope you don't mind."

Will raised eyebrows and waited.

"Just why are you doing this? I mean you can't want neighbours. It's so peaceful here."

"That depends on the neighbours. I told you. It's the work. I'm getting a little too old for all this, but I'm not ready to leave yet. I can't bear to give it up. Not at the moment." He allowed himself a smile. "The grass, as I said, has been running my life."

Looks rippled between them. One of the girls—Flute!—spluttered with laughter that sounded rude.

Will's face became an interrogation mark. "Did I say something?"

"Grass," Bo explained kindly. "It's pot. Dope." He grinned rather stupidly. "Marijuana."

"Oh," Will said stiffly, "of course. I've heard the term. Well, not that sort, not that sort at all."

It was another fortnight before they moved up. Where he had vaguely expected thumbprints or trembling X's on the lease, (Groper, his mark!) he found signatures that were firm and in one case, florid. There was reluctance about the disclosure of surnames but then, Will thought, who could check the veracity of whatever names they offered? When his solicitor demanded driving licences and social security numbers, Will was the only one embarrassed.

They took over the old drying shed and for a week or so the river calm was ripped open by the noise of hammer and saw. Sporadic, too, Will observed with cynical smilings. He drove up to the Cape for a few days, leaving them to it. It was time for mowing, anyway, and he mentioned this to Bo before he left.

"Just testing," he said to Connie.

When he returned the garden was magnificently shaved. In the late afternoon he strolled across to the shed to compliment them and found the place transformed by tacked-on bamboo blind walls, a hand-hewn sink counter, large areas of brick paving outside and old repainted cane furniture.

Melting towards them. Melting.

They made coffee on their gas cylinder cooker, twanged a guitar, and packed him off with some homemade bread Shark had baked in a camp oven they found abandoned in the shed.

On his return to the house, its emptiness assailed him, but right on five he played Delius to his sundowner and promised his lawn-liberated self he would extend his nursery. And maybe after that there would be time to start messing about with paint again or his violin or . . . or . . . if only to satisfy a curious emptiness he now found in his palms.

Crazy stuff, that. Just to be able to sit, read, without aching. (Did the skin itch?)

The family, as he began to think of them, were dutiful with their next mowing and their next. I should have done this sooner, Will told himself. They were unintrusive as well. He enjoyed the occasional contact, the sound of laughter from beyond the bamboos. After five months Will noticed certain areas were looking a little too lush. There were patches that had been missed, patches strategically distant from veranda spy-posts. He wondered how to word his reproach. Straight accusation of slackness? Polite circumlocution? He gave them an-other month. This time the shaggy areas had increased. Annoyance bounced him over to the shed where he told Bo without preamble that they'd missed a few sections. The place wasn't up to scratch.

The four of them were lolling around after lunch on homemade bamboo deck chairs strung with a web of vine. They had developed a small dog. There was a strangely sweet odour through the shed, the essence of hay. He could not name the smell with any exactness, only observe the business of Groper who, at Will's entry, began nipping out a clumsy-looking cigarette.

"You mustn't get obsessive, man," Groper said. His blue eyes, usually so sharp, were glassy and wandering.

Will was enraged. "Look," he began, speaking too loudly, "you're not—"

"Easy now. Easy." Groper might have been addressing the dog.

"Let me show you. Relax. Relax. You got to get rid of those hassles."
He'd finished nipping the end of the cigarette and had replaced it
carefully in his shirt pocket. "You ever rolled in the hay, man, eh?
You ever tossed yourself down into thick green tussocks and just
rolled yourself crazy and felt how good it was?" It was black Sambo
talk. A parody of rhythms.

Flute started to giggle. Will looked at each of them in turn. They all
had that dazed unfocused look about their faces as if life had somehow
become oblique. Behind the hair on Bo's face there was a dreamy
grin.

Will sat down on the steps and took out his own cigarettes.

"You know," he tried to soften his words, "you're not keeping up
the conditions of the lease."

Groper ignored the remark. "Come on man, *have* you? Have you
ever taken that roll?"

Will could sense his anger being blocked. He drew on his own
cigarette and clutched at calm. Finally he managed, "Not for a long
time. A long time if you must know."

They were all smiling at him so pleasantly. Flute had stopped
giggling and was holding out a plate of misshapen brownies. What the
hell could he do?

"Well you ought," Groper said. "You really ought, man. When it
gets a bit cooler we'll all go out and do it. How about that, eh? All of
us rolling to glory, shedding a few heavies. That's what it's all about,
man. That's what it's all about."

Will found the drone of this rubbish hypnotic. Time flowed. Shark
had placed a mug of coffee at his elbow. He glared hopelessly at them
and fumbled for another cigarette. He was just about to light it when
Groper reached across and ever so gently removed it from his lips.
"Pardon me, man. Oh pardon me. But don't light up. Look, try one of
these."

Groper's fingers were suddenly busy again rolling a fat cylinder of
leaf crumbs, packing them carefully in paper. Delicately he tongued
one edge and pressed it into position.

"I'm right," Will said. "Don't use your supply."

There was laughter at this, giddy spirals, and something behind the
laughter he wasn't sure of.

157

"Try it, man," Groper urged, holding it out. "Peace pipe. Friendship. Okay?"

There were four sets of eyes on him now. He felt conscious of his age, old-maidish, spinsterish, every variation. He felt . . .

"All right." Aware of his elderly spotted hands. "But I want to discuss . . ."

Groper had applied a match and automatically Will inhaled. Why in God's name were they all watching him so closely? There was a certain amused—yes, malice—in Flute's sparkler eyes now narrowed in concentration. The rejected stub was rescued from Groper's pocket and re-lit. Groper sucked deeply on it and to Will's surprise handed it directly to Bo.

He inhaled again himself. The sickly fumes rose and then drifted out to the river.

"Like it?" someone asked.

Will replied obediently, "Very pleasant. It's not tobacco, is it? Tastes different somehow."

They all roared with laughter. Too much roaring. Too much laughter. Flute could have had a seizure she rolled round so much. "Have another brownie," she gasped.

"It's grass," Groper said. And they roared again. "It's grass, man, grass. Your special thing."

"Recycling, eh?" Will said.

Flute shrieked so unhingedly at this she had a coughing attack that nearly choked her.

"Cut it out!" Bo ordered, frowning.

Will drew on his fat cigarette again and asked, "What's so funny?"

He was peeved but strangely not nearly as annoyed as he normally would have been. Irritation would seem foolish in the face of such good humour. He knew he should be reprimanding them about the garden but the urgency seemed to be receding as he took another deep pull on the cigarette. Blandness was taking over landscape and air. Taking over self. That, mainly. Self.

"That's it," Bo explained kindly. "That's what you're smoking. Grass. Pot."

Will took in only the edges of the answer. He found he didn't care much. It was agreeable to be sitting there watching the river, feeling the heat peel back as the sun drooped. He inhaled fully again and blew the smoke out of his nostrils in peaceful grey tusks. He was getting to like that sweetness. The abrading taste of his own tobacco was aggressive in comparison with this syrupy sliding inhalation. Relaxed. That was how he felt. Relaxed.

Bo had rolled another joint and given it to Shark who drew on it and passed it to Flute.

"Quite a party, eh?" Groper said. "We call this thing a joint. You know that word?"

"Joint," Will repeated. "No. But I do now, my friends, I do now." This delighted them.

"Right on!" Groper said. "Joint holding, you see. Get it, man? Share and share about. Like, it's for all of us. Very democratic."

Will heard himself say "but not hygienic" and giggle. My God, was he giggling? He tried to pull his thoughts together, looking at the four of them made benign by smoke haze.

"There was something I wanted to have out with you. The garden . . ."

"Yes?"

Shark refilled his coffee mug. "Yes?" she asked sweetly as well.

"Oh God," Will said, "it doesn't matter. Look, this is so pleasant, I must say. Can't spoil it, can I? Did I tell you how splendid you've made the shed look? Really splendid."

More smiles. It was idiotic, the sheer listlessness that dominated the last quarter of daylight, the torpor—he could call it nothing else—of his body. Was he realising his age at last?

Some time later Groper asked, beadily keen, "Like another?"

"Well . . ."

Even later than that he remembered one of the girls handing him more of those strange-tasting brownies and his sucking on the second joint like a dependable dummy. A glow of amiability suffused him.

But nothing explained how, in the granulated evening, he found himself with the four of them rolling about in one of the thickest patches of his unmowed garden, sinking, twisting, wallowing, burying his face in grass and snuffing up a rich stew of earth smells and early dew and the very stench of greenness and growing, and rocking with laughter along with the others when they fell on their backs panting to stare up into twilight.

How had he got there?

He couldn't remember.

The grass tickled his ears and whirred. His hands paddled in the stuff to his wrists. He was bathing in grass on his shaggy acres and savouring the unkemptness. Not drowning, but swimming! He couldn't believe it.

How? How?

Could he hear the lawned acres sighing with relief from the despotism of four-stroke tyrants? Or crying for it?

If he heard, he didn't care either way, not about anything.

The day Billy Mumbler was released from gaol where he had done six weeks with hard labour for tax evasion, he had only the clothes he stood up in. They were jeans, a t-shirt, a torn cotton zip-through windbreaker, and thongs. He realised he would have to walk back to the coast. Seven months before he'd gone west past Flystrike for mustering on one of the stations. His earnings for the five months he was there amounted to only a few thousand dollars, but the taxation people were charging him provisional tax and he didn't understand.

How could Billy Mumbler be a tax dodger?

Boong, no-hoper, river-tribe layabout.

But while Billy was a boong, he was none of the other things.

After the mustering was over, the station boss offered him a few weeks' work fencing. He was a hard worker and the rest of the men liked him.

Billy had never seen a tax-return form until the arresting copper showed him one and even though he could read and wasn't as stupid as whites wanted to believe, he was troubled by the questions.

The elastic clauses of the form stretched to mind's breaking point.

"It's like this, Billy," the copper said patiently. And he tried to explain.

"Don't give me no explain," Billy said. "Them buggers rooked me anyway."

"What buggers?"

"Them station people. Shoulda been a whole lot more. A whole lot."

"Well, I don't know about that," the copper said. "But you earn, you pay. It's the law. Anyway you must have something tucked away."

"Sent it all home," Billy said. "Well, most, anyway. Anyway, how'd they know?" He marvelled. "How'd they know about me way down there?" He meant Canberra or Brisbane or any big town he'd never seen.

"Gawd knows!" the copper said. "They've got these computers now."

Billy didn't know what a computer was. He asked other people. How'd they know?

He asked the visiting parson who came to him in the remand cell.

"Not a sparrow falls," the parson said. He was low-Church Anglican and the answer was only what might have been expected.

At the magistrate's hearing Billy raised his hand before sentence was pronounced.

He was ignored for two minutes. His arm ached.

"Yes?" the magistrate snapped finally, looking at Billy over the tops of his glasses.

"How'd they know?"

"The computer," the magistrate said.

Later a cellmate explained. They were jogging round the exercise yard of Flystrike gaol, melting in the vivid heat.

"Not a sparrow falls," Billy said bitterly.

Now the copper was asking him, "Got your bus fare? Train?"

Billy couldn't be bothered answering. He scowled into the hot morning.

"Guess you'll have to walk then," the copper said, pleased with something in the day. "It's illegal to hitch, mate, but maybe I'll turn me other eye." He winked, showing how his eye would turn. "Okay then, Billy. On yer way. You got a long walk."

The sky was heavy with unshed rain. The morning lay over the town like a plastic skin.

Billy wandered down the road from the gaol and squatted under a tree to read again the one letter he'd received since he'd been inside. It had arrived only a few days before and already was grimy with rereading. He could see the copper standing back at the lock-up watching him.

Dear Billy, his mum wrote, when you get out that place you better get back soon, you dads on a drunk charge and Eldon done workin on the raleway, no ones hear but me an Mable an we finding it hard no man about, enyway you Loo sez she not goin wait to long you come back, all reddy she got eyes goin fast that big Garfeel from the ilans. Not much fish in river till las week, plenty then you should see. Water come up real high. Them white folks other side was cut off. You come soon, you homes hear, its rainin in Mango.

He read it again. And then again. An ant started crawling across the paper. He crushed it neatly, folded the letter and shoved it back in his jacket pocket, wiggled his toes and contemplated the blacktop running out of town. Miles and miles and miles. Jesus, he thought, all that bloody way. While he sat there wriggling his toes and slapping at flies, the copper came sauntering along the road to him.

"Don't want to leave us, Billy?" The irony was as leaden as the weather. "Sticking around, eh? Waiting for something to turn up? That's the trouble with being nice to you Murris. Never know when it's time to leave the party."

Billy shrugged and looked at his feet and wiped flies away.

The copper frowned. He didn't want to start anything. He wasn't a bad fellow, it was just the bloody climate, and Billy had been no trouble. "You'd better get going," he advised, or they'd have to throw another charge at him, loitering, being without means of support. "Get you on a vag charge, eh? I don't want to do that, not right now, not when you've just left us."

"I'm goin' home," Billy said. "It's rainin' in Mango."

The copper looked at Billy sitting there, a natural part of the dusty sidewalk. The morning sun munched ravenously at them both. "Try the garage, mate, the last one as you leave town. There's a bloke going through to the Taws. Maybe he'll give you a lift."

Billy uncurled and wandered off along the street past the hot little shops and the drinkers who'd started already because it was thirsty country, and was overtaken by the copper in his police car just before he came by the last houses. By the time he reached the garage, the copper was arguing with a truckie whose fridgemobile was pulled in at the bowser.

Billy stood back a little and the truckie kept looking over at him and he could tell his color was being hated.

"Ah, come on, mate," the copper was saying. "He's a good black. Not a real crim. Just a tax dodger like the rest of us." He winked. "Never gave any trouble and anyway we want him out of town. Got enough on our plates already with Christmas coming up and the rodeo. Don't want any extra. You'll be doing us a favour. It won't go unnoticed, mate."

The truckie strode over to Billy and fixed him with a hard stare. His eyes travelled up from Billy's thongs to his curly skull and then slowly travelled to the feet again.

"Okay," he said at last. "You can hop up. But no trouble, mind. First bit of trouble and you're off. I don't care where it is. Get it?"

"Thanks, mister," Billy said. He moved round to the passenger side of the cabin and began to open the door.

"Wait a sec," the copper said as Billy got one foot on the step. "Jesus, I must be getting soft. Here. Take this. You'll need some tucker." He handed Billy a two-dollar note.

The truck reached the Taws in under eight hours. The driver was a large hard-bodied man of few words. He drove relentlessly fast through claypan and bulldust country boring past coast-bound traffic as if it weren't on the road. Billy kept quiet. It was always best to keep quiet. Country-and-western tunes screamed out of the cassette player. The cabin throbbed.

As they drew near the Taws, rain began spitting on the windscreen, becoming increasingly heavy until it challenged the wipers. In the main street, gutters were awash.

"I'd take you on," the truckie said, speaking round his cigarette, "but I'm stopping off here for the night. Got to pick up another load of carcases. You'll be right here. There's plenty of stuff moving up the coast. Try at one of the pubs."

Billy squeezed the note in his pocket and scuttled through rain to a hotel directly across the road. On the veranda a couple of old-timers sat drinking and speculating on the weather, gummy men who watched him all the way up the steps and into the bar. Inside there were a couple of blacks down one end playing darts and four or five pensioners propped against the polished wood in the high malt-stinking gloom.

The barman paused in his wiping and regarded Billy.

Then he looked past him and spoke to the truckie who had come in behind, shaking water from his hair like a dog. "What'll it be, mate?"

Billy waited patiently, rubbing one thonged foot against the other, practising easily the humility he had known all his life. When the truckie had taken his beer off to a corner, giving the tiniest of nods, Billy gave his order to the back of the barman's head.

The next minute he found a beer planked down in front of him and an extended hand open on the length of towelling damp-cloth that stretched along the bar counter. The barman's hand seemed not to belong to his body, for his head was turned indifferently while he chiacked with a lounger at the other end.

Billy put his note in the hand, which closed over it, clamlike. He drank slowly. The room seemed filled with eyes. He licked his dark lips nervously. Finally he addressed the room at large. "Any trucks goin' up the coast tonight?"

There was nothing but the violence of rain slamming the iron roof.

Then the mumbling resumed, aged quacks, grating coughs, nasal suckings, and the barman turned up the radio.

Billy gulped his beer down.

"What about me change, mister?" he called to the barman.

The barman pivoted slowly and fixed him with an outraged eye.

"You talking to me, mate?"

"I said what about me change?"

"I put it there, mate, right in front of you."

They both inspected the sodden towelling.

"No you didn't."

The barman turned back to the radio and began twiddling knobs.

"No you didn't," Billy shouted. "You didn't give me no change."

The barman's eyes swept the room, gathered them all in and then rested on Billy.

"You calling me a liar?"

"Ain't no change there," Billy persisted. "You never put no change."

The barman walked slowly over and leaned both hands on the bar and stuck his face up close to Billy.

"Think you better go, boy," he said softly. His breath smelt of steak and Quickeze.

"I want me change," Billy said.

"You know what you are?" the barman asked slowly and clearly. "You're a troublemaker. A real troublemaker. You get yourself out of here quick-smart or I'll have the police in."

Billy looked wildly round the room. The other blacks dropped their eyes. "He never!" he cried. "He never put no change there. You see him put me change?"

Unfriendly eyes regarded him. The truckie rose from his table and wandered over, casually, and took Billy's arm in an iron grip.

"Come on now," he ordered. "You better get going." He steered Billy across the room and onto the veranda. The rain was so dense it screened the shops across the street. "You won't win, mate," he advised confidentially. The empty town was weeping in their faces. "No way. You know what these places are. Better get going and write it down to experience. You'll pick up a hitch all right." He gave Billy a friendly little shove. "You get going before there's any trouble."

Billy yanked his arm angrily away and walked into the rain.

It was storm-dark outside and the road out of town rippled like a river.

Billy swore, but under his breath, hitched his jeans, took off his thongs and stuffed them in his back pocket, and began walking.

The circle might be perfect, containing its own finality.

The nobility of the forward line his great-grandfather Bidiggi had advised in the tribal language he had almost forgotten now except as sounds that picked at his dreams. The forward line.

He was travelling that way through the rain to Mango.

Cars and trucks raced past his paddling figure and splashed him from head to foot. Not that it mattered. The rain had already obliterated the meaning of his thin clothes. Head down, eyes on sloshing feet, he merely slapped one bare foot after another.

No matter what, Billy thought angrily, no matter what he did! There was only this paralysing sense of effort in an imprecise landscape, like the heights of failure he'd clambered over and over again from the primary school where he never did well enough, to high school, for one year. His uniform fell to bits. Everyone laughed at him. "Me mum hasn't an iron," he explained to an uninterested form master. "She got to wash me stuff in the river." How the kids had roared. Like animals, he hated, like fuckin animals, the lot of us, jus livin like animals, remembering his uncle gone rotten with the trembles, hands clutched round the flagons dropped illegally outside the mission grounds and sneaked in at night. His mum with her eyes blacked fighting that Loo, not a full-blood mum, once a pretty quarter-caste working round the hotels in Reeftown cleaning the rooms, and then got into trouble and went back up the coast, a kind of punishment till Charley Mumbler became her man, legally spliced by the minister and everything, one of them hearties with God-given muscle strength and moral purpose that pervaded the should-be idyll of beach and jungle clearing like a holy stain. Billy knew about that stain. Just like the purple dye they used in the harbour to show where the crap flowed. He couldn't help grinning.

The grin cheered him. After two hours he understood only the technology of feet. His face ran like a beach.

About eight miles out a bunch of coast-bound hippies pulled up beside him in their van and took him on board, made space for him amongst the junk of tools, old timber and a dead bed-base that cluttered the tray. They took him all the way up the coast to Reeftown, huddled with three of them under their canvas tarp, and set him down on the esplanade in a night fluid with frogs and mosquitoes.

His big splayed toes met the sodden turf with the same indifference with which he'd padded through bulldust slush along the highway. He made his way to the public toilets, stripped off his soaking clothes and hung them over the cubicle wall to dry, and fell asleep in a coiled-up ball on the filthy cement floor.

Later, a hammering on the door woke him. The sound separated itself from the noise of rain and he dragged on his wet jeans and pulled the door open to a brotherly bottle thrust into his face. He went out into the night and found the rain had stopped. There was a group of black men under one of the figs near the water and he sat with them and drank and slept again, curled up this time between the buttresses of the tree, a disturbed sleep of brawls and shouts and whacked flesh and curses and a police round-up from which he woke in a summer-sick cell, the bucket knocked over, the stench rising and a Palm islander moaning on the other board bunk. His windcheater and shirt were rolled up in one corner.

"Not good enough, Billy," the sergeant in the cell doorway pronounced. "We know all about you. Flystrike said you'd be on your way. There's nothing we don't know."

"Like God, eh?"

"Now don't be cheeky," the sergeant said, the morning at his back, throwing his shadow long and menacing over the concrete floor and the urine puddles. "Come and get a mop and clean up that stinking mess."

Later, sick with belly cramps, Billy walked out of town, cutting through cane fields to the railway line in the foothills. The morning rail-motor had already gone up the range and he had the track to himself. He still had his mum's letter in his pocket, unreadable now, the ink run and the paper wadded, but he could remember it by heart. Bits kept talking to him. *Not much fish in river till las week . . . water come up real high . . . its rainin in Mango.*

Halfway up the range, his thighs aching from striding sleeper to sleeper, the rain started again. A goods train lumbering by to Tobaccotown slowed enough near tunnel nine for him to slip over the side of one of the cars and when he finally reached the whistle stop near the settlement the afternoon had turned black with storm-cloud.

As he trudged up the track from the little station, guinea grass dragged at his knees. Behind him the river snarled white and the wind kept turning over the raggy banana leaves outside the shacks as if it were reading them. He wavered outside his own doorway, seeing lamp-flicker in the gusty air, hearing the kids screaming themselves stupid with delight at his homecoming, feeling the arms hugging and the hands touching, smelling his wife's hot familiar smell and his mother screeching "You got me letter? Got me letter?"

He pulled the damp wad of paper from his pocket and put it down on the table and wanted to howl.

"I got it," he said.

Three days before Christmas late afternoon he was walking into Mango township with his father, the two of them head down to the blustering weather, when old Will Laffey from the place upriver overtook them and gave them a lift. The steam from their bodies rose in a fug in the closed space of the van. Wind spun branches and leaves across the road. The windscreen wipers tore at glass.

"Hello Charley. Hello Billy," Will Laffey said pleasantly. "Christmas shopping?"

"Christmas drink more like," Billy said. He grinned.

"I hope you'll have one with me," Will said.

"Okay," Billy said. "Loo's in town with the kids. She been shoppin'. I'm goin' to give her a hand, put her on train back. Then I'm stayin' on a bit."

The top pub was jammed with drinkers. Television screamed above the racket. They walked down the road to the bottom pub where Loo waited patiently, an old pram piled high with groceries. The two boys chased each other endlessly up and down the footpath. Will insisted that Loo join them, at least for one drink. She wheeled her rickety pram into a corner near the door and the three of them crammed in at a table amongst the timber workers and concreters from the new shopping complex.

"What'll it be?" Will asked. "Beers all round?"

Outside the kids kept dodging up and down, squealing shrilly as the rain swiped at them, catapulting into the doorway and hurling themselves against their mother's hip.

"Them kids," Loo complained.

The noise of the rain made talk difficult. The air was curdled with breath and steaming clothing. Billy tried to tell Will about the fencing job and gave up. He sat next to his father and stared gloomily into the rainwashed street, watching now and again the four big bruisers from the building site who were drinking at a table near the door. He felt strange, back in town again, strange sitting here with Loo, and the kids yelling outside, and his father and old Laffey. He kept seeing the hard earth of the exercise yard and not even the beer chased away resentment. The kids kept rushing in, rushing out, their yelps cutting through even the rain-hammer.

After a while one of the concreters got up and lunged towards the door, roaring at the kids to shut up. The older boy stopped dead with fright, rolled his eyes, giggled nervously and went scooting up the path to the other entrance. But in a moment he'd forgotten and was back, wriggling and shrieking at the one spot where he could see his dad's and mum's comforting backsides. The concreter hoisted himself again from his chair and boomed, "I said give it a rest, willya?" He reached behind him for his beer. "You bloody deaf, kid?" Then he swung his arm forward in a vicious arc and launched his beer right into the boy's goggling face.

For a moment the kid simply stared, then his face, running with snot and beer, crumpled up and he yowled his head off. Loo squeezed her way out and began cuddling the boy while Billy pushed his chair back and slammed across to the other table.

"Watcher do that for, eh? Watcher do that for?"

The concreter eyed Billy insolently for a few seconds and then shoved past him with his empty glass, pausing to lean over Will. He breathed hard. "Mate of yours?"

"Hey lissen! You lissen!" Billy was elbowing and pushing to get at the man, stumbling over legs, knocking chairs. "You don't throw no drink on my kid, see? You don't do that to my kid."

The Block pulled himself up and looked down on the runty little black bugger.

"You talkin' to me?"

"Yeah. You don't throw no drink on my kid."

"Who're you saying 'don't' to, mate?"

To cries of "Shove it, Block! Siddown, mate!" he took a step forward, looming above Billy, his sun-spoiled mug, with its untidy collection of features, clouded. He gave Billy a contemptuous shove and the crowd stiffened, waiting for the fight. At the end of the room four murris playing snooker stopped their game. Will found his protesting hand shaken like a fly off Block's arm. The whole room went quiet, leaving space to rain and television riot, and the pub owner, who hated blacks but loved their welfare cheques, watched from behind the bar with horrible interest.

Billy went down with the table at his back. Drinkers cursed and grabbed at their glasses but Billy unknitted his feet, scrambled up and swung a punch that caught the surprised Block on the gristle of his nose.

"Why, you little shit! You lousy little black shit!"

He began to rave and hurled his drunkenness forward, lashing out brutally with clubbing fists. Billy ducked. One of the watching murris slipped quickly through the stilled room and as Block, carried by his own air-punishing weight, lurched forward out of control, he shoved out a skinny leg and sent the concreter thudding over it to crash messily between the tables.

170

The pub roared: concreters, timber workers, blacks, even the barman, all hauled high on the relief of laughter. Billy began to strut a
little as Block heaved himself up, fingering a pulped and bloody
mouth. He strutted right out the door after Loo, heading safe for the
train now with the kids, not hearing the screamed threats. Three
drinking mates were holding Block back, dabbing at the ruined face,
pouring another beer into him, drowning the rantings, the threats of
payback, of punching the stupid black bastard out of his brain.

Old Charley Mumbler wished for invisibility.

Two days after Christmas a cyclone crossed the coast at Port, tore
roofs off like wrapping paper, uprooted trees, flung boats about like
driftwood and swung out to sea again. The Wet settled in. Mango's
streets ran like drains. The shacks at the settlement leaked, dripped
with damp and the timbers swelled. All that week the river, fed by
creeks higher up the tablelands, kept rising, and just before the new
year Billy Mumbler trudged back into Mango with his cousin Clive to
relive his victory at the pub.

In the main street leftover bursts of wind were still socking water
into doorways and against shop-window fronts. The little town had
emptied of tourists. The cafes were closed, the outdoor tables stacked
inside for the next season. Inside the pub there was a kind of animal
cheer, the false and resonant babble of beery goodwill. Billy felt
comfortable. He knew the faces. There was Eldon playing snooker
with that Garfield. His old man was drinking out the back with Niggy
Pawpaw. That Mister Laffey was reading the paper down one end. No
kids. No Loo. No worries. He was walled by voices.

He wriggled his muddy feet and giggled at something Clive said
and tossed his beer down fast and went back to the bar to buy two
more.

"Set 'em up, Perce," he said cheekily to the barman, and stood
surveying the room while he waited. He even hummed a little tune.
Then, in the angle leading to the front veranda of the pub, he thought
he saw a familiar shape. He stepped away from the bar to see better,
and, "Christ," he whispered, "oh Christ." Block. Grabbing the
glasses, he slopped his way back to Clive. Bloody hell. "Think we
ought to push off after this, man," he said. "Them. They're back.
Great load of 'em."

"Oh bull!" Clive said. He was a husky young man, half islander. He lived for the day. "I didn walk all that way for nothin. Drink up an stop lookin, eh? You doan make no trouble, they won't."

"There's a mob," Billy insisted. "Fuckin great mob."

"Okay," Clive said. "Well okay." He pushed his glass aside and got up and went down the room and looked at the crowd of men drinking in the angle. There was a speculative and waiting tension about the massed force of blue singlet and belly-stretched shorts. There was a lot of muscle exposure. Clive couldn't help grinning at his own thoughts as he went back to Billy. "Pretty big, eh, some of 'em! Them blokes soon gunna have piccaninny!" He rolled about at his own joke.

"Shut up," Billy hissed. "Don't draw attention. Them blokes has come to get me, I bet."

Just along from them was a group of hippies, all hair and beads and the confidence that comes from paid worklessness. They were packed into the space between old Will Laffey and the bar and Billy could hear some of them talking earnestly among themselves about a—what was it? A raid? Payback? He edged his chair back and listened, picking up rumour and part rumour of a hit pack organised in Reeftown now on its way up the range despite rain and rockfalls, to beat hell out of the boongs. He sneaked a look at the speakers and found faces that registered a lot of soft horrified expectation.

Billy fancied the room began to sizzle.

"You hear that?" he asked Clive. "You hear that, eh?"

"Sit still," Clive ordered. "You bloody imagine."

Billy felt as if he were stuck to his stool. He wanted to pee. His inside heaved.

But nothing happened. That was what was so terrible. Nothing happened.

The clock hands swung through the hours to closing time.

Billy was too drunk now to care or notice much but he saw one of the hippies go up to the barman and start talking hard, and when the kid returned he heard someone else say, "Police. We need the police."

Nothing happened.

Then another one plunged into the rainy dark and came back full of outrage. *The point-head*, he reported, meaning the copper, *had*

shoved his minimal skull round his minimal door and said it was his
night off, for God's sake, and gone back to his video.

They were all waiting for a move.

No move. Not yet.

When? How?

Billy felt his slaughtered forebears shiver through his bones.

Why didn't he leave?

The pub was not cosy, not any more, but it had the props of cosy—
light glinting on scores of bottles as if this earthly supply of liquor
would never diminish; the unbroken roar of voices that told, even if
they didn't communicate; the thud from a dartboard; the crack of
snooker balls; the shudder of the television screen. The whole prism
was a fortress against darkness and rain.

It was a watering-hole and the animals were all there, playing
Happy Arks, a cheer-spot on the map where people met and thought
they loved people. Don't count the ones who'd left to stagger their
drunken disappointment up Main Street or lurchers on the way to
vomit their realised loneliness in washroom cubicles or just-reached
doorways. Don't count any of that. Just look at those moving mouths,
those grinning gawpers. It's cosy. You know it's cosy. But just wait,
cobber, just hang in there till the barman calls time.

That old phrase came honeyed with malt. This evening it had an
edge to it.

At a minute off the hour, the barman's smoky voice cracked out a
couple of times and the wall of din split down its centre like dust-
stiffened curtains as drinkers swilled recklessly, lousily frightened to
leave a drop. There was a general movement to the doors and isolated
sounds surfaced as the telly was snapped off, the bar cloth slapped
along the counter, the snooker balls and cues slotted away.

"Please," the barman roared. He said, "Gentlemen." He said,
"Please."

Billy smacked down his emptied glass and wobbled away without
waiting for Clive. Will Laffey folded his paper and saw Billy Mumbler
hesitate in the light on the sidewalk. In three minutes the room was
almost empty except for two old blacks sitting deafly at the bar angle.
Charley Mumbler and Niggy Pawpaw were stranded by their bones.
"Okay you two," the barman said. "Speed it up."

Billy was suddenly worried for his dad. He loitered out of the light, nervously aware of a knotted mob on the footpath, men who watched the door, watched the night, noted the streaked yellow of departing car lights.

"What about your ole man?" Clive asked softly. "You better wait, eh?"

The men at the doorway looked at them both, winkled them out in the shadows, then looked back into the lighted pub room just as Charley Mumbler and his tottering mate made their stumbling way to the door behind Will Laffey.

Suddenly, chaos.

Block headed the pack. He sprang from nowhere under the knowing eye of the barman, and, grabbing a stool, slung it whistling straight over Laffey's head at old Charley. A leg caught an eye and a scream, bounced off and crashed into the bar rail. The other men raced behind him mashing the air with sticks and fists. Billy saw his father fall beneath the surge of bodies, saw Will Laffey run at the mob protesting until a fist gummed his mouth shut, and saw Niggy Pawpaw drummed backwards under a table.

Sobbing, Billy ran back in to the flattened shapes and was felled by Block, who had been winding up another stool like a spring. He was a madman, screaming as he flailed. There were four bodies on the floor now and the kicking had begun.

Where was the barman?

Where were the police?

Clive had slunk off under the mango trees.

Billy kept coughing out bits of teeth and blood. Next to him a leg was doing fancy bootwork on Niggy Pawpaw's head. He could hear the slobbery whimpers of his father who sat up in the middle of the massacre, one wrinkled black paw to a gushing socket. His own fingers had been chopped across the knuckles and through smears of blood he saw bone glistening white through red. Nearby Will Laffey crawled along the floor out of the scrum, still clutching his paper and trying to pull himself up by one of the tables. Fists beat him back.

For five minutes it was a slaughterhouse. No one could stop the frightful impulse that seemed to have its own momentum. No one tried. Billy, his face mopping up dust and sputum and beer slop on the floor, played dead. There was still the contempt of boots.

Outside in the street came the sound of running, of feet slapping wet bitumen. Had someone tried for help again? At the thought of the law Billy Mumbler smiled savagely through blood.

By the time the sergeant arrived, uniform dragged on over pyjamas for this late-night show, the pack had pulled out, revving their trucks defiantly and blasting their horns before vanishing down the range road. The barman crept out from his bolt-hole in Gents and became busy with the evidence, lugging the flattened victims outside to prop them on the street wall of the pub. Billy Mumbler wrestled with him and was tipped in the gutter.

He looked up from all this slush and saw old Mister Laffey holding a hanky to his father's jellied eye. Their blood mingled and ran into mud. Niggy Pawpaw fell sideways from the wall and was beyond words.

Will Laffey broke off his dabbing and tried to tell the sergeant what had happened, stuttering and coughing.

"I'll do the talking," Sergeant Purdy said crisply.

He straddled the path, feet wide apart. Carlights slid away behind the triangle of his legs. From inside the pub came the clatter of broken glass being swept into piles. The hippies from up the river near the settlement hung under the mango dark waiting for justice. Ignoring their protests Purdy ordered them on, and ignoring his order they stepped back a few paces until the darkness shielded them, then moved quietly back.

The sergeant surveyed the scene, knowing he must be careful. He'd been warned this would happen a week before. When he spoke his voice was full of long-suffering at the trouble caused, full of the realisation of his own irony and unfairness. He saw the doctor paddle in from the rain, a thin young man new to the district and stuffed with stupid ideals. Already he was bending over Charley Mumbler's eye with an expression of disgusted compassion.

"Just a minute, you," the sergeant said. "I want to get the facts right."

"This can't wait," the young man said without looking up. "He'll lose his eye."

"I said hold it," the sergeant ordered.

Billy raised his head from the gutter and saw the two men staring each other out, faces full of distrust.

175

"They near killed my ole man," he squawked through broken teeth. "Them bastards near killed him."

The sergeant's self-hate reached out to settle on this mud-covered shape at the edge of the picture.

He looked from him to the men lying against the wall, at the doctor bending over them, and back to this mashed face struggling to stand by the side of the road, and he felt it had all got beyond him.

"All right, Billy," he decided at last. "All right."

He wanted out of this quickly.

Pin a culprit, that was it. Pin one.

It was in order to blame a blackskin. The easy way out.

"Can't keep out of trouble, can you? Lousing up everyone's new year. I'm taking you in for disturbing the peace and inciting to riot."

There was a lot of windy laughter from the trees behind him. The darkness began scoffing as he went over to Billy and jerked him roughly to his feet. The handcuffs rattled.

Billy stood dumbly while the links clasped him. He looked over at the three against the wall.

The mauled faces, the pulped eye, the battered ribs.

The doctor's hands were moving gently from one man to the other. He heard his father moan and saw old Laffey's face twist as he swallowed words. And even as the sergeant began to haul him off to the wagon, the dark under the mango trees came alive with movement as kinder shapes moved in from the rain.

OLD MAN
IN A
DRY MONTH

"Conversation," he says, stretched out on this strange pub veranda, muffled by mosquito netting that the stars still stab through, "should be tasted, drawn out like gum or rubber to snapping point. Rubber time."

No one answers.

He's talking to himself in the buzzing dark. The world hangs heavy. Mango trees around the pub are great blots of inky leaf. The township has dropped into its own four A.M. black hole and a dog yelping from a yard down by the river says more.

"Tasted," he repeats. "Savoured."

Will's waiting for another Wet and he's tired of waiting. He's tired of a lot of things but mainly his lost self. His sleeplessness is shot all through with remembered follies. His latest flaps bat wings. *When Buckle sings*, he doesn't want to remember, *his voice is full of dust*. Music, words, throat—all grating with dust. The powdered country blows through his mouth, through the harmonica he occasionally plays. Once, when Will saw him, he was wearing a ho-hum t-shirt, and the words "Another Shitty Day in Paradise" stretched taut across his sunburnt back. The hem of the shirt flapped its shrunken edges outside soiled jeans as if the phrase really meant what it said.

Strolling along the tacit boundary between his place and the family's shack, Will had paused, standing motionless where the fenceline held the dark up, to catch Buckle's voice as it wound through a welter of other voices—river, leaf, bamboo—and the whole ambience emotionally up-ended him as if he had never been part of it before. *Perhaps*, he speculates now under mosquito netting, *I was seduced by revelation: Buckle reveals the cities of the world! The actuality of Eden!*

177

"Is it that shitty?" he had asked the singer.

Buckle had pondered this, harmonica held away from grin.

"It's the heat," he said. "It's like swimming. Even thinking's an effort. Even saying 'ho hum.' We just gasp and sprawl and sweat out all this paradisal stuff—hey, it is paradisal, isn't it?—because, well, because it's all too much to contain. Too heavy. It weighs."

"You mean we're not fit for it?"

"Maybe. I'm not into ethics." Then the harmonica trailed the ribbon of a mournful tune into the dark and Will walked on.

He'd had the habit over the last two years of drifting down to their shed for a morning chinwag, lending a hand with the new house they were building out of recycled country churches, being agreeable about the amateur basketry and leatherwork they flogged, overpriced, at Mango's markets. Their presence dropped disturbing colour into the day. They irritated. They absorbed. And Buckle's face remained clear in those hours he spent alone. The easy talent of him made Will lust after talent too. That unhurried easy talent.

Too late. Everything too late.

Will abandons slumber. He gropes for cigarettes, tugs the mosquito net aside and sits on the edge of his stretcher in the dark drawing in smoke while out beyond the veranda rail fire-flies throb and pulse with light in response.

Sexual transmissions.

He hates the irony of it.

He could sob.

He'd never come to terms with his loneliness. Until now. He had posed the brave face. Until now. Everything worried him: age, fastidiousness, failure. He knew he'd failed. He wanted to blame his generation, the war, missed chances. He'd tried to talk to Connie, who thought she understood, but the words fell like isolated clues that could never be assembled to a pattern. At the fag-end of his life, this. He thinks of Buckle.

When Buckle sings, his voice is full of dust.

His apt monosyllables club ideas. *I wanted friendship only*, Will lies in the friendless dark. He sorts back over the relationship and dredges up hurts. Familiarity had ultimately bred contempt. There had been bored or arrogant rejection of the most tentative suggestion or reproof. Will thinks of that. Was he, he asks himself now, so prickly, so rude to his elders? He remembers little of his father except as a vigorous and kindly brown eye watching him over a post-hole digger, the wire-strainer hanging from a curled leather belt, sunlight catching the fence-wire and igniting it to a line of barbed light a moment before his father dropped across it.

Someone had gone screeching up to the house? Was it himself? The collapse into a fuss of black arms and racing feet.

Connie remembered more. She remembers father talking of the Bathurst Bay cyclone when hundreds of ships went down, himself on one of them in his first attempt to escape the pub at Port, George who always loved the sea dumped into it until it vomited him up on some sand-drained battered beach vowing never to go back. He'd bought this place and settled, not marrying until he was nearly fifty.

Another bachelor, Will thinks. Another. Despite marriage.

And his mother? Only a smile remained for him, a smile that faded in a flu epidemic, the rooms reeking of eucalyptus oil and the stuffy odour of wrung-out hot flannels and father, oh shocking, howling like a kid over an unmoving shape in the front room.

His life began again at Swiper's Creek. Surrogates took over. His tears were dried by the strenuousness of the buggy ride over the range and at the end of it Jessica Olive and Clytie fussing with restraint, caring but concealing. When he thinks of Jessica Olive he sees only a worn Sunday missal and horn rosary beads, smells a wistful fragrance of violet on skin fine as pressed paper. Nana, he thinks in the dark with the fireflies, dying bolt upright at breakfast as she asks for more rosella jam. His five-year-old grief spent itself more vigorously then than for the kindly brown eyes inspecting him across the fence wire or the unexpected stilling of his mother's singing.

"Eighty," they had all said mourning Jessica Olive. "She had a good innings."

"She had a lousy innings," Aunt Clytie had refuted vigorously, paining the refinement of griefstricken neighbours. "There's something about this family that goes in for rotten innings. A vagabond husband who walked out on all of them. A lost daughter. Decades of hard work. What do you mean 'a good innings?'" She had glared at Uncle Harry who had winked at the small boy and walked away from implicit accusations, taking his big tea mug onto the veranda. No one had the courage to protest further. Not even young Father

Rassini, recent parish appointment whom she detested but endured for the requiem Mass. "Upstart," she described him. "He'd patronise God."

Will could still hear those words. Why wasn't he like Uncle Harry, able to walk away? For two years he couldn't eat rosella jam. He thinks of that. And he thinks of Buckle and the ingratitude of youth and his resentment becomes turbulent with Buckle's physical presence, that amused and knowing smile, the quick lithe body whose hands move surely and confidently about the garden, about radios, generators, car engines and the innards of pumps.

Once he had tried to impress his own tastes on the boy. "If you'd only listen," he had pleaded. "Just listen." And fussily he had selected a tape, but Mozart's spring-rain gusts served only to douse. Buckle tolerated five minutes, six, before sliding from his chair to edge doorwards with "so-so" hand gestures, backing across the veranda, where his body came to life again and he'd bounded, yes bounded, down the freedom steps and loped away across the garden.

Buckle's skin glistened like tanned silk. Will resisted touching that skin though his fingers ached. His hand still recalls resting briefly on a shoulder and his own palm bearing the memory of muscle and warmth. Buckle had looked at him, grinning. And the grin knew.

Will groans at it all. Never again.

Foolishly he'd maintained a cultural persistence, foisting his own interests until he began to feel like a payola tout. Buckle was unmoved. Will couldn't analyse his feelings. Perhaps he didn't dare. His infatuation rendered him mindless.

What a fool I looked, Will thinks, watching the fools of fireflies winking back at his cigarette, those times I tried to play along with his tastes, hanger-on to the family at rock-fests, discos ("My shout," says generous Will), the oldest swinger in the country, trying to find what they found but unable to tap, click, jerk, make shudder moves with stricken shoulders.

"You really hate this stuff," Buckle had said. "It's not your scene. Why do you try?"

"It's bloody mindless!" Will had cried, goaded by a smirk from Flute. "And it's not music."

"Then," Buckle said, looking sideways at him, "why come?"

Bo had looked at him with such compassion he blushed.

Will kills his cigarette butt savagely with his heel and stares into nothing.

Grubbing for dignity, he gave up trying.

His mind kept revolving the whole nasty litany. One morning when he returned from visiting Connie and discovered his tape deck missing, along with fifty dollars in cash that had been left carelessly on a kitchen shelf, he endured all the pangs of the victim.

"Only a loan, man," Buckle said when challenged. "It wasn't for me. It was for Bo. His kid's coming back. And I borrowed your tape deck to run through a few new ones we've got. Ours has packed it in."

"Was the money really for Bo or for the tapes?"

Buckle smiled disarmingly. He put a hand on the older man's arm for a moment. "Look, you weren't here. You were up at the Cape. We didn't know when you'd be back. It's just a loan, Will. Don't make such a heavy scene. I'll work it out. Money really doesn't interest us. You know that. What would you like me to do?"

What?

They both looked at Buckle's hand resting on the worn check sleeve and then the hand slid off and Will had gone outside and drowned in heat.

"Conversation," Will tells himself once more, "should be tasted, mutually sipped."

There had been that monstrous fortnight a year ago when he had taken Buckle down to Sydney at Christmas, moved by pleas the kid had made, some vague wish to see his folks. "Sure I've got folks," he'd said, to Will's amusement.

"You lot," Will countered, "seem to have sprung fully aged from the womb."

It had been a disaster. With all the madness of a lover he had imagined shared pleasures of concert, theatre, meals. Buckle had vanished for most of the fortnight to a pad in Balmain while Will stewed it out in a motel at the Cross, reliving the loneliness of his previous visit. The only time Buckle came to life in his presence was one steaming day at the surfline, Will roasting on Bondi beach, thin, edgy, constantly wiping smudged lenses, harassed by transistors and flung sand, the loud squeals of cavorting youth.

At departure time Buckle became sullen and slept gracelessly on the flight north.

Fool, Will calls himself. Fool.

The termination of things has the angularity of a knife onto which he is plunging.

He thinks of much and little. His sixty-odd years have shrunk to a seed. What has he got to show for it all? A Trappist might ask as much.

He thinks of Bougainville and Corker and a stretcher-bearer running.

He thinks of Cassidy and Brisbane in sunshine.

He thinks of Connie. He has almost forgotten the poignancy of that unexplained moment by the beach.

He thinks of Buckle. *When Buckle sings his voice is full of dust.*

The sky is lightening, a watery red washing up from the east, and the mango trees are establishing their brooding identity. Will stares and still sees emptiness. He wonders just what he is doing on the veranda of this beaten-up pub outside Tobaccotown, miles from anywhere. He knows the reason and he hates it.

. . . *it concentrates his mind wonderfully*—how did that quotation begin? *When a man knows he is to be hanged* . . . He knows. He has always known and it terrifies him to put the two pieces together. But the concentration! The past keeps rolling in.

Waiting for the Wet, this Wet, "I can't bear it," they all said one after another at the commune.

"It's like—it's like, well, waiting for your period," Flute complained. "That awful heavy feeling as if something's going to burst. The build-up. That's exactly what it's like."

It was hardly a commune. It had grown by two if you counted Waitawhile, Bo's monstrous, head-shaven, pot-smoking eleven-year-old, and Buckle. Waitawhile had been passed back to his father from a group at the Roads where Moth, his mother, still unable to find herself, had decided on a self-discovery trip to Borneo.

Buckle had sauntered into the beach commune two years before, be-palled in a Reeftown bazaar where he was busking with his mouth organ and a borrowed mike. After Bo moved to Mango, Buckle came for what was meant as a brief visit and enchantment kept him there. He wore levis cut off at the knees, aphoristic sweatshirts, and kept his harmonica in a hip pocket where it bulged like a gun. His thick yellow straight hair dangled a royal family flop below whose sunny thatch his private-school face gazed out at the world with stunning candour. He had marvellous teeth. He'd been spoilt stupid, you could tell, by both sexes, but he used that material for laughs. He was cool, laid-back, and, for the first months of any new acquaintance, meticulously civil.

"Should I go up and introduce myself to the old guy?" he had asked the others that first sizzler week.

Will had been away a few days.

"Why not?" Flute agreed too bluntly. "Go charm him, Buckle. You never know when it might come in handy. Ask him over."

Buckle looked sharply at her, his features losing their ingenuousness for a moment, but he detected nothing in her abstracted profile. Engagingly he grinned with an I-did-it-sir-let-me-take-the-blame guilelessness that wrapped itself round the hearts of old ladies and small children. "Okay," he agreed, and sauntered beautifully into the distance.

That night the family was throwing a party to farewell a Kiwi hipster who had sweated it out in Mango for a year and had failed to scratch the social surface. He was a middle-aged babblemouth who talked computers and fad diets remorselessly, seasoning his monologues with plod monosyllables—Jung, Bach, Proust—managing to give them the intellectual weight of Ping-Pong balls. He bored everyone. But the easy courtesy of the tropics demanded he be sent off in the easy manner with which he had been received.

"At least we'll make sure he's actually gone," Bo said.

Waitawhile suggested he was a freak.

"Right on, son," Groper said. "And he's intellectually passé."

"What's that mean?"

"Ask me when it's cooler," Groper said.

But it never was.

Shark made a whole-meal carrot cake the texture of flannel. Flute spent a listless hour chopping raw vegetables into a puddle of oil. "Is this Pritikin enough?" she asked, wiping oil and hair in one weary movement. They were doubtful about the oil. Groper worried about the grog. "Is there enough? There never seems to be enough for the Hacker."

"That's because he's such a dedicated vegetarian," Flute commented sourly. She added raw potato to the salad. "He demands vegetable juices."

The new house was decorated with banana leaves and trails of allamanda. Bo shoved art deco arrangements of twig into old wine flagons. Waitawhile sat perched on the rail smoking and spying the landscape. He'd grown beyond excitement by seven and was evilly calm. "Here comes pretty boy," he said. "He's solved the grog problem, as if you wouldn't know."

Just before sundown, guests began drifting in. The grass slope between Will's place and the commune jammed up with trucks and vans. Hacker brought his girlfriend, soon to be dispensed with, a bold-eyed, barefoot macramé genius with a flair for discomforting silences. Drinks began to circulate and Bo, operating the tape deck, split the heavy rainless night open.

Round about seven Will went over. If he went to the centre of the noise, he imagined, like the eye of any cyclone, there would be utter stillness. He was loaded with more beer cartons, his years and a rush of timidity. Into one pocket along with his antacid tablets, he had slipped a little Debussy.

Why was he going?

He'd avoided their parties before, conscious of the age gap, their polite tolerance.

Was it merely the flattering insistence of yellow-thatch who had appeared with charming diffidence at his afternoon door, lots of deference and the occasional Mister Laffey shot in for social punctuation?

Could he have imagined the conversation had been opened with an old-fashioned "sir"?

Yet when he arrived, despite the crowd, the liquor, the elemental rote from the tape deck, the party appeared to be dying. Bo waved him up. "Pink Floyd," he said, explaining the beat. "Pink what?" Will had asked. Was it a guest? He looked around. There was a kind of sated boredom behind the music, behind the marijuana fumes. His fears that he might be out of place were more or less accurate despite

184

the presence of a few gnarled old-timers who had driven down from
the Roads. They, too, used the vocabulary of time-warp. In one
corner of the room Hacker held a group captive. They looked ready to
die of ennui. Words like *software*, *McLuhan*, *floppy disc* and *Marcuse*
had the buoyancy of dud balloons.

Then, with altar-boy tact, Buckle was offering a plate of lumpy
salad. Will found himself bemused by the engaging flop of hair, the
grammar-school face. He was shouting his thanks above the racket of
music when the tape cut off suddenly and despite pre-party vows of
tolerance he found himself saying, "Thank God that noise has stopped
for a bit."

"You didn't like it?" Buckle looked as if he really wanted to know.

Will made a wry mouth. "Can't say I did. It's too violent. It agitates
me, jangles. Do you know what I mean?"

"That's what it's meant to do."

Buckle was all smiles.

"Did you bring over any of your own tapes?" he asked.

How admit? "A bit of Debussy."

"Debussy?"

"Yes. Modern French. Well, fairly modern French."

"I dig Bach," the boy said. There was that smile again. "I even
play Bach." He drew his harmonica from his back pocket, shook it,
gave a preparatory blow and launched into a gigue.

"Oh God," Flute declaimed, loud enough for those around to hear,
"there he goes, laying the foundations. A great little builder, that
one."

"What of?" various listeners inquired.

"We must just wait and see, mustn't we?"

Groper was semaphoring large winks to any receiving post.

And Buckle played. After a while someone picked up
a guitar and strummed along with the mouth organ, and
Will moved away from the players to lean anonymously against the
railing and watch clouds ride sky against a quarter moon. There was
competence of a kind in the music-making, but the freshness lay in
the homemade quality, and he was fifty years away at one of Aunt
Clytie's evenings. "You have to sing," an adult would order. "Or
play. Or recite." And they did, Will dragging his bow across his

violin while Connie at the piano gave a sly upward smile meant only for him. "No accidentals," she would whisper. And the two of them would play wickedly on, agonising the adults while they made themselves nearly sick with choked-back laughter, and Clytie hissing at them, "I'll murder you two later" during the dutiful applause. *Those days!* he regretted. *God, to have them back!* He turned to see Buckle blowing a storm, hands curved lovingly about the little mouth organ.

They'd all stopped talking to listen, even Hacker, and after awhile, on some not quite resolved phrase, Buckle lowered his instrument and the guitar went on alone, liquid and wistful in the night air. Buckle sang along with it, attractively hoarse. He held himself limply against a veranda post, hair flopping, eyes not quite catching those of the group, head just a bit—that minuscule fraction—to one side. Dust blew through the words.

How not succumb? *The answer*, Buckle told them, *is blowing in the wind, the answer is blowing in the wind*.

Sixties' tune. Eighties' party.

Too much! Shark was crying. They were all crying, uttering grief sounds the singer mounted. They wanted it that way, that mood. When Buckle began playing again and plaintive Dylan tunes floated mournfully into the purple air, it was all too much—the river, rain forest, bamboos, the greyer light behind the lighted rooms. Nothing is as sad, Will thought, as a mouth organ played in the bush at night. He remembered the canecutters up for the season, the reedy sounds coming from their barracks in the evening, the flickering of campfire. His mood and that of the party fused. Some of the guests sang along with Buckle but most of them held their glasses and stared into the past. Groper longed for the sea again and Bo thought mournfully of his lost girl, Moth. Shark kept seeing her folks in Idaho, while Hacker wondered if leaving were the right thing after all. Even Flute found herself stroking Waitawhile's bristle-head. They were rejecting the words of the ballad. They were all thinking twice and for some it wasn't all right. But the moment of sadness was unrepeatable, perfect, a pocket of beautifully staged nostalgia.

Buckle could have looked into the curved shells of his hands and found the party, shrunken, there.

Leaning into the night across the rail Will found his own decades-dry eyes wet with unspilled tears. He was too old for exposure. He slipped quietly away into the garden and walked back to his house through heavy dew with the sounds of the mouth organ chasing him.

Catharsis? Maybe, he supposed. After that, things were never the same.

"Play for me, Buckle," Will would ask late afternoons when he broke the habit of years and the Delius remained mute on the tape deck.

He longed for those trembling diminuendos on reeds.

In those first probationary weeks while Buckle was still probing what might and might not be used, he played willingly enough.

Buckle was a user, accepting with the confidence and ingratitude of a cat. And when Will, in the first movements of his besotted gavotte, would head off to Reeftown to load his van with articles the family might use, sometimes practical and needed, sometimes merely extravagant and amusing, Buckle recognised, despite the general nature of the gifts, their particularity.

In direct ratio to the insanity of Will's abundance, Buckle became, over the months, less available, was absent during Will's early-morning coffee saunters shamelessly prolonged in hope.

Flute made little cracks. Bo tried clumsy comfort. Waitawhile blew smoke over all of them and watched closely.

"Where's the court musician?" Will would inquire with ponderous levity. Blankness. "Where's the muso?" he tried for the second time that week in an ugly parody of their jargon, embarrassingly chipper.

"Gone to town, man. Needed some wire."

"Gone to town, man. The generator needs a new part."

"Gone to town, man. Distributor head."

Will learnt to bite off the automatic "You should have asked me." And then Buckle would reappear at Will's door one morning as if there had never been an absence, yellow hair flopping, smile golden and relaxed.

"How about a coffee, Will?" he'd ask. "And a spot of Bach. Don't mind if you play me some Bach. I'd like that."

Will would rush about with the nervousness of a reprieved lover while Buckle flexed his limbs and stretched out on the planter chair.

The odium of it!

Will sensed he was dropping into an enticing void whose emptiness would never manage to engulf.

"It's the Wet," he would offer as an explanation for all transgression. He sipped his coffee slowly to prolong this small moment. "The build-up. We'll all feel better with the Wet. It's late this year."

Buckle yawned. "The Wet. God, the Wet. I've never known people get so involved with weather, not till I came here. They compare Wets like racehorses or football finals, discussing form. Does it mean all that much?"

Bach kept raining down on them.

"It's hard to explain," Will began. His cup rattled on its saucer. "Up here it's—well—it's a release. You have to live through a lot of summers here to understand."

"I guess I'll never get to know then," Buckle said callously.

Will felt his face stiffen. He forced himself to sit rigid. "Thinking of moving on?" But the question came out wrong.

Buckle's sunny head turned slowly and his eyes swept coolly over Will and past him. "Maybe."

Will heard fatuous words slither from his mouth. Youth. Restlessness.

His mawkishness got the silence it deserved.

Someone was calling from beyond the bamboos. Flute's voice slashed shrilly through golden groves of restless cane, prodding Buckle into movement, and unteachable Will found himself stupidly trying to detain the kid for yet another five minutes, two, a half.

"We're off up the coast," Buckle said, easing himself languorously from the planter chair. "God, that Flute's a drag!" He stretched like a cat. "They need me to sort the camping gear. All that shit."

"Going for long?" Did the anxiety show?

Buckle said carelessly, "A few days. Who knows?"

In his solitude later that week, Will moped around the emptiness of acres that had once been solace. Two years ago he had welcomed their departures. It was different now. He turned lackey during their absence, weeded their vegetable patch, cleaned their water-tank filter, deep-watered the fruit trees. The day they returned in a riot of honkings and "hiya" waves, skidding too fast into the drive and across the lower slope, Will was almost nauseated with relief.

*　　*　　*

Trouble was coming to the Cape. The local politician known affection-
ately as the Member for Cannabis had proclaimed a road through
virgin forest and was preparing to hack his way north. Protesters were
arriving from all over the country. A blockade was planned.

A few days before confrontation, the little commune on Will's river
flats once again made preparations to leave.

Will felt excluded. His years were stale blankets.

Jealously he observed their stratagems, their illegal plottings, and
became aware that his morning visits brought a chill on the group.
Waitawhile challenged him when he sauntered in across the gardens.

"They're like busy, man," the checky watchdog would advise, jaw
truculent. "They don't want to be hassled."

Flute was more explicit. "There's not much you could do," she told
him, "except make a contribution to the fighting fund."

"What sort of a contribution?"

"Large," she said, "not to put too fine a point on it."

He handed over lots of dollars.

Prodding Will's infatuation, she spent a lot of time hanging obviously off Buckle's arm or rubbing lingering hands about his waist.
She was brittle with smilings. Will had to look away. These days he
feared that the lot of them might up stakes impulsively and he would
be left stranded on the banks of the river gasping for the sort of air
they provided, even their hostility. The powdery tones of Buckle's
voice and the plaintive harmonics of his mouth organ overcame un-
friendliness.

He was humble with them.

He sickened himself hearing the humility in his voice.

Two days before their van took off, his tape deck vanished again,
and a wallet. Waitawhile had been an insolent prowler on the perimeters, plucking passion fruit, raiding his pawpaw trees. A further
search revealed tools missing, a sleeping bag and folding bed he'd
kept in a lean-to behind the house. A gas cylinder cooker was gone.

He was crippled by betrayal.

"You might have asked," he accused Flute, Groper, Shark and Bo.
He avoided Buckle's eye. Waitawhile watched him unblinking.

They all smiled at his anger. As they indifferently inspected his
offended face, their sextet achieved unity.

"You were out," Buckle said. "You'd gone into Mango. We had to get the stuff packed, man. We knew you wouldn't mind. You've been asking all the time what you could do to help and this is really important."

"But I do mind," Will said. "I mind very much that you make assumptions that always favor your wants and indulge your selfishness. It's not the bloody *things*. It's your manners. If you'd asked, if you'd just had the courtesy to wait and *ask*, for God's sake, of course I would have said yes. But you go on like barbarians."

Their eyes were cold above fixed smiles.

"Don't you listen, man?" Groper said. "You deaf or something? We've told you why we couldn't ask."

"Does that reason cover taking my wallet, too?"

"Oh shit, man," Flute said with all the contempt she could spit out, "it's only bread. You're making a fuss about a bit of bread."

Was he the guilty one?

He was terrified he'd whine.

"I'm not making a fuss." *Keep the voice level. Hold in.* "And if I were there'd be plenty of reason." Suddenly, seeing Waitawhile wink, he lost control. "You're totally arrogant, the lot of you. You're lazy. You're entirely wrapped up in your own needs. All this brotherly love you go on about. You don't give a shit, to use one of your favourite words, about anyone except yourselves. You put nothing in. You contribute nothing. Nothing!" His voice was becoming shrill. He was swept on by rage. "You simply take. You're only off on this tree-saving caper because you're bored witless. There's nothing in your day that's fruitful. You sit around like a bunch of bums wanking away at your egos with a mush of pseudo-enlightened yap about sharing and love. You're full of cant and philosophic garbage all learned from your brothers in bummery. You bludge on society and now you're breaking all the rules and bludging on me."

He could feel his mouth quiver. His whole body shook.

"You finished, man?" Groper asked.

Will's mouth opened but nothing came.

"You're full of crap, man," Groper went on. "Full of crap."

Flute leaned forward. "Come on," she asked, squinting at him, "what's really bugging you? It's not your crummy money or your lousy tape deck, is it, or the other bits and pieces? It's not that at all, is it?

Is it?" She smiled mockingly and challengingly. "Well, *is* it?"

Her eyes slid from his, rested on Buckle and slid back.

Will's eyes were dragged to and fro with hers. Waitawhile eyed him with such smirking insolence he wanted to hit.

"It's him, isn't it?" Flute cooed softly. "It's Buckle. You've got the hots for him, haven't you, mister? Oh oh oh, a real case of the hots. And it isn't any good, is it, because you're not making any play, are you? He doesn't come across, does he? You ought to hear the things he says about you! God, you're a laugh!"

Will felt the blood drain from his head and he swayed.

"Shut up, Flute!" Bo was protesting, his face as stricken as Will's. "Just shut up, eh?"

Will turned his back on the group and began stumbling away over the grass, hearing Groper's grating laugh and the mad arpeggio of Flute. Oh God, he thought. Oh God oh God oh God. His elderly legs wobbled at his steps, his hand fumbled stair-rail and although he heard someone running after him and Bo's rumbling kindly voice he dared not turn.

He sat in the kitchen, face plunged into hands, ignoring a rapping at his open door, plugging his ears to Bo's tentative calls. He could not endure the shaming. Could not. Could not. His throat croaked with something like sobbing but the tears wouldn't come, only a racked pain-cry that ate him from the heart outwards.

That evening no lights shone from the shed by the river or the gingerbread house they had built alongside. Will forced himself to prowl bush-pole alleyways of allamanda whose butter-yellow bells hung ghostly in the dusk.

It was as if the humanity had gone from his garden, as if he had lost, after a lifetime of search, the other half of his equation. He shook his head free of that nonsense. He was every vile moment of his sixty-odd years. That neutrality, he asked himself, that kept you cockahoop for so long, where is it? Determinedly he went up to the brick terrace in front of the drying shed and lit a cigarette, urging himself towards reason, rejecting rejection, rationalising thievery, insolence, selfishness. All the vices, he kept insisting with each draw on his cigarette. Not one missing. Officer material!

Nothing helped. He traipsed the mournful regions of heartache. It was weeks since he had played his crepuscular serenade to the gardens, his definition of the close of any day. As if it mattered, he told himself bitterly. How could it matter in this limited darkening river glade where the absence of light and voice made his own presence more insubstantial. The antithesis they provided subtracted meaning. He had shrunk.

Back in his kitchen he made a meal of sorts, scrambling food together in a skillet, eating without savour. He shoved his dirty plate in the sink, poured himself a whisky and took it outside, offering himself to mosquito and moth. The racket of frogs oppressed him and he drank in night sky and rain forest and the two empty shacks, drank again and again under the unexpected percussion of rain striding in from the coast and battering the canopy. He gulped that as well, wanting to drown the lot.

There was a sodden morning waking, desolate on a canvas deck chair, his face swollen with mosquito bites, his head thickened, his mouth putrid. The day, so crammed with driving water, loomed empty.

He had resolved nothing. Actions imposed themselves. He could not stop himself if he tried. He showered and shaved. Deliberately. He cleaned up his kitchen. He looked at his resurrected self in the mirror and hated himself. Yet rehearsing every variation of phony excuse he prepared to follow the family to the Cape. They would stare through the transparency of his reasons to examine his dwarfed apologetic self. He knew this. He still could not stop himself. He stuffed the back of his van with groceries even as he wondered cynically why they hadn't taken that as well. He packed a battery radio, flagons of water, extra bedding and spare torches. As an afterthought he added his rifle.

Then deliberately he drove off after them.

Why? he asked as the van skidded in the slush of the track. Why?

Fool, reason said to self. Here's tears for those decades of dogged aloneness, for the stubborn refusal to admit others.

Until now.

Why now?

Why near the end of it all should he founder like this, wanting, if not the physical closeness of others (and he admitted at last that he wanted that too), then their mental approval?

And of such a group? The youth he never remembered being.

Senile? he asked himself pumping the van through rain squall. Is that it? The final silliness of an old man?

And when he got there, when they met, what then?

It was worse than he could have imagined.

It was a flaying from a mere four words.

The blockade had been running three days now.

Up the coastal track beyond Connie's farmlet a barricade of shag wagons, trucks, greenies buried to the necks in man-holes and weighted down by lumps of concrete chained to their feet, others roped in the top branches of trees.

At the southern end of the proposed road a tent village had sprung up. Police and bulldozer drivers conferred. The Member for Cannabis, crazy for tree-killing, moved about like a gadfly. Hippies sang, speechified and remained passively goodhumoured. Offshore, a yacht stood by to transmit information on enemy movement to the protesters. Chant and his followers had appeared for one brief afternoon and prayed for a miracle. Conservationists from southern states came in relays. So did the rain.

When Will drove up to the southern end he was in time to see infuriated 'dozer men attacking protester-bearing trees with chainsaws until screams from above and below forced the police to move in. He looked along the track. There was Reever wearing only the skirt he had lately begun to affect, dangling fifty feet up.

Where was Connie?

He shoved his way through chanters and moved onto the new section of road. Farther along it he saw his own lost family with arms linked in front of a 'dozer that had started its motor again and was edging them forward inch by muddy inch. Will squelched out into the morass and although someone grabbed his arm he flung them off and clumped forward, each boot lifting a sticky clay other. He began to yell.

The family went on singing.

The rain had stopped for the moment and the whole area steamed up in razoring sun. Will floundered down the road towards them, lurching through the freshly turned earth. On either side the rain forest raised its own barricade a hundred feet and just beyond this brutalised section he could glimpse rags of sea, grey and speckled. His ugly agony, his smashed pride, wallowed through mud like a bug.

That thought didn't stop him. Not now. He was heading to the final humiliation with the inflexibility of a martyr. The six of them had seen him and refused to acknowledge his cries, his waves. They swayed, arms linked, voices linked, and looked through and past him.

Will looked up. Reever was shouting and waving. He would witness the ultimate debasement as well.

The thought didn't stop him. He could be longing for it.

Listen, he heard himself gabble as he drew alongside. *Listen*. Their eyes refused his. He strained to shout above the roar of the 'dozer. "Listen. I've brought you kids some extra gear!" Did he say that? Was he yelling? His voice sounded to himself like a distant scream. Two policemen were ploughing through the mud towards him. "Listen," he kept trying. "Listen. I'm sorry about yesterday."

The chanting went on.

He screamed apologies. He reached out a longing hand.

Then one of the police had grabbed his shirt sleeve and was dragging him back and he kept uttering his *confiteor* over and over. *Pitiful*. He knew he was pitiful. Thin grey hair stuck with sweat, his lined face mired.

The dozer-man cut his motor and climbed down from the cabin to watch in the stunning silence. Will was hauled backwards to the side of the forming track still lumping out words.

Even the family stopped chanting.

Buckle swung his sunny head towards Will, his eyes glittering with refusals.

"Piss off, old man," he shouted. "Piss off."

The other five kept their heads averted. Bo seemed to be concentrating on the future. Flute's lips curled in the tiniest of smiles. Even the coppers stopped in shock.

Will's face jerked as if slapped. He knew his mouth was opening again in anguish as his tongue laboured over repeated contritions but no words seemed to erupt, nothing that would make sense.

Buckle's spangled eyes bored into his and the distance between the two of them was now so great Will knew a lifetime would never allow him to bridge those miles and miles.

"You hear me, old man?" Buckle bawled again, his voice carrying beyond the stopped machine to the mob of protesters. "You hear me? *Piss off*."

When he turned away, Connie was standing there.

She sat watching him across her kitchen table. His face appeared to have been pummelled sideways. A nerve kept jumping under one eye.

Looking at the furrows in the once-chubby cheeks, the awkwardness of his constricted mouth, she wanted to nurse his old head against her own older shoulder. *I love you, Con*, he had said all those years back but she had defused his sentiment. She'd encouraged the brittle jauntiness that became an unbreachable carapace secreting God knows what quirks, kindnesses, despairs. Seeing Will juxtaposed against the tearaway canvas of his Mango family, she had always wondered how he dealt with dropouts. Even though he was more or less one himself, he was veneered with attitudes of another era, traditional, basically conventional.

"Dear Will," she said, putting a hand on her brother's arm, "listen to me."

He shook his head. The sounds of forest being ripped apart had resumed. The rain had become a drizzle.

"I've stopped wanting to listen to anything."

Connie patted his arm. "Don't be like that. Nothing matters. Listen, I mean, to the days ticking over. The weeks. We've lasted hundreds of them. Thousands of days. Don't, Will, don't let the last days we have get at you. Please don't."

"It's simply that they *are* the last."

"I know," Con said softly. Her face beneath plaited grey hair was softened and vague. "I know, Will. You've left your run too late. You'll have to accept that. You've let friendship and what the world calls love go by the board. I know. I've watched you do it. Maybe I should have tried. I don't know."

"And what can you see now for us? Tell me that. What can you see now?"

"I can't see anything. That's the trouble. An awful space. Don't explain what happened down there. You don't have to. I know."

"Do you?"

"There's always me, Will. Me and Reever. We're here. It's family."

"You're not enough," he said. "I don't know what it is." He knew she knew. "It's as if I've caught some virus peculiar to old age."

"There's no fool," she said, and regretted the words immediately.

"You're right," he agreed. "But it doesn't help knowing it."

"Sixty years of passivity, Will. Well, it wasn't even that, was it? More like indifference."

"And that's the way I'd like it to go on. If it could. Right to the end. I don't like what's happening inside me. It's as if all my nerve centres have been wired up again and wrong. Hell, Con, I don't want to go on like this."

Ineffectuality bogged her down.

She gazed about a room that held most of their childhood. Rocklike it had resisted all attempts to change its character—coats of paint, windows cut wide, walls knocked out. Nothing altered its substance. She could hear the sawdust of decades raining insidiously from every ceiling. A stubborn house clutching its essence from the moment Uncle Harry had built it. Too many loved objects still usable, still beautiful, obliterated the disposable tawdry of the decade's plastic rubbish. On the table was a fruit bowl Jessica Olive had taken on the first long journey to Charco, bounced by water, by bullock dray, amazingly intact except for the faintest crazing on its sepia glaze.

She put her hand gently on the bowl's rim. "Look, Will," she said. "Look here."

"I know. And that." He nodded up at the lampshade above their heads, a coloured glass hemisphere Jessica Olive's crusty barrister father had brought from Ireland over a hundred years before, bequeathing ungraciously as he lay dying. "Take what you like, Jessica. You always did."

They both looked at it, remembering. "Oh unfair," the old lady had sobbed to the six-year-old Constance, the four-year-old Will, cuddling her grandchildren for comfort on returning from the funeral in Sydney. Her father's accusation had made her reject everything from the paternal home except that one object. Its crazy lozenges of glass with imbrications of leaves and birds was her sole inheritance. "Nothing," she told the children she had told the lawyers, her mouth reliving its former unforgiving lines. She had looked at her father's bony public face. "I've been self-sufficient for years now, without the aid of your sex. Oh yes, I know you helped with George and Harry, but that's all I've ever asked. And now this is the only piece of flippancy I wish to indulge." Then she had wrestled the lampshade in her father's living-room from the gas mantle and stalked out, a rustling mass of indignant black silk. She acted her indignation out for them. Will and Connie watched adoringly. "So cross I was!" Her brother, she told them, had rumbled after her, protesting and bleating. Jessica Olive protested and bleated while Connie and Will squealed their delight. "Have the lot," she told them she told him. "What a watchdog you turned out to be!"

Still there, mantling an electric bulb fed by the generator.

The room was crammed with the marginalia of six decades.

Often, now, Connie felt she was Jessica Olive as Will felt he was George.

"I keep going back," Connie said. "I go back and back. There's safety there. Today is yesterday already. Doesn't that help?"

"I'd like to believe that," Will replied. "I'd truly like to believe it." He found his fingers stroking the fruit bowl. "These days, it's always today. I can't move out of this stinking present. Especially now. This day, Con, seems the culmination of all the other lousy days I've ever had. The day I ran away from school, the day I stopped a bullet in Bougainville, the morning my buddy was blown apart, the day I left Brisbane and came north and came north and came . . ."

"I thought that was one of the good days."

"Which?"

"Coming north."

"Overall," he said. "Overall. It's the same with the good spots. They make one tiny part. They're so few."

Connie got up and walked over to the window. She could still catch glimpses of her middle-aged son negating his years in the top of the celerywood tree. The restless munching of the 'dozers agitated her, and the crashing as trees dropped. She couldn't cope with this double worry. She wandered over to the sideboard and found herself picking up one thing after another, inspecting, replacing.

"Do you identify backwards?" she asked.

"I don't know what you mean."

"Will, I've lost my identity up here. Sometimes I'm Nana on that bucking dray going to Maytown. I'm camping by the river. I *see* it. I'm waking up to find grandpa gone. I'm Nadine rocking out to sea from that house in Sunbird Street. There's an enormous tonnage of feather-weight past I carry myself and I tell you, Will, it's all become meaningless. In the whole range of things, none of it matters a damn. I'm Reever up that tree, the silly fellow, and it isn't going to matter."

"Those 'dozers," Will cried suddenly as if she hadn't spoken. "It's those 'dozers. I've got to get out of here."

He went over to where she stood and took her hand. The fingers were starting to knobble with arthritis but the face she turned up to his was still bright, still youthful with her ancestors behind the minute alterations of time.

"Stay," she asked as she had asked once before.

"I can't."

"Just for tonight."

He shook his head.

She tried to hold him there with words but he turned, went out of the kitchen and down to his van.

It was what he did next that frightened her.

Had he really done it?

He stopped halfway through opening the van door and came back up the stairs to where she stood on the veranda. He raced up the steps quickly, lightly, as if he were twenty again and had come to some decision, and, putting his arms round her, hugged her tightly and warmly and said, "I love you, Con."

This day was that day, that night, forty years ago.

It frightened her stupid.

What am I? Will wonders. *No tough centre like Con's, like father's.*

Take father as the centre of my circle and swing a curve that has the perfection of its arc broken only by the beach north of Swiper's. The radius is one hundred miles. Distance doesn't matter up here. The equatorial diameter of the world is 7926.4 miles. Applying the formula Brother Pythagoras (they called him that) drummed in so intensely it is more meaningful than the tattoo of an arrow-pierced heart, the circum-ference would be twice πr, *a piddling twenty-five thousand miles more or less.* "Wrong," Brother Pythagoras whispers. "You're dealing with a solid, boy. A sphere." "More or less," Will argues. "More or less."

Its tininess appals. *Dear little planet,* Will hopes, *you affirm my belief in a God who can retain within his mind's kindly eye the personal history of every human, animal, plant, the ultimate proof of an all-seeing God. If machines made by man can cope (Hi there, Hacker!) then how much easier for Him. I feel better believing. It's like a salve on my whole raw being.*

Will flicks his cigarette into a shower of sparks across the pic-caninny dawn. The damp grass douses it.

When Buckle sang, he doesn't want to remember, *his voice was full of dust.*

He tries not to think of Buckle. He tries not to remember.

He whistles a little Schubert, waiting for the sun, and realises it is "The Winter Journey" and recalls how often over the years, all those years, he had sat listening to Schubert and waiting for the Wet. Listening and waiting. The renewal process, the regeneration of water. It was the same for him with the permanent freshness of any creative moment. When the hands of the artist-creator moved back at last from the created object and the heart said "There!" hailing com-pletion—that was the moment Keats stumbled on. A water-jug in the atrium of some Roman villa, a bust for the Hapsburgs, a Monet landscape—all complete, perfect, pulsating beside "Der Greise Kopf" which now he mumbles to himself. Despite himself. *Auf dieser ganzen Reise,* he sings softly, *on this whole journey, on this whole journey.*

Will bunches the mosquito netting untidily and tiptoes along the pub veranda, across the grass strip and onto the road. The fence is made of dawn light and he leans on dawn light, frail as the rosy bar that crosses his body.

The trees crowd in out of the sunrise and he hears Buckle's voice cutting him down like a tree.

The bills paid. Each store. Newsagent. Grocery. Chemist. Hard-ware. Connie seen, visited, farewelled. Did she know it?

And then he'd said, "I'm off now, Con."

And she'd said, "Where?"

"Just off," he'd said.

As if unwanted knowledge bit her, she persisted, "I said 'where,' Will?"

He thought of a quick and acceptable lie.

"Maxie Tripp's."

"You're not ill," she had said with a desperate vehemence. "You are not ill. You don't need Maxie."

"It's a kind of illness," he said. "Con."

"When are you going?" It was as if her foolish questions aimed at holding him. Her folly paralleled his own. Oh he knew all about it. How he knew.

"Now," he replied. "I think now."

He thought of adding, years, ages later, "I love you, Con." But simply all he did was drive away from her, from the old homestead, from the salt-ruined piano with the resurrected photograph of mutton-chopped Cornelius aboard alongside the pompadour waves of Jessica Olive, ringleted Nadine and sailor-suited George trapped in the eye of the man with the tripod.

As he is driving now.

She will never hear the shot.

"**J**esus, man, you've got a square cock," Malloy says to Reever.

Reever looks down. He's given skirts away these days and lives in bathing trunks. Where else for the wallet when he hits town?

Since the blockade the zest seems to have gone out of things. The bite is missing. Connie has put a clean broom through Will's place and flung out the family. The property is up for sale. "I don't want to remember it," she says to her son, "not even as a memorial to Will."

"It's time to be pushing on," Reever says to Malloy.

"Where to?"

"You're the one with the boat," Reever counters. "Hell, no, I won't saddle you with me. I'll think of something. I'm thinking of walking back to my source."

"And where's that, mate?" Malloy asks kindly.

Reever doesn't answer. Already he's heading for the Swiper's Arms and midday oblivion.

The day they hauled him down from his tree he overheard one of the workmen say virtuously, "He's a nut and his mother's a nut and so's her bloody brother. Whole fuckin' family of nutters."

"You're missing a couple," Reever said. "You've missed my great-grandparents, my grandparents, and an aunt. Great nutters, all of them."

"Why don't you shut up?" the 'dozer-man said. "Why don't you just shut up?"

He begins a finger-tally of nutters. Clytie, Reever recalls, heading backwards through waves of malt. Clytie who, one evening of raucous metal rock in this very pub from a visiting band of cone-heads, all thrusting groin and amplification that threatened the rotting walls, had whirled her seventy-plus years up the road and demanded that the pub owner quiet it down. The pub owner feigned deafness. *What's that, lady?* the devious fellow kept asking, hand cupped to ear. *What's that you say?* In reply Clytie had quietly gone behind the bandstand and reefed power lines from wall sockets as if she were winding wool. *Jesus*, they had all screamed into the marvellous silence. *Jesus*. No one could believe it. She caused five hundred dollars' worth of damage to guitars whose delicate sexual engagement parts were mutilated by the abrupt termination of juice. She looked too frail to knock down. When the sergeant came he was terrified by a ninety-pound fury of chalk bones and white hair. He drove her home.

That's my girl, Reever murmurs to his beer glass. *That is definitely my girl*.

He was forty. He was fourteen. He was four.

Where's dad, mum? he had asked at intervals through his small boyhood. *Where's dad?*

How can I tell you, Connie had said, nuzzling his sweaty rosy neck. *How?* Once upon a time, she said, there was this girl, born the wrong sex and too late. *How do you mean?* he had asked. *Just listen*, she had said. She was eighteen and still plaited, imagine, when she went to a khaki Brisbane, bound for the same university you might go to yourself one day. Eighteen. Her round eager face shone like a schoolgirl's. The plaits were braided round it. Let them down, let those plaits down, her friends urged, and then you'll look like the child wonder. Let them hang.

She was the child wonder. She tore Bach partitas apart, scribbled dazzling last-minute essays, hiked with her friends into the mountains, sang with them along the coast road to Surfers and swam out past the lot of them into deeper and deeper blue.

Despite her happiness she felt there must be something else. Something bigger. The war had changed things. After she kissed her brother goodbye as he went off to the Pacific, she fled back to her college room and wept. Then more and slicker khaki poured into Brisbane. The town filled up with servicemen with *largamente* vowels. *What's that?* Reever asked. *A drawl*, Connie said. *I'm trying to improve your vocabulary*. One afternoon after lectures she allowed herself to be picked up by an American naval officer at the corner of George and Queen Streets. He was bemused by her dangling plaits.

202

He called her Rapunzel. Later as he stared at her across the linoleum topped table in some terrible Brisbane caff, he couldn't bring himself to concoct the usual lies.

He was thirty and seemed older. When this girl looked at him she was reminded, as she watched his mouth for untruths, of another man she once met in a library in Reeftown and the grotesque maturity of her first insistent kissing on the veranda looking out to bay waters. The shock of tongues. This American drove her everywhere. They sped up and down the coast. They danced. They held hands. Finally they went to bed together.

I'm a virgin, she announced at some crucial moment in a dying back-country hotel. She was also missing a lecture on Milton's prosody and another on the Franco-Prussian war.

Honey, the American murmured.

I do not, the girl announced, stripping off the last of her clothing and standing magnificently revealed under the irony of her plaits, want to become pregnant.

What's pregnant? Reever had asked. *Hush,* Connie had whispered, *just be quiet and you'll discover.*

Of course not, the American soothed. Honey . . . honey . . . of course you don't.

She bled quite a lot. *Why?* Reever asked. *I'll explain later,* Connie said.

Is that all? the girl asked afterwards.

So you really are a virgin? he said.

What do you mean "really?"

Well, that's what they all say. Anyway, what do you mean, "Is that all?"

Just that, she said. Is that all?

Let's try again, he suggested.

Moonlight pasted itself all over the little bedroom, trapped spots of light on the bone of the water jug, shafted into the wardrobe whose door wouldn't quite close. *Like mine,* Reever had said sleepily. Outside, she went on, the leopard trees and willows along the town's small street breathed out dust and pollen and made this girl feel alien to the breathy vows and panted compliments of the naked man in her bed.

Better? the man inquired later.

203

The girl examined that question from all angles. Better than what? Than hand-holding, hugging, kissing? *Than ice-cream*, Reever gurgled. *Yes. Certainly than ice-cream*, Connie had said. Than swimming out into blue and deeper blue? Than the first time?

Truthfully, she had said, I'm not sure.

The American sighed. Well, we'll just have to make you sure, won't we. Just give me a little time.

They spent more than a little time washing blood stains from sheets. Is this normal? the American asked. I mean, I've never slept with a virgin before, obviously.

"I don't know," the girl said. She was sleepy. Perhaps from loss of blood. She turned her back and went to sleep with a towel packed under her. Maybe she would bleed to death. It didn't seem to matter.

In the morning he tried as he had promised to make her sure. No, don't do that, he protested as she began unbraiding her plaits. It looks marvellous like that, honey. Marvellous.

There was a lot of nuzzling and plait-stroking at the start. There was a deal of baby talk.

"I'd rather," she said, "you loved me for myself alone, and not my yellow hair."

"Shit," he said. "Yeats!"

And afterwards when he asked her was it better that time she spoilt everything by saying yes, she didn't know he read.

He persisted with his attentions for another fortnight until his ship was due to leave for the Pacific. There had been times when he speculated as to the nature of their parting and had tried to imagine her as a possible wife. He thought of his parents in Boston and could sense their disapproval at thirteen thousand miles. The plaits? Bohemian. Unconventional, anyway. The candour? Appalling. The intellectual jibes? Well, well, well. There didn't seem to be much money there. He sensed a background of rurality exotic to the point of screwball. Okie stuff. Hill country. Talented, yes. But for the wrong things. She played piano far too well. She could swim like a fish. Her good health was outrageous.

"Honey," he said on their last night together after some awkward manipulation in a borrowed jeep, "I hate to say this but I think maybe—well, look, don't be hurt—you're frigid."

The girl wrenched herself vigorously from underneath him, her eyes bright with rage. She'd spent the last fortnight reading Havelock Ellis.

"Me?" she cried. "Me?" Her voice shook the dark of River Terrace apart. "It's you. You aren't a good lover."

"My God," he said, "how would you know?"

"I know," she said. "You're a selfish lover, did you know that? You're only interested in your own orgasm. Not mine. Not me."

His fine American face grew stiff. He adjusted all loose clothing, put the jeep into gear and drove her down River Terrace to the college.

"Well, say something," she demanded. Bullied.

"Honey," he said leaning across to help her out and get rid of her, "I never thought I'd hear a girl use words like that."

"Words like what?" She was nearly obliterated by the shadow of camphor laurel trees, but her voice shot out like a ray of light. "Words like what, for God's sake?"

"This is terrible," the American said. "Oh my God, I didn't mean us to part like this."

"Words—like—what?" she bellowed.

He looked at her bleakly, saluted, and drove up the Terrace and out of her life.

This is a serial, Connie would say to Reever.

The girl went back north. She threw away her university course as I hope you won't. It took weeks to get a permit to board a train and in the end she submitted to national workforce rules and gave herself up to train as a nurse in Townsville. For a few days before Manpower seized her, she stayed with her uncle and aunt on their sugar farm. Well, it wasn't really her uncle. He was her cousin. But that's another story. The farm seemed to have shrunk, perhaps because her brother was in the south Pacific.

You'll be a hopeless nurse, her aunt told her. You're too scatty.

The girl smiled. You can't be too scatty for bedpans.

She responded to the rigours of training with better grace than she had imagined possessing. It felt like boarding school all over again but this time there was a sense of purpose even in the most menial of disciplines. By the end of the year she wondered if she had ever had any other life.

In the middle of the Wet, dodging from awning to awning in Flinders Street during a morning off, she met her second American. With the unseemly speed of wartime she found herself engaged within a fortnight and married within a week of that to a dark intense young drawler from Washington whose own university course had been interrupted by the draft. By the time he had flown out, the confetti still pasted sodden on the cathedral footpath, the memory of a two-day honeymoon on Magnetic Island fading, she was pregnant.

Neither she nor her sturdy son were to see the second lieutenant again.

Is that all? Reever always asked.

Forty years later, as she watched a documentary of the marines landing at Iwo Jima, the cameras showed Bucky to her washing back and forth in his own blood in a totally lyric tropic sea.

Reever, sitting across the room from Connie, noticed his mother's face grow thin, tensing, pointing like an agitated dog's.

"What's up?" he asked.

"There," she said, pointing to the wavering screen. "That's your father."

But not really my source, Reever thinks, hunched on his bar stool in the Swiper's Arms. *I'm too like Cornelius, Nana, Harry, Nadine.* Connie had investigated that source when he was five. He remembered Washington under snow and his mother crying with homesickness and cards every Christmas that finally stopped coming. *My source is here, in the north, inextricably.*

He thinks of Nadine, bobbing out to sea on cyclonic waters, who might have been saved by a client with powerful breast-stroke. He grins at the possibility, and Malloy, who has tracked him down and sidled onto the next bar stool, swings his weathered body closer and asks, "What's the joke?"

Reever just shakes his head. He has come to believe in silence and the authority of stillness, its power to move.

"I don't mind running you up the coast," Malloy says after a while.

"The excitement's all gone these days. I'll take you further if you like. The towns here are going rotten."

Reever keeps swimming through malt but listening. Malloy's right. Everything has changed. Charco, Mango, Swiper's. There's a smell of hot wallet when once it was the thing, yes, the very thing, to make nonworking an art form. The towns are packed with perma-press tourists and joy-spots have broken out like a rash. They're selling the tourists beads and mirrors as if *they* were the natives, with an admixture of twentieth century technology in the form of malfunctioning ballpoints or shrinkable sweatshirts inscribed "Mango" or "Reeftown" or "Charco" on their spurious surfaces.

"I'm going to walk," Reever says after a long while.

"Walk? Walk where?"

"Right up the coast. Right up to Charco and in to the Palmer."

"You're nuts," Malloy says. "Mind if I watch?"

"It all started there," Reever says. "I'd like to take Billy Mumbler along."

Malloy laughs. "Doing an early explorer, eh? A Kennedy complete with Jacky-Jacky. You've got a hope. He's into Stevie Wonder plaits and sharp cool-dude clothes these days since his dad copped it. Maybe he thinks it's protective colouring."

"Leave it," Reever says. "Just leave it."

"Okay," Malloy says. "If that's the way you feel."

"It's the way I feel."

He drove his van back to the house at the Cape and spent three days cleaning up his shack. Connie was still grieving for Will. He sank his own tears in work. He mowed, scythed, pruned. He cleaned roof gutters, unblocked storm drains and swept cobwebs from windows. Then he went up to the big house and did the same for Connie.

"I am Jessica Olive," he heard her say absent-mindedly over breakfast. "I am Cornelius and Nadine and George."

"So am I," Reever says as he flings muscle about the house. "So am I."

He packs a roll, the smallest feasible: pup tent, blanket, frying-pan and a couple of plastic containers of food. He crams his pocket with matches. He throws in a hand line. No printing press, he mock-salutes Cornelius, and adds a notebook and ballpoint. Then he straps his bundle up tight.

Connie looks at it. "I saw a man go through with less," she says.

"When?"

"Years ago. He wanted to walk off the map."

"I don't. Not yet. I'm not ready for that."

"I am," Connie says. "I wish I were going with you."

"You're too young," Reever says, pushing his grey hair back. "I couldn't keep up."

She smiles as he intended her to. But even at the end of things, she is still looking for a reason.

"What will you do when you get there?" she asks.

"I'll leave my footprints, that first," Reever says. "And I'll stand and see and be satisfied."

"That won't be enough," Connie says. "You'll want to stay and start the whole cycle all over again."

"Maybe," Reever says. "I don't think so. Who knows? Keep a light burning."

Then he goes back to his shack, closes the door, pats the veranda rail as if he's saying goodbye to a friend, and heads off up the track where only a few weeks before Malloy had chained himself Christ-like to a cross in protest.

He pauses beneath the tree where he had been roped in the canopy. They'd spared it. He can't help grinning. Spared it. He can still see Connie watching him from the veranda through binoculars and he waves back to the corner of her house that's still visible. He waves and he sees Will broken in a spiritual two beside the path where he's standing, Will, ankle-deep in mud, pleading for something.

"Hello, Will," he says. "We'll do this together."

But Will is shaking his thin worried head at him and saying, *No, not this time. No.*

"Whatever," Reever says. "Whatever."

He finds he is close to weeping and the morning is too beautiful for that.

He shakes his head free of everything, shoulders his pack a little higher, turns his face north and starts walking.